Illusive Flame

Illusive Flame

Dara Girard

ARABESQUE®

ILLUSIVE FLAME

An Arabesque novel

ISBN 1-58314-629-6

© 2006 by Sade Odubiyi

www.kimanipress.com

Printed in U.S.A.

*To my grandmother who was an inspiration for Victoria.
Also to my parents—your support is priceless.*

CHAPTER ONE

Flames clawed at the walls. Only Victoria Spenser could hear their murderous rampage. She glanced around the simple bedroom, knowing there was nothing in it to encourage such a vision. But the fire still snapped, dancing through the darkness as it spread its red cloak-like wings. She didn't know where the image came from only that something burned. That a fire lived.

It called to her, haunted her, and seduced her. Its tongue of flames whispering the words only she could hear, casting a spell as it burned and destroyed. She could see the pumpkin-colored flames carrying the taint of evil. Victoria understood the language of arson—manmade destruction as though the spirit of the fire starter had been trapped inside the flames.

She couldn't afford another vision tonight, though. She was in America now. Her life would be different here. It had to be. A normal life was within reach and she wouldn't do anything to jeopardize that. She tried desperately to build a shield so the firestarter's emotions would not become her own, but his emotions were strong. He was too potent to block out. The fire fueled him. He took pride in the merciless rage of his fire.

She blindly picked up the clothes from her suitcase and placed them on the bed. *Focus, focus. It's not more powerful than you.* Still, the sensations threatened to consume her with their ferocious violence. She could see the flames snapping at the darkened sky; feel the fury and desperation of the man who'd started it.

She dropped to her knees, succumbing to the force of her vision. Her breathing grew shallow, her throat tightened. Flames swallowed up the building, eating everything in its path. It was the manifestation of a man's passion—one man's hatred. She could feel the intense heat of the blaze. She could feel it now burning her skin, blurring her vision. Was he burning himself or someone else? The sensations were too intertwined for her to tell the difference.

"Victoria!"

She heard the harsh snap of her Aunt's voice as though it came from the end of a tunnel. She struggled to reply. Her tongue lay heavy in her mouth. She knew she had to act normal. "Yes, Aunty Janet?"

"Are you finished unpacking?"

"Soon." She hardly heard her own reply. She wiped the sweat on her forehead with trembling fingers. *Focus, focus.* Why couldn't she block it out? It threatened to overwhelm her. For a brief, desperate moment she let herself succumb and connected to the mind of the arsonist. He was a fire linguist and had created a riddle. The investigators would have a hard time deciphering this puzzle. He was no amateur. He'd done this before. His fire was cunning, cleverly eating all the evidence of its cause.

"Victoria, did you hear me?"

She squeezed her eyes shut. "I'll be there in a moment."

He was at the site watching the building burn or he was burning. Why couldn't she tell which? She smelled the scent of melting plastic, burning wood. She saw a door laying yards away blown off its hinges. She felt no panic yet her skin felt ripped apart, exposed. Usually the fire-starter and victim were separate. Tonight they felt like one.

Suddenly, a hand gripped her arm. She cried out and turned.

Her aunt stared down at her with dark, assessing eyes then said, "Come on." She dragged her to the bathroom then held her head over the sink and splashed cold water on her face. Victoria felt the grip of the vision fade as the icy water struck her. Her aunt cupped her chin, forcing Victoria to face her. "Better?"

She felt exhausted, but relieved. "I'm just tired from the journey."

Janet folded her arms and for a moment didn't say anything. A tall sturdy woman with graying black hair and skin the color of warm chestnuts, she usually waited to speak opposed to filling any silence with useless chatter. "I didn't know they were like this. I thought being away might…" She let her hands fall. "Perhaps you shouldn't have come."

"But it was nothing really," Victoria said quickly. "Probably just a small garbage fire. I'm so tired it felt like more." She could sense her aunt's hesitation and managed a smile to reassure her. "It's nothing really." She was desperate to stay. There was no one in Jamaica who would claim her. No job that would hire her once they found out about her past. Her aunt was all she had. "It was small flames eating garbage." She watched her aunt closely. How well she could lie. How easily. She swallowed, feeling a layer of guilt that she had to start her new life based on a lie, but lying had become a part of her survival.

Janet frowned at her. "Perhaps you are tired."

She relaxed.

"But change your blouse, anyway. We're going out."

A few moments later, Janet studied her critically when Victoria emerged from the bedroom. "Is that all you have?"

She knew that the blouse was a bit tight, but she'd grown fast and didn't have money for new clothes. It was one of her best. She'd starched and ironed it too. "Yes, Aunty."

Janet drew in her lips, thoughtful. "Hmm. When they said you were a big girl I never imagined this." She shook her head. "You watch yourself. Men get ideas. Understand?"

"Yes."

"Do you have a hat?"

"No."

"Never mind. I always keep an extra one in the car. Come on."

Victoria didn't ask questions as her aunt navigated her classy black Lincoln through the traffic. Few cars crowded the two-lane road and streetlights only dotted the side leaving long stretches of darkness. She felt as though the were floating on a twisting, winding black river. Her heart began to pound when she saw a white building with a tall spire in the distance.

She gripped her aunt's arm, now understanding the need for the hat. A Jamaican church. She knew what that meant. "Please. Please don't."

Janet yanked her arm away. "Stop this foolishness. It's for your own good."

Victoria let her gaze fall, knowing pleading was useless. Dejected, she steeled herself as her aunt parked the car. Her aunt stepped out and opened the trunk. "Choose a hat," she said.

Victoria looked at the selection and frowned. "They're too big."

Janet waved her hand with growing impatience. "Pick something, *nuh*. You can't go into the church without a hat."

She sighed and selected a purple boater hat with two green feathers on the side. She knew she looked ridiculous, but said nothing.

Victoria walked with stiff legs across the cement parking lot; dread becoming more present with each step. In the distance, she heard the soft hush of cars driving past. The church was not large. It looked like one of those buildings you'd find as part of a railway set. A few bushes lined the side and concrete steps lead to the front door. She saw the door open and a beam of welcoming light spilled through the darkness onto the ground. A small silhouette figure stood in the doorway.

Victoria felt her heart lift. Perhaps this time would be different. Perhaps everything would be different. This was her new life. These people didn't know anything. She could start afresh. She walked toward the building with growing confidence. The silhouette became an older woman in a peach pillbox hat, paisley dress and polished brown shoes. Victoria would have considered her a handsome woman, if her face didn't look as though it were trying to suck in her lips.

"Sister Spenser," the woman greeted with a thin layer of censure. "You don't usually come during the week."

"No, I don't," Janet replied unaffected by the tone. "Sister Brown," she said, turning to Victoria. "This is my niece."

"Yes, we know who you are." Her dark eyes hardened. There was no tone of welcome. "Victoria Spenser."

Victoria's insides grew cold. She'd heard that tone many times before. They knew. Her past had preceded her.

"We'd like to see Pastor Fenton," Janet said.

"*You* may see him." She jerked her head in Victoria's direction. "But we don't want her in the church."

"This is the house of the Lord not yours. He'll have to tell me to leave."

Sister Brown pointed at Victoria, her voice rose. "She'd been touched by the devil. The very fires of hell run through her blood."

Janet stiffened. "I said—"

Victoria spoke up, taking a step back. "I want to stay outside anyway. You *gawan* without me." She saw the woman's mouth pinch up some more. She knew her accent defined her background. She'd been practicing to improve it. "I mean go on."

Janet tugged on her arm. "No, it's not for man to

judge, but for God." She turned back to the woman. "Sister Brown, I suggest you move before I knock you out of my way."

The woman made a move as though ready to do battle, then kissed her teeth and shifted aside. Janet and Victoria walked past her and stepped inside the church. It smelled of worn hymnals and perfume. A collective gasp escaped the group when they saw them. The group consisted of mostly older women. One younger man in his late thirties sat behind a piano and openly stared at her. Victoria felt the tiny hairs rise on the back of her neck. An older man offered a brief smile, as did a teenager in full headgear—though it may have been a grimace, she wasn't sure.

Janet pulled her down the aisle toward the man at the front. Pastor Fenton stood tall behind the podium, his hands gripping the sides. He kept his expression passive, his deep-set eyes giving nothing away. Victoria wanted to pull free from her aunt's grasp to hide from the scrutiny, from their condemnation. She wanted to scream *I'm a good person* to combat the stings of their silent scorn piercing her heart, but she walked instead with her head high as though their opinion meant nothing.

Pastor Fenton spoke to the group in a deep soothing voice, looking to the man at the piano. "Brother Rodgers will take over." He lowered his voice and said to them, "Follow me."

He led them to his office, a surprisingly large room for such a tiny church. Bookshelves lined the room as did three bulletins boards and pictures of various church members. He gestured to two seats then sat behind a desk and clasped his hands together. "What brings you here?"

Janet rested her handbag on her lap. "I think that's obvious, Pastor."

"Yes." He nodded. "Victoria Spenser is finally on U.S. soil again. A pleasure to meet you, my dear."

Victoria held out her hand. "Is it?" The corner of her mouth quirked with a bit of malice when she saw a moment of unease enter his gaze, but he hesitated only briefly before shaking her hand.

When he released her grip, he rubbed his hands together. Either to rid himself of her touch or from nervous energy she couldn't tell.

"I want you to bless her," Janet said.

He cleared his throat. "Well, I—"

"Do you not think me worthy of a blessing?" Victoria asked sensing his discomfort.

"Every child of God is precious to his Father."

"Then I suppose the question is, am I His child?"

He coughed; Janet sent her a sharp look. Victoria ignored it keeping a steady gaze on the man in front of her.

"No," he said. "That is not the question, but I am careful in situations like these." He rested his hands on the desk. "There may be a reason for this. It is not always wise to interfere with God's will."

"How do we know it's God's will?" Janet said. "Just one prayer please, if it can't be a blessing. Something to guide her during her stay here."

Pastor Fenton paused a moment then said, "Okay. I will pray for her." He stood and placed a heavy hand on Victoria's head. He clasped her head in such a strong grip she thought he would crush her skull. He closed his eyes and leaned his head back. Janet lowered her head and closed her eyes. Victoria kept her eyes open. She'd been prayed for so many times she'd lost faith anyone was listening, but she respectfully kept still and watched a spider using its gossamer string to descend from the ceiling and land on the computer monitor.

"Dear Lord!" the pastor said with such vehemence Victoria jumped. "Help this poor woman. She is one of your own. We will not question your reason for cursing her so. We only ask that you help her to carry the burden you've given her. We ask that you help to guide her on the path that is righteous. That you lead her to the way that is good. Dear Lord, only you can wash clean the blood of evil that runs through her veins. We ask that you strike out this demon of fire that has taken its claim in her heart."

Victoria clenched her teeth, trembling from anger and shame. His prayer was no different than the rest. They all thought she was evil. Cursed, something to be reviled. Maybe they were right, but there was something in her, an unyielding defiance, that refused to believe them. She was a good person no matter what they said. She clenched her hands until her knuckles paled. She wanted to leave, but the pastor's strong grip held her hostage. It absently yanked her head side to side as he shook with the conviction of his words.

"Lord bless her new life," he continued. "Make her useful. Make her good. Make her one of your own…"

He continued, but Victoria blocked him out until she heard her Aunt's final, "Amen." She loosened her fists.

"Thank you, pastor," Janet said.

He sat at his desk looking weary. "I did my best." He looked at Victoria and let his eyes trail the length of her. "But the sins of the father—"

"Yes, I know the verse," Victoria cut in. "Exodus 34:7. However, I hope God has a more forgiving heart than yours."

Pastor Fenton smiled cruelly. "A woman with a sharp tongue. How the sound must grate on the Father that made you. You are a woman. Honey should be the flavor of your words." He shook his head. " But you cannot help it. You are a pathetic creature to be pitied. Until you change no man will have you and you will bear no children. Therefore, it is your life's work to repent and seek forgiveness. Such passion is not normal in a woman of good breeding. I hope that one day your coarse ways will be smoothed."

Janet could feel Victoria's anger and spoke up. "Thank you for your time."

He leaned forward and lowered his voice. "I think it best you don't bring her here again. Not that I don't want her, but she may be in danger from others. Scared people do foolish things." He stood and nodded towards Victoria. "I will continue to pray for you. "

Victoria stood and held out her hand. When he grasped it, she gripped his hand until he winced. She spoke in a low tone. "And I will pray that your hypocrisy never be held against you."

He visibly blanched.

Janet turned to her shocked. "Victoria, how dare you show such disrespect?"

She released his hand and looked at her aunt. "I only

disrespect him because he disrespects me." She shot him a glance. "He is lying."

"A preacher doesn't lie."

She sniffed. "A preacher is a man and men lie. And he did so right inna me face. He speaks as though the congregation doesn't want me in this church, but he's the one who doesn't want me here. He who is given the power to sway people could have tried to welcome me. To push past the prejudices of his people. The people he leads in the path of righteousness. Instead he shuttles me away into his grand office and prays for me so no one can hear." She rested her hands on the desk and leaned forward, meeting his gaze in challenge. "You pray that I will be good, but how do you know I'm bad?"

His eyes became flat, his voice heavy with disgust. "Because we know what you did."

She straightened as though he'd struck her, feeling the potent sting of his words.

"She was only a child," Janet said.

"Yes, her father's child," he said. "She will always be her father's child."

Victoria swallowed determined to maintain her composure. "Yes, of course." She smiled bitterly. "See Aunty? He will not pray for me. In his eyes I'm already condemned." She folded her arms. "Pastor, I will pray for you because you will need it. You need to know that truth is more sacred than popularity."

Victoria abruptly turned then stormed out of the office, into the main hall. The congregation's praise song fell silent. She walked proudly down the aisle. Halfway to the door she halted and slowly turned. "Please don't stop. If you have such faith in God why should you fear me? You are to be the light of the world, correct? Shining brightly in a world full of darkness. It's such a shame that your flame is so cold."

The old man who'd smiled at her before, grabbed her arm before she could pass. "Don't be so angry, child. The world is unfair. People can be cruel, but anger eats at your soul."

Victoria felt tears spring to her eyes, feeling the warmth of his compassion, but unable to welcome it. "There are other things that eat at your soul." She escaped his grasp and darted into the cool night air. Once again she heard the flames; saw them reaching the sky. The scent of ash filled the air around her. Danger lingered so close and only she knew it.

"Hey," someone said.

She spun on her heel and saw the young man from behind the piano. He stopped in front of her. He smiled, but she did not trust the expression. "Good evening," he said.

She stared at him uncertain. "What do you want?"

He struck her with the back of his hand, knocking her to the ground. "To do that. One day you will be taught humility."

Victoria blinked stunned then began to laugh. He was so afraid he had to strike out in anger. She felt sorry for him.

He shook angered by her laughter. "Who are you to judge anyone?"

She stood and bit her lip, not wanting to upset him more. "I do not judge. I merely see."

"And what do you see?" he demanded.

"Your fear."

"What do I have to be afraid of?" He moved close.

She took a step back until she bumped into the side of her aunt's car. She could feel his anger rise to something more dangerous. She knew she needed to leave. "It doesn't matter."

He rested an arm on either side of her, trapping her against the car. "There's no use struggling. You're a sinner. Do not pretend to be pure. Especially when you tempt men with a body like this." His voice deepened as his hand skimmed down her side. He covered her mouth with an angry, punishing kiss. She bit his lip. He leaped back and swore. "Whore. Don't play games. I know why you were flaunting yourself in there. You know your power. But you will not hold that power over me." He grabbed her hands and lowered his head to kiss her again.

"Brother Rogers," Janet said. "You're needed inside."

He hastily stepped back from Victoria and went inside the church.

Janet sent Victoria a knowing look. "I told you to be careful."

She wiped her mouth with the back of her hand. "I was. You can believe what you will. I will no longer waste my breath trying to defend myself."

Janet opened the car door. Victoria was about to get inside when Pastor Fenton ran out of the church. "A moment please," he said breathless.

Victoria gripped the doorframe ready for another battle. She relaxed her grip when she saw the look of remorse on his face.

"Tonight I will ask God's forgiveness, but first I will ask for yours." He took a deep breath. "You were right. Mendacity is my sin. This is the first church of my own. I do want to please them so they will continue to trust me, but I cannot seek to please them and lead them at the same time. You taught me to be truthful in my ways and in my speech." He grabbed her hands. "I don't understand what you are, but God bless you."

She felt her inside crumble and fought against tears. "Thank you."

"I'll continue to pray for you."

She shook her head. "No. If you are to pray, don't pray for me. Pray for the soul of a firestarter who's all ready to set this county ablaze."

CHAPTER TWO

Robert Braxton watched the crimson flames of the building's blaze clash with the flashing red and white lights of fire trucks. The group of fire engines and ladder trucks continued to swarm into the maze of warehouses. The smell of acrid, bitter smoke coursed through the air. An enormous vertical tower of black smoke twisting like a captured arm of a raging fire monster fastened itself to the flat roof, eating away at the concrete block structure.

He watched the firefighters battling the flames, hoping there would be no casualties. He'd lost a friend to such a blaze, but could not become emotionally involved in what he saw. He had to concentrate and put his skills of observation to use. He had to understand his enemy to defeat it. The sound inside the warehouse roared like a rocket ready to launch or the furious cry of a dragon ready to devour. Flames escaped through the roof, blowing out of the cracks, clawing and cracking at the sky.

Firefighters continued to rush toward the building dressed in their alienlike gear and began laying pipes and setting up ladders. They had to stop the flames from attacking the building next door. The fire could demolish the entire warehouse district if they failed to tame it. At least there was no residence nearby.

They knew they had a mean enemy on their hands. It breathed the oxygen the building structure provided. Air vents, heating and air condition ducts, and crawl spaces all helped the fire to travel, acting as journey routes and smoke shafts, taunting them as it sped past doors, snapping through the roof and office windows tossing ash everywhere.

It soon created its own source of energy, sucking in oxygen, feeding on papers and other debris across the docking yards, and maintaining its voracious appetite. They had to find the tail and teeth of this dragon to know how to handle and capture it.

Robert turned his attention to the crowd. He liked to arrive early to a suspicious fire to observe the onlookers. He could sometimes pick out the culprit. A pyromaniac always looked more intense than other casual spectators—their eyes as bright as the blaze. He looked for two extremes— an individual either oblivious to others around him or desperate to seek attention from anyone who was willing to listen to him. He also looked for guys with their hands in their pockets—masturbating; however, he didn't see any of that sort in this group.

He couldn't understand pyros. He should, considering his advanced degrees in psychology, but the psychological profile of a pyromaniac was beyond him. That's why he'd switched careers from psychology to investigation. There was just too much about people he didn't understand.

"Hey Braxton," called detective Grant Elliot. "Early as usual." He folded his arms and watched the action. A black man of average height and on the slim side, he gave the impression of being the exact opposite, with limitless energy and a quick mind.

"Hello, Elliot."

"Damn inconsiderate of the bastard to start a fire at this time of night."

Robert glanced at his watch. It was nearly morning; fighters had been trying to tame the flame for hours with no relief. It felt as though the fire would last forever. "You don't know if it's arson. Could be accidental."

Grant sniffed. "Right and my middle name is Frederica."

Robert patted him on the back. "Really? I didn't know."

Grant frowned at him.

"I'll call you Freddy from now on..." his voice faltered when he saw two firefighters helped into an ambulance. "I wonder what's going on."

"Something about the fumes is making them sick."

He softly swore.

"I agree." Grant put a cigarette in his mouth and pulled out a lighter.

Robert glared at him. "You planning on going up in flames too?"

Grant looked at the lighter chagrined. "I was a smoker even before I was assigned to arson."

"Think about quitting. It doesn't look good lighting up a cigarette at a fire scene."

He pushed the lighter in his jacket pocket. "I guess you're right."

They turned. A flash of light briefly blinded them. Robert blinked a few times before making out the light of a news camera. His eyes fell on an attractive brunette with too much makeup, holding out a microphone. "Captain Braxton, I'm Susannah Rhodes of the Channel Six news. Could you say a few words about this?"

"Yes." He paused thoughtful. "It appears to be a fire. Excuse me." He walked to his car.

The pair followed. "Witnesses say they heard an explosion," she said. "Do you think this is a bomb? Perhaps the work of terrorists?"

"No." He jumped into his car.

Grant moved to the other side and said," When we have information you'll be the first to know." He got in the car and chuckled as Robert sped away. "You should be nicer to reporters. It's not good PR."

"So? Their goal is to get a story. They call it trying to inform the public, which basically means scaring them."

"Do you think the public should be scared?"

Robert thought about the blaze. His first thought was to say, *no*, but until he investigated he couldn't be sure. He shrugged. "I don't know."

They stopped at a nearby diner. The smell of sizzling bacon, frying eggs, and butter melting on a heap of mashed potatoes hit them when they stepped inside. They sat at a booth and grabbed the menu. The waitress on duty noticed the familiar pair and took their table. "Morning boys," she said. Her nametag said Anna-Jane, she kept her pepper red hair tied back with a rubber band while bold cat shaped earrings hit her cheeks.

"Morning," they said.

"I heard that explosion in the warehouse district all the way here. I could see fire shooting into the air."

"Hmm," Robert said.

"So what do you think caused it?"

"Don't know," Grant said not in the mood to talk about work before eating. "Can I have the Brady Special?"

Robert set his menu aside. "I'll have a hamburger. Well done. Dark, but not blackened."

Grant smiled. "He doesn't like his food burnt."

Robert shot him a look. "You're a sick—"

His smile widened. "Yea, I know." He looked at the waitress. "Hey sweetie, also give me a cup of coffee. Better yet bring me the pot."

She hesitated. "We don't usually—"

He winked. "We'll make it worth your while." He jerked his finger at Robert. "At least he will. He's got money to burn."

Robert dismissed the jab, taking out a pen and pad from inside his jacket. He nodded. "We'll pay the price."

She smiled and left.

Grant lit up a cigarette and studied his companion. He'd worked with him for a couple of years now. Except for the fact that Braxton wore two-hundred-dollar ties and owned three homes, he could be considered a regular guy. He had enough money to do nothing for the rest of his life; instead, he'd become an arson investigator and now sat in a cheap diner waiting for a fire to cool.

Grant knew the job was the right fit for him. Braxton

was too clever just to sit around. He already could see his mind working. Grant took a long drag and exhaled. "So what do you think?"

"We know three things at the start."

Grant nodded. "Yep. Number one. Huge blazes in warehouses are always suspect."

"Right and the building was almost totally engulfed in flames. Second the smell of the fire overcame some of the firefighters. Which meant the fire had a chemical taste to it."

"Hmm. Also witnesses said the fire started with an explosion."

Robert frowned and tapped the pad. "Or so they say. Some people hear exploding glass and think bomb."

The waitress came back with the food. Robert thanked her then lifted up his hamburger bun. He swore. "What the hell is this?"

Grant looked at Robert's plate and laughed.

The chef had put a piece of burnt meat and charcoal on his bun. "Get the chef out here."

AnnaJane shook her head. "I'm not sure he can—"

"He can."

A few moments later, the chef emerged from the back—a willowy guy with huge glasses. He raised his brows looking innocent. "Is there a problem, sir?"

"Sebastian, one day this building's going to go up in flames and I'll be the first to cry arson."

The look of innocence vanished. "You know I hate well done. You want to taste the meat not cook out the entire flavor. I like to cook my food, not destroy it. Try—"

"I like well done."

"But—"

Robert folded his arms. "Get me what I want."

Sebastian yanked off his hat and crumpled it in his hands. "You want to give me a heart attack."

He merely stared at him.

Sebastian sighed and returned to the back. Grant stubbed out his cigarette and looked at his companion. "You two like giving each other a hard time, don't you?"

Robert didn't reply, but a smile spread on his face.

They returned to the scene of the fire a few hours later. The cloudless morning shone down on the floating black lake that had once been a building. Robert controlled his initial eagerness. He had to do things methodically if he wanted to trace the trail back to the crime. If it was one.

"Look out," Grant said annoyed. "There's Arson ready to screw somebody out of their claim."

Robert looked at the man across the parking lot. His name wasn't really *Arson*. It was Allen Caprican. He earned the nickname "Arson" because that's what he liked to prove most cases. That way the insurance company he worked for didn't have to pay. His company loved him because he knew how to work the system. Arson investigation was not an exact science, and it could be easily misconstrued.

Robert put on a pair of gloves.

Grant noticed. "What are you doing?"

"I don't want to leave marks around his neck."

Allen approached them. He reached Grant's shoulder, but didn't feel intimidated by the pair. The morning light made his slick black hair look onyx. "Captain Braxton, nice to see you here. Ready to make a little pocket change?"

Grant frowned. "Lay off, Caprican."

"I'm just curious, Elliot. I mean you'd think a guy like him would be able to find another hobby to fill his time. He's got a nice big house and a lot of cash, why doesn't he give this job to someone who really needs the money? You know like helping his people instead of taking jobs away from them?"

Robert folded his arms and smiled. A dangerous smile. "Keep going. You might succeed at making me angry."

"Is that a threat?"

He blinked. He didn't need to make threats and Caprican knew it.

Allen stared at him for a moment then turned. "I've got work to do."

Grant called after him. "You've got to wait until it cools or did you forget procedure?"

He flashed them a crude gesture.

"Bastard."

Robert nodded. "Yea, and he knows it. That's why he's so upset."

Grant laughed then glanced around. "Doesn't seem like the monster's going to cool off anytime soon. We'd better—"

"Hold on." Robert walked away and picked up an object. "Look at this."

Grant studied the walkie-talkie. "Well, that's a nice sign."

"Hmm." It was a sign, but could mean different

things. Radios could be used for communication between the firestarter and his look out, or be used as a detonating device.

"Unfortunately, not a big enough sign unless it's got a name scrawled on it."

Robert turned it over. "No such luck."

"The building still needs to cool. We'd better go home."

Grant patted Robert on the back as he stared at the walkie-talkie. "I'm not worried. If it's arson-for-profit we'll have this case solved in no time."

Robert sighed, wishing he could agree.

CHAPTER THREE

The uniform squeezed her like a boa constrictor. Victoria scowled at her reflection, resting her hands on her hips, careful not to move too quickly in case the material tore. She wanted to make a good impression. Right now she wasn't sure she would. Red eyes stared back at her and makeup barely covered the bruise on her jaw. She hadn't slept well and the lost hours showed on her face. However, the uniform was the worse.

If she hoped to persuade Mr. Braxton to hire her as a housekeeper she had to look smart, not as though she were an overstuffed beef patty. She stared at the black shift dress with white lace butterfly collar and blue apron. It had been kind of her aunt to loan it to her, however she would have to make adjustments.

She let out the hem, so it fell to her knees, and folded in the collar. She glanced at herself again and frowned. Unfortunately, nothing could be done about the rest of it. She cautiously lifted her arms above her head. At least the fabric was flexible. She wouldn't embarrass herself by ripping anything.

She went to the stairs, glanced around, and then slid down the rail to the bottom. She met her aunt in the living room.

"I suppose you'll do," she said, giving Victoria a brief inspection.

"Don't worry Aunty, I will impress Mr. Braxton."

The scent of banana cake teased her nose as she passed the living room. She looked at the vanilla colored wallpaper, shiny wooden floors, and the cream sofa with matching chair stuffed with cotton yellow pillows. She was happy to call it her new home.

"Come on you can daydream later. Here." She handed her something wrapped in a napkin and a thermos. "You must be hungry." She opened the door, ushering Victoria ahead of her.

Victoria stepped outside and glanced up at the little stone carriage house with green shutters where her aunt lived. Huge, sweet scented peonies, bleeding hearts and mounds of bushes lined the walk path.

She was pleased her aunt hadn't mention anything about last night. She wouldn't return to the church. She was certain there was nobody here who knew about her past. That meant she was safe. "You have a lovely garden," she said.

Janet nodded. "Purely by accident, I assure you. I rarely tend to it."

"Now that I'm here, I can do that for you," she said eager to please.

"You'll have plenty to do at the main house. Come along."

With a snack of Jamaican spiced bun and cheese and chamomile tea in hand, Victoria walked the massive grounds and listened as her aunt described her duties. As the head housekeeper of the Braxton estate, Janet felt privileged that she could offer her niece possible employment.

"What is he like?" Victoria asked.

Janet hesitated then said, "Mr. Robert Braxton is an investigator, but he started out as a respected psychologist. He has written award-winning books and lectures all over the world. He is called 'doctor' in professional circles."

"Yes, but what is he *like*?"

Janet moved her shoulders with impatience. "Never mind that. It doesn't do good worrying about someone you're suppose to work for. Good or bad, you do your duties and that's the end of it."

Victoria couldn't help the wicked grin that touched her mouth. "Well, depending on how good or bad he is affects how well I do my duties."

Janet's lips thinned. "I will not have that kind of talk Victoria."

She nodded.

They walked along the gravel drive towards the main house. A row of Bradford pear trees, their white flowers in full bloom, guided their path like spring brides. The path ended at a greenhouse whose wide glass windows

shone like polished silver. Inside lush plants peeked
through the windows with their colorful faces. Her aunt
Margaret's little flower shop in Jamaica never had such
a variety of blossoms. She had to keep reminding herself
she was in America now.

Victoria gasped when the main house came into
view, showing off two white columns, large curved
windows gleaming in the sun, and a sweeping balcony
that laced the second story like an iron skirt with ivy
piercing through like green thread. The house sat
among bushes hinting the promise of spring with buds
yet to open. A brick path wove its way to the front
steps with a preponderance of purple coneflowers,
violas and golden marguerites. Brilliant green grass
covered the lawn and the rolling hills in the distance.
Trees loomed behind the house.

Victoria toyed with the bird-shaped earrings
dangling against her neck with nervous fingers. They
were her good-luck charms and the one constant in
her life, a gift from her mother. She hoped they would
offer her luck now. This is where he lived: A man who
had the power to alter her future. She stared at the
house, determined. She would not fail; she would
convince Mr. Braxton to hire her.

"You haven't mentioned a Mrs. Braxton," she said.

"There isn't one."

She widened her eyes. "He lives in this big, big house
all by himself?"

"He is divorced, but frequently entertains guests, and
his family visits often."

"Oh." It still seemed strange that one man could own so

much, but she would not question it. She spotted a golden retriever under a maple his head resting languidly on his paws. She walked towards the animal. "I didn't know you had a dog."

"I don't," Janet said, appalled at the suggestion. "It belongs to the house or rather Mr. Braxton. He used to always hang 'round Mr. Braxton until…"

"Until what?"

"He now favors the gardener." She pointed to the greenhouse. "He's busy right now getting the plants in top shape. In a couple of months, they'll have the garden show. Mr. Braxton should win."

"Hmm." Victoria stared at the dog wondering why it looked so sad with so much field for it to run about in. She moved towards the dog; it began to growl. "What's this?"

Janet kept her distance. "It has a nasty temper that one."

"And I'll have a nasty one too if you bite me," she warned the animal. "You're just in a bad mood because you need some attention." She slipped him a piece of bun and patted him.

Janet folded her arms in disapproval. "Are you going to give him your tea as well?"

"We've only just met. That will be another time." She stroked the dog's head then stood. "Poor thing. He looks so sad. Perhaps he's lonely. I'll have to take care of him."

Janet glanced at her watch, choosing not to comment. "It's time to get to work. You will mop the kitchen floor. Mr. Braxton isn't home presently and if he sees your work, he might be more likely to hire you. Cook is also out, but if you happen to meet her, be courteous. It does good to stay on her friendly side. She can cook almost anything."

Victoria's face perked up. "Solomon Grundy?"

Janet sent her a look. "I said almost."

The kitchen was the size of the first floor of the carriage house. Copper pots hung above a cooking island, mingling with drying herbs that scented the air. Once her aunt left her alone, Victoria ran her hand over the counter. She peeked inside the large steel fridge, marveled at the china dishes lined in the wooden racks, and glanced at the breakfast nook surrounded by large windows that afforded such a grand view of the lawn it looked like a painting.

She picked up the broom and began to sweep, thinking of how to convince Mr. Braxton to keep her. Unfortunately, she wasn't the greatest of cooks and making beds wasn't a particular talent of hers. She would find something she could do exceptionally well. Perhaps she could polish the furniture in the sitting room or dust the books in the library. She liked books. They'd helped her to escape when life seemed unbearable, and working in there would give her the opportunity to sneak a quick peek at a few.

An hour later, she leaned against the mop and stared proudly at the gleaming tile floor. Suddenly, an older sandy haired man in trousers and pressed green shirt entered the room. He walked past her then stopped and turned. He stared at her his soft blue eyes curious. "Hello?"

She smiled. "Hello."

"You're new here."

"Yes."

He leaned against the island. "What's your name?"

"Victoria."

"Janet's niece?"

"Yes."

He held out his hand. "It's a pleasure to have you here."

She shook his hand and continued to smile until her cheeks ached. "Thank you."

His watch beeped. He straightened. "Got to dash." He glanced at the floor. "Great job."

Victoria watched him leave and sighed with relief. She'd impressed Mr. Braxton. He thought she'd done a great job and nothing like the cold, distant gentleman she'd imagined. She'd have no trouble working for such a man. He suited this beautiful house perfectly.

The heavy thunder of footsteps soon interrupted her thoughts and cut through the quiet of the house. She pushed the mop and bucket aside as the footsteps approached.

A man stormed into the kitchen his striking profile marred with irritation. Eyes the color of dark molasses swept through the kitchen with annoyance then briefly landed on her.

He headed towards the hall. "You'll have to prepare the rooms," he said in a voice so deep it seemed to vibrate within her. "You know the ones. It seems Nicholas and Patrice are coming for one of their famous visits. When? I don't know. But knowing them it will be sooner rather than later. You know how delightful their visits are, so be prepared."

She caught her breath as he passed by her. He smelled like the earth and had a scent purely his own. Her eyes drank him in. They slid down his impressive back, which stretched his red chambray shirt, falling to his solid legs clad in worn jeans. Then she glanced down and noticed the large muddy footprints. Her awe turned to outrage.

"Not one more step," she said in a quiet voice that shot through the room like a released arrow.

Her words hit their target. The man spun on his heels and glared at her. "I beg your pardon?"

"You should not be begging for my pardon. You should be begging for your life." She placed a hand on her hip. "Is what kind of man walks through a nice clean floor with shoes not fit for the gutter?"

His tone grew soft as her voice rose. "Madam," he said in an ironic tone. "Do you know who I am?"

"Yes. A man who obviously can't fly. So if you wish to walk further you'll take off your shoes and apologize."

"Do you want me to do both at the same time or one after the other?"

"Whichever you can manage. I don't expect much."

He lifted a challenging black brow. His piercing dark eyes focused fully on her. The remoteness never left them, but something unreadable mingled there. "And who would I be apologizing to?"

"Ms. Spenser."

"Ms. Spenser? You don't have a first name?"

"It's no concern of yours."

"Why not?"

"You won't be using it."

He offered her a quick unflattering glance; taking in her altered uniform and interesting face. "Yes, that's true." He turned and walked out, leaving more muddy prints.

Incensed, she grabbed her mop and followed him down the hall, mindless of the dripping water that followed her. "Do you think I speak for your entertainment?"

He stopped, glanced up at the ceiling as if gathering patience then slowly turned.

Victoria took an involuntary step back. From across the room he hadn't appeared so large or so fierce. She had found his face striking, but on closer inspection that description didn't seem to fit. Although he had high cheekbones, a sensuous bottom lip and brown eyes surrounded by curling lashes, his attractive features seemed to mask a more predatory nature.

"You're lucky I do find you entertaining, Ms. Spenser. I'm a busy man. What do you want?"

"I expect an apology."

"For what?"

"I just told you."

He folded his arms; Victoria tried not to notice how the motion put an extra strain on his shirt. "Refresh my memory. If something's not important I usually forget about it."

She clenched her teeth. "I spent an hour wiping that floor you just mucked up."

"Right now you're making a fine mess of your own." He nodded to her mop.

She shoved the mop at him, pleased when it dripped on his shoes. "Good. Then you can do the hallway too, Mr.—."

He lowered his voice as he gripped the mop. "Braxton."

"Mr. Braxton and I…" Her anger froze as his name registered. "Braxton? You're Mr. Braxton?"

He began to smile, a smile as genuine as crocodile tears. "Yes."

Her insides began to melt. Whether from his smile or his words she was unsure. She swallowed and said his name carefully, hoping she was wrong. "Mr. Robert Braxton?"

His smile widened.

"But you can't be. That other man—"

"What other man?" He frowned then suddenly nodded. "Oh yes my white impersonator. He likes to come over every once in a while and confuse the help." When she stared at him blank he said, "He's my assistant, Foster."

"Oh."

Her temper hovered over a layer of dismay. Here he was. The man who was to hire her, the man she was supposed to impress. Here was the one obstacle that stood between her working here or somewhere in town, and she'd gone after him like a fishwife. If she'd paid more attention, she would have noticed that no hired hand would have had such arrogance surrounding him unless he could afford to be dismissed. He had plenty of arrogance, too, that filled every line of his handsome face and cloaked a body as magnificent as his land.

Robert watched in reluctant admiration when she quickly tucked away her anger. Actually, he was surprised to find a lot to admire about her. She had a compelling face, though it would not be described as conventional beauty, and more body than he usually liked on a woman, but it was her eyes that caught most of his attention. Her brown eyes flashed with an intelligence that kept him transfixed.

He tapped his foot, annoyed. He must be more exhausted than he thought if he was responding to a woman this way. He rubbed his tired eyes and took control of his wandering thoughts. "What's your name again?"

"Ms. Spenser."

"I already have a Spenser. I don't remember hiring another one."

An icy river of fear crept up her spine. She pushed away her pride and met his gaze boldly. "That's because you haven't hired me yet."

"Yes, I haven't hired you." He nodded thoughtfully. "That sounds about right."

"But you will."

"And why would I hire you?"

"Because you want to."

He moved closer to her and rested his chin on the top of the mop handle. "I think you'll need to be a little more convincing than that."

His intense gaze made her speechless. He was a clever one. She knew no amount of feminine manipulation, no matter how subtle, would go over smoothly. She would have to find something that would appeal completely to his intellect. She raced through her thoughts trying to think of an answer. "Give me three weeks no pay and I'll prove to you that I'm worth the cost."

"Three weeks no pay?" He shook his head. "Slavery's dead, darling." He lowered his eyes and Victoria breathed a sigh of relief now that she was free of his gaze. "If you can keep your tongue in order, you're hired." He looked at her. "Think you can manage that?"

She nodded.

He handed her the mop. "I doubt you'll succeed," he muttered. "But no one would confuse me with an optimist."

She clutched the mop until her palm burned then spun on her heel.

He grabbed her apron string and pulled her back. "I'm not finished."

She counted to five before she looked at him. "Yes?"

"What are you wearing?" He waved away a reply. "Never mind." He took out his wallet and handed her a few bills. "Tell your aunt to get you a uniform that fits."

She felt her face burn. "I will, sir."

He shook his head. "No need for the *sir* part. Just call me Mr. Braxton."

"Yes, Mr. Braxton."

"Very good." He pushed his wallet in his back pocket. "Sorry about the kitchen, but next time try to make the floor shine so I'll know the difference." He flashed a quick grin and turned. He raised one hand as he walked away. "Close your mouth, Ms. Spenser. You'll only say something you'll regret."

Victoria snapped her mouth shut and bit her lip as his pounding footsteps echoed down the hall.

***

"What did you think?" Foster asked when Robert passed him on the way to the stairs.

Robert stopped and looked at him." What did I think of what?"

"You know."

He headed up the stairs. "No, I don't know."

Foster followed him. "The new girl."

"I'm letting her stay." He turned into his bedroom. "And that's the end of this conversation." He closed the door.

Foster sighed disappointed, but not surprised. He knew Braxton kept his life organized. There was his work, his house, and his personal life. The three never mixed. Foster turned to the stairs unable to stop a grin. He had a feeling things were about to get interesting.

CHAPTER FOUR

Victoria let loose a string of *patios* as she marched back to the kitchen, creating, in her mind, the most colorful and creative insults regarding his character.

"We don't use that kind of language here," a woman said.

Victoria spun around and saw a striking brown-skinned woman at the end of the hall. Victoria resisted the temptation to curtsy.

"My name is Katherine Anderson," she said in a lovely educated Caribbean lilt.

"Victoria Spenser."

"Nice to meet you."

She stood a little straighter impressed by the woman's regal carriage. "Likewise."

"I'm from Barbados. So many Americans think I'm from Jamaica that I thought I should make it clear now in case anyone asks you. No, you don't need to tell me from where you come. I know."

"Oh."

"I'm in charge of personal matters about the house, such as guest and visitors."

Victoria frowned confused. "Aren't they the same thing?"

"No, and do not make the mistake of confusing the two. One is welcome and the other is not. However, both must be handled with due importance and grace."

"I see," she said though she did not.

"It's important that you present yourself accordingly. Never show your dissatisfaction. You work here. That's what you're paid to do; that's all you're paid to do." She measured Victoria in one sweeping look. "Just a little advice. Good morning." She left.

Victoria's high opinion of the woman disappeared as she watched her leave. She shook her head amazed. She'd met two unpleasant people within five minutes. Victoria muttered unflattering comments about both and shoved open the kitchen doors.

"What are you upset about?" Janet asked as she checked items off her clipboard. The cook, Dana Meadows, stood at the counter. A hearty middle-aged woman with curly blonde hair and plenty of laugh lines from years of gossip and finding pleasure in the misfortunes of others.

"She must have met the boss," Dana said with a smirk.

And someone else equally unpleasant, she thought. Victoria could find no humor in the situation. "Codeh! Look at my floor." She gestured to the large footprints.

Janet frowned. "I am looking at it. Dirty as a prostitute's knickers. I thought you were cleaning it."

"It was beautiful before that Mr. Braxton tromped

through it with him big high head. I worked so hard to make it look clean."

"He never pays attention to us," Dana explained, taking food out of the bags. "You'd think everything in this house happened through automation by the amount of notice he gives us. I remember when I was first here I thought I'd impress him with gourmet meals, but he'd give me no more credit than if I'd made macaroni and cheese. One maid tried to get him to notice her so she fainted. He just walked right over her body." She opened a cupboard and began putting things away. "The young ones always have it the worse. Natalie was a college student working during the summer and ended up falling in love with him, poor girl. She left with a broken heart."

"He didn't encourage it," Janet reminded her.

"True, but he did nothing to discourage it either. Every man has an ego." She pointed a finger at Victoria. "I gave my assistant, Trish, the same message so listen up. He's handsome, he's rich, he's charming...and he's totally off limits. I'm telling you this now to prevent you from forming any hopeful ideas."

Victoria rested the mop against the wall. "The only ideas I could entertain would involve a shovel and soft ground."

"Victoria!" Janet said.

Dana laughed. "Ah, leave her alone. The more she dislikes him, the better off she'll be. Keep up that attitude and I think you'll do well here. The best thing to do is pretend that he's a robot. It won't be too hard since he comes pretty close to acting like one. He won't ever notice you're around, so you do the same. Personally, I think those science types are naturally absent-minded. I worked for one woman who was so particular about everything I wanted to pull my hair out. I tell you, I'd rather be ignored any day."

"I believe you think too highly of yourself," Victoria said. "If you think he'd go out of his way to ignore you. He's just selfish."

"He's preoccupied."

"That's one word for it."

"Never mind his habits," Janet said. "You'll have to start over."

Victoria shook her head in disgust. "And that woman."

"What woman?"

"Ms. Anderson from Barbados. Mind you don't say she comes from anywhere else like the backside of a—"

Janet sent her a warning look. "Victoria!"

"She's awful."

Janet and Dana shared a glance. "Best you do as she says," Janet said. "She means well and she's good at what she does."

"I know Mr. Braxton already has an assistant. So what exactly does she do? Besides create differences where there are none?"

"Mr. Braxton runs his home very efficiently. Ms. Anderson is involved with his personal affairs, events, family issues etc.… Foster takes care of his business like trips and conferences, and I am in charge of the household. The system runs well."

"I can't imagine all these people working for one man."

"Be nice," Dana said. "This man keeps food in our mouths."

"But his manners—"

"Never mind his manners," Janet said. "Besides, I'm sure this was an accident."

Victoria picked up her broom and began to sweep. "It won't happen again. I told him off."

The two women stopped and stared at her.

Janet put down her clipboard. "Good Lord, you can't go on telling people off. I don't want any trouble Victoria. You must keep to your temper." She tapped the counter. "It is his house and his floor. If him want to mess it up you clean it up again and again and again. It's what you're paid for. You're in no position for high ideals. A poor man never vex anyone, especially if he expects to have a job in the morning."

"Don't worry." She squeezed her aunt's hand, seeing the worry in her eyes. "I will behave. I have too many plans to let that creature get in my way."

Her lips thinned. "Victoria."

"Never mind, Aunty. I'll only call him names behind his back. However, your secret is out. Now I know why you didn't describe him. There's nothing pleasant you could say. There's only so many ways you can say *bastard* before you have to search for words in other languages. He is absolutely—"

"Be quiet!"

"No, let her finish," Robert said amiably as he walked into the room. He rested against a cupboard and sent Victoria an amused grin. "Go on. We're all waiting. He's absolutely what?"

She sent him a cool glance; her eyes finishing her sentence better than any words could. She would not be provoked and risk getting fired. The shame to her aunt would be too much. She continued to sweep, and noticed he'd changed his shoes: fine black Italian leather. She swept in his direction, letting some dirt mar the black polish.

He held out one shoe. "You missed a spot."

"I'm afraid you're too big to sweep out of here."

Janet cleared her throat. "Victoria."

"Don't worry, Aunty. Mr. Braxton has a sense of humor. He understands my little jokes." She smiled sweetly at him. "Don't you?" She didn't wait for a reply. She turned to the storage cupboard.

Robert studied her a moment, annoyed that he still found her fascinating, despite the fact that she probably hated him. He pulled out a stool from under the island and turned to her aunt. "Ms. Janet, you should have warned me about her."

"Warnings belong on product labels, Mr. Braxton. People can only be experienced."

He rested his arms on the table. "Did Ms. Spenser mention my good news?"

Dana turned; Janet glanced at Victoria then him. "No."

"I'll be expecting Nicholas and Patrice."

Dana began to protest, staring at the bags on the counter. "But I haven't—"

He held up a hand in reassurance. "Don't worry they won't be arriving today. Just sometime in the near future so be prepared. I need the rooms to be made up and the kitchen stocked with their favorites. The regular routine."

"Will they be staying long?" Janet asked.

"A week perhaps two. Maybe more." He reached for an apple. "You know how they are."

"Nicholas is rather fond of Chablis," Dana said.

Robert examined the apple a moment as if it could give him the answer. "Pick it up then. I trust your judgment, Dana. They've never complained of staying here before, so we must be doing something right. Since I'm hardly here I know where to apply the credit."

Dana blushed at the casual praise; Janet nodded. "Thank you, Mr. Braxton. We are always pleased when our work is appreciated."

He stood, tossing the apple in the air. "Well ladies, don't let me keep you." He inclined his head in a little bow then left.

"That was strange," Dana said after he'd gone.

Janet pushed the stool back under the island. "What was strange about that?"

"He's never sat in the kitchen with us before, and in all my time here he's never spoken to me directly. Let alone said my name." She sank against the counter in shock. "I wasn't even aware that he knew it."

"Mr. Braxton has always been cordial to me," Janet said primly.

Dana laid a hand over her heart like a star-struck groupie. "He actually paid me a compliment. I can hardly believe it."

"Well, enough about him. We have Nicholas and Patrice arriving."

Dana pushed herself off the counter and groaned. "That is a damper."

"Why?" Victoria asked.

"Because they're—"

"You need to finish the kitchen floor and find another time to gossip," Janet cut in. "We'll leave the kitchen free so that you can complete it." She picked up her clipboard. "Come along, Dana, this will give you a break before dinner."

So the bastard could be civil, Victoria thought as she swept the mop across the floor. Civil to anyone but her. Dana didn't need to warn her. She'd fallen victim to one man's charms and would not do so again. Unfortunately, he did have something oddly magnetic about him that made her curious about what thoughts went on behind those eyes. Even as he talked and smiled the remote expression never left them. She recognized the look. She's seen the same expression in the mirror when her mother died.

She was six when her mother died in a car crash on her way into the city. Victoria was quickly shepherd into the company of her mother's brother, Uncle William and his family—a wife on constant imaginary bed rest and her two obnoxious sons, who used to pull her hair and pressed lit matches against her skin. She stayed with them until they kicked her out. She eventually wound up with Uncle Winston and his wife Margaret, who hated her on sight.

They had no children of their own and found Victoria useful for doing both household chores, and for working in the flower shop they owned. Unfortunately, being young, she still got into trouble (disappearing into the alluring Caribbean Sea with its water as blue as her favorite snow cone; relaxing under a coconut tree, letting coconut water quench her thirst and slide down her chin when she should be getting fish for Friday's dinner). She had caused a lot of mischief.

The fire, however, had not been her fault, though it was rumored that it was. Trevor, the local transient, had gotten drunk and carelessly dropped a cigarette, burning up the store and her aunt and uncle's financial security, as well as all of her dreams. In her nightmares she could still see the flames eating the little blue shop she had hoped to inherit one day. She was soon told that she would have to find a new place to stay because her aunt and uncle were moving in with relatives who had no space for her.

She quickly dashed off letters to all the relatives she could think of. The one positive reply was from her father's sister, Janet Marie Spenser, who had immigrated to America and secured an enviable position on a grand estate.

Victoria smiled remembering the letter that changed her life. She would make sure her aunt had no cause to regret sending for her. She glanced around the kitchen and sighed at her good fortune and slowly slipped into a hint of melancholy. She missed being outdoors. The home was grand, but she felt hemmed in. At home she would work in the garden until the very soil seemed to melt into her hands. It wouldn't do to stay indoors.

She felt free in nature. Normal. There were so few

places were she felt that. Nor did she want to encourage any more incidents with her boss. She knew that she could only hold her tongue for so long before it seemed to move of its own accord. She would have to seek out the gardener and persuade him to allow her to help him. She wasn't exactly an expert about plants, but she did have a healthy knowledge and could work outdoors all day. With that plan in mind, she quickly finished her chores.

Two hours later, Victoria walked down the dark paneled hall of the east wing of the house hoping to find her aunt so that she could assist her. Heavy, giant pictures of family members past and present hung on the walls in gilt frames. In spite of the smiling faces, it had the warmth of a museum and she felt no desire to linger. She turned and walked upstairs.

She saw a room decorated for a young girl. Clouds and flowers plastered the wall and a cartoon character draped the windows and covered the single bed. She didn't know he had a daughter. Why hadn't her aunt mentioned it before? Victoria pushed down any curiosity, determined not to be distracted. She lost the battle when she saw a light click off in the closet. She crept closer and opened the door.

Two almond-shaped brown eyes stared up at her with careful regard. Victoria opened her mouth to ask the girl what she was doing in there, but the girl put a finger to her lips and pointed to the door of her bedroom. She nodded in understanding and closed the door. The girl stood and came out of her hiding place. She was an extraordinary looking child plucked right out of an English novel. She wore a school uniform (blue skirt, white blouse), a dour expression as if she had already found the world rather tedious, and two braids falling down her back in neat rows. She checked her watch and nodded. "Good, I'm right on schedule."

"What were you doing in there?"

"Hiding," she said as though the answer were obvious.

"Why were you hiding?"

"Music lessons. I absolutely hate them. Everybody knows I don't go except Uncle Robert, so I just stay out of the way until they are over." She paused. "So who are you anyway?"

"Victoria Spenser."

"I'm Amanda Hargrove." She sat on the bed. "You're not going to tell Uncle about this, right?"

Because that would involve speaking to him, the answer was clear. "No."

She began to swing her legs. "Good. It took me a while to persuade Ms. Dana and Ms. Katherine, but they finally came around. I did tell Uncle that I didn't like the lessons, but he wouldn't listen so…" She shrugged, feeling there was no other explanation.

"I'm sure he just wanted you to have something to do."

She lifted her nose with her forefinger. "He wants me to be refined." She rolled her eyes, making it clear what she thought of the idea. "It's my mother's fault really. She has her little brother wrapped around her finger."

"Are your parents on vacation?"

"Constantly. She and Dad are too busy traveling the world to look after me. So they just tell Uncle what to do with me and he does it."

"But what do they do?"

"Do?"

"For work?"

"They don't do anything. They don't have to." Sh sighed and cupped her chin. "Lucky dogs. I can't wa until I'm old enough to do nothing."

Victoria sat next to her. "I'm sure that they do som thing. You just don't know what it is."

She studied her. "You have an accent like Ms. Janet."

"That's because I'm her niece."

"Oh."

"So what instrument don't you want to play?"

She gestured to a thin black case in the close "The flute."

"And why wouldn't you want to learn the flute?"

She looked at Victoria with all the disdain that a nine year-old could muster. "Because it's boring."

Victoria retrieved the case and deftly put the instrumer together. "Instruments aren't boring...only their player In Jamaica music is part of the essence of your soul." Sh picked up the instrument and began to play. Soon the so sound of light notes fell around them like confetti in a da: zlingly array of colors.

Amanda smiled. "That was pretty."

"I taught myself to play." She handed her the instru ment. "Don't bother yourself too much with the note and the rules. The music is all that matters."

The door opened and Dana peeked her head inside "I didn't think it was you that played so well," she said t Amanda. "Come down and get your snack."

"Thanks Ms. Victoria." Amanda took the flute an

headed downstairs. Loud squeaks and missed notes following behind her.

Dana grimaced. "Now you've done it. She'll drive us all into an asylum. I remember when my brother was trying to learn the violin. God what an awful sound."

"She'll learn. At least this will encourage her to go to her lessons instead of hiding in closets."

"True. But watch out for that one. She's got a heavy dose of the Braxton charm and before you know it you'll start thinking you are family and forget why you're really here."

Recognizing the hint, she stood and left the room.

Late that afternoon, Victoria tossed a fashion magazine down on the side table and glanced longingly towards the front door of the carriage house. The only long conversation they'd had was when her aunt had taken her up to a strange, windowless room with a hidden door.

"This is what Mr. Braxton calls the Safe Room," Janet said. "It is meant to guard us against burglars or other intruders. Anything that threatens the safety of this household. It is soundproof and has all the supplies one would need, but it is meant for a limited time only. If anyone were to break in here, there is a trapdoor." She squatted and lifted a secret panel.

Victoria stared down into the dark tunnel. Although hearing about the Safe Room and its trapdoor was supposed to provide her with a sense of safety, Victoria felt a cold chill travel up her arms. "I doubt I'll ever have a need for it."

Janet nodded. "Yes, I hope so, too." She looked at her aunt, who sat with her reading glasses at the tip of her nose engrossed in a novel. When she'd asked what it was about, Janet only peered up long enough to "shush" her. She let her gaze drift around the room until it fell on a photograph of an older man that sat on the side table.

She picked it up. "Who is this?"

"Mr. Braxton the former."

"Former? He's dead?"

"Yes, he was Mr. Braxton's grandfather."

Victoria studied the picture then placed it down. "Handsome man."

"He has the typical Braxton features," Janet said simply.

"Must have skipped a generation."

Janet sent her a warning look.

"Did you know him well?"

"Yes. The former Mr. Braxton used to live here. Myself and another woman used to occupy the upstairs, so that we would be on hand in case he needed anything. When he died, I was allowed to stay and live in it."

"What about the other woman?"

"She left. Have you settled in?"

"Oh, yes." She loved her room. It wasn't a storage cupboard turned into one, but a real room with ivory colored walls and an iron bed that squeaked with delightful abandon covered in a brightly colored quilt.

Victoria rested her head back and sighed as her aunt returned to her book. Her duties were over; she was supposed to relax. They'd gone out and bought her a new uniform, had a delicious lunch of chicken and rice, discussed the day's activities and plans for the evening.

and finally fallen into a companionable silence, but a sense of restlessness lingered. She knew restlessness was always a bad thing.

CHAPTER FIVE

Robert drummed his fingers against his thigh. The woman was dangerous and he knew something about danger—he'd studied addictive personalities for eight years and he'd seen that there were dangers less obvious than those that lurked on side streets, lived in dark alleys, and slept in bars. There were those of the mind—unchecked thoughts that could lead to a temptation that sent its victim to his own destruction.

Right now his destruction lay in the form of a tantalizing woman humming to herself in the cool glow of a setting sun as she set the dinner table. He watched as her graceful arms reached to straighten a place setting and her expert fingers turned napkins into fans.

He was used to watching people. His profession made it essential to be an expert observer, but he knew there was nothing scientific or cerebral about what he was doing now. He'd never hid in a doorway and watched one of his employees' work, but there was something about her that led him to do this, a vitality about her that drew him, that made his body respond to her in ways that irritated him.

Was it her temper? No, he'd met plenty of women with that unpleasant flaw and they had only annoyed him. Was it her beauty? She was pretty, but not beautiful. She was a big woman and looked like she could survive a strong force, but he knew there was something delicate—vulnerable—about her. A vulnerability she was desperate to hide.

Perhaps it was just his imagination. Something meant to make sense of his attraction to her. No attraction was too simple a word. His entire body responded to the sight of her. He felt a tightness in his groin just peering at her breasts. He could imagine how they would feel in his hands, how her rear would feel pressed against him. His analytical mind could find no logic in his emotions.

He shifted, trying to loosen the tension in his trousers. He was just bored, tired. He knew temptations easily encumbered a mind at rest. He had to find things to occupy himself. He knew the dangers of temptation. His ex-wife had taught him well and he'd learned his lesson.

The next day Robert parked in front of the burn site and stepped out of his car.

"Bad night?" Grant asked him.

Robert scanned the area. The scent of charred wood and melted steel surrounded them. The warehouse was still too hot and needed to be cleared before they could investigate. "I hired a new employee," he said absently.

"Another servant?"

He turned to him annoyed. "I don't have servants. What century do you think this is?"

Grant tried not to grin, he liked to bug him. "So what's wrong?"

"She's a nuisance."

"Pretty."

"Does it matter?"

Grant sent him a significant look.

He shrugged nonchalant and looked at the building again. "Yea, I guess. I haven't paid attention."

"How old?"

"Why?"

"I might find use for a housekeeper."

Robert ignored him. "Where are we with this anyway?"

Grant scowled. "Great," he said in disgust. "Our baby-sitters are here."

Robert saw ATF agents Melinda Brenner and Carroll Chancy. Melinda, a slender light-skinned woman with reddish brown hair, glanced in their direction, but made no acknowledgment. Carroll, his white hair sticking up as though he'd just gotten out of bed, waved to them. Robert waved back; Grant nodded his head.

Robert didn't have the same disdain for working with the government as Grant did. He wanted fire investigation to be seen as a legitimate science, and the ATF agents helped that image. The bureau's laboratory had pioneered techniques that had helped them to reconstruct scenes.

It was their behavioral science unit, however, that he most admired. If you wanted a psychological profile of a firestarter, they could give it to you.

"They're here to help," Robert said. "This is a big fire."

"We'll solve it before they get through the red tape."

"I doubt it."

"Pessimist," Grant mumbled as the pair approached them.

Robert nodded. "I know."

Carroll stopped in front of them and glanced at the building. "What a mess."

"Yes, it is." Robert said.

Melinda rested her hands on her hips. "I've already assembled a response team."

Grant curled his lip. "Lucky us."

She pierced him with a glance. "Got a problem, Elliot?"

"Of course not. We always welcome your intrusion."

She smiled coldly. "Glad to hear it."

"Come on," Robert said, hitting Grant in the chest to break the tension. "We need to find some witnesses."

Grant bowed to Melinda with mock humility. "If that's okay with you."

Robert pushed him forward and muttered, "Careful, she might think you like her."

Grant sent him an ugly look and got in the car.

A couple hours later they sat facing a teenager who ran errands for a local company hoping he saw anything that night.

The teenager sat in the doily-crowded living room with sweat dripping down face. His Adam's apple bobbed as his knee bounced up and down. His mother stood in the kitchen doorway.

Grant spoke, "We'd like to know—"

"I admit I did it," he said his voice cracking.

Grant looked at Robert amazed. No way it could be this easy.

Robert spoke with caution. "What did you do?"

"I took the old man's Jag for a spin. He always said he'd lock me up if I ever touched his car. I thought he was bluffing, you know." He swallowed his eyes widening more. "What will he charge me with? Theft? Think I can get off on bail?"

"Um—"

"Do you think I'll get a couple years in juvie?"

Robert sighed. The poor kid was a victim of too much TV.

"That's not why we're here."

"No?"

"No."

He saw his mother's face and swore. He turned back to them. "Could you forget what I just said?"

His mother hit him on the back of his head. "What did you think you were doing?" She hit him again. "You no good—"

Robert raised his hand. "Ma'am, do you mind letting us ask your son a few questions?" *Before you lower his IQ a couple more points?*

She narrowed her eyes and pointed a finger at the teenager." You're going to get it from me later." She looked at the two men and her face softened. "Would you like anything to drink?"

"No, thanks," Grant said then directed his attention to the teen.

The boy looked glum. "Pop's gonna murder me."

Grant agreed, glancing at a family photo. The man in

the picture looked like he ate nails for snack. "Did you see anything strange yesterday morning?"

"No."

"You're certain?"

"Yea."

They asked a few more questions that went nowhere, then stood. "Thanks for your time." Grant handed him his card. "In case anything comes to mind."

"Hey, my name is Randy," he said as they opened the door. "You know, just in case I go missing."

Once outside, Grant shook his head as he got in the car. "What did you think of that kid?"

"Make a wild guess."

"Imagine taking your Dad's Jag." He looked at Robert then rolled his eyes. "Oh, I forgot. You wouldn't have to," he grumbled. "You probably got one for your birthday.

Robert only smiled.

Later that day they spoke to a gas attendant at a nearby station.

He laughed, sporting a silver tooth. "Did I see anything strange last night? Ask me if I ever see anything *normal.* The weirdoes that come out at night, man. Once I saw a guy in a giant chicken suit without the feet. I mean how can you be a real chicken without the feet? And then there was this girl with one leg. Now I've got nothing against people with handicaps and all, but she was carrying the fake leg under her arm. Using a crutch then—"

"Yes, we get the picture," Robert said. "You see strange things. What we mean is, did you see anything suspicious?"

"You want to know suspicious?" He began to tell them another story. Robert interrupted him and thanked him for his time. He turned to leave and saw Grant reading a tabloid. "Let's go."

Grant held up the tabloid. "Hey a psychic channeled a sixteenth-century peasant girl."

Robert frowned. "Put that crap back."

Grant shot him a glance surprised by his vehemence. "It's a harmless—"

"Harmless my ass. Psychics are the biggest frauds of this century."

"In front of politicians?"

He pushed open the front doors of the gas station and left.

Grant replaced the tabloid and followed. "It's just a story and all psychics aren't fakes."

Robert sat in the car. Yes, they were. He knew from experience. His ex-wife had spent most of his money on charlatans and even convinced herself she had innate powers of ESP. Then she got his mother to believe in psychics. His mother ended up spending more than one hundred thousand dollars trying to contact her dead husband and a sister she'd lost in childhood. Robert made sure they closed business fast. Psychics were vultures preying on people's needs for answers. He didn't have tolerance for that kind of deception.

Evening descended as Grant and Robert stood in front of the home of Annabelle Warren, the owner of the burned warehouse. Because they'd found no useful witnesses, the owner seemed a good choice. The owner of a burned building was always the first suspect anyway. From the size of her home, it seemed business was good.

Grant rang the doorbell, then looked at Robert. "Hmm looks like one of your summer homes."

Robert surveyed the grand home then shook his head. "Too small."

A blonde woman with dark circles under her green eyes opened the door, draped in a bright orange caftan that was a striking contrast to her pale skin. "Ms. Warren?" Grant asked.

"No, that's my sister," she said in a strong Caribbean accent.

They introduced themselves. "We called your business emergency number early this morning to the report the fire at your building," Grant said. "But no representative from your company has yet shown up that we know of."

She stared at them, making no move to invite them inside. "My sister is out of town. She was upset to hear about the fire and will return as soon as she can."

"When did she leave?"

"Yesterday morning."

"When will she return?"

She blinked as though gathering patience. "As I said, she will return as soon as she can." She shrugged. "Perhaps tonight or early tomorrow morning."

"Are you familiar with the contents of the warehouse?" Grant asked.

"No."

"Perhaps you're acquainted with any clients who had merchandise stored there—"

"No."

"Like electronics, radios—"

She blinked again then said slowly, "I don't know. I couldn't care less about the business. I have other interests."

Grant persisted. "Do you know of anyone who might have carried a two way radio like a watchman perhaps or—"

"There is no reason for anyone to stay after closing."

Grant gave up and pulled out his card. "Have your sister call me when she gets back."

Robert and Grant returned to the car. "So the owner is out of town," Grant said pulling on his seatbelt. "Vacation, business—"

"Or alibi?" They looked at each other then Robert put the car in gear.

CHAPTER SIX

Victoria's heart raced. The sense of restlessness kept growing stronger. She could still feel a high from the previous fire and a need for something more. The feeling was so familiar if she weren't used to these episodes she would have confused them for her own, but she knew they weren't hers. They belonged to the firestarter. He was confident of his skill. He would not make mistakes. He would only become more dangerous as his confidence soared. He would strike again soon and she was helpless to stop him.

She curled up on the couch, rocking a little to ease herself into a soothing rhythm. She hummed, but when that didn't help she turned on the TV hoping the various images would push the sensations away. Suddenly, the title of a show grabbed her attention: *Psychic Detectives*. She watched in amazement about a case of a police department using the services of a psychic to solve a murder. She let her feet fall to the ground feeling rejuvenated.

Perhaps if she told them what he was like they could know what to look for.

Later that day Victoria sat in the police department looking across at an officer with heavy jowls and small eyes. He stared at her with careful regard. "What did you say?"

Victoria fought not to squirm in her chair and spoke slowly so he could understand her. "I think I can help with information about the warehouse fire."

He took out a pad. "You were there?"

"No."

"Someone said something to you?"

She shook her head. "No."

"You saw something?"

"In a way."

"What does that mean?"

"I saw it," she said in a rush. "In a vision."

He sighed and muttered, "How come I always get the nuts?"

She pretended not to hear him. "It's a man of medium height," she said. "I can see from his viewpoint at times. He watched the fire. Perhaps he wasn't involved but took satisfaction in it, so I think he set someone else up to do it, though personally he's taking credit for it. He's a professional. This isn't for money. He's gaining strength from this fire and it's not his first."

The officer looked bored. "Uh, huh. Give me your name and address and we'll be in contact."

"It's very important how you handle this. He's going to get more dangerous."

"What's your name?"

"You have to—"

His tone hardened. "I said what's your name?"

Another man came into the room. He smelled of cigarettes and aftershave. "There's no need to shout at the poor woman."

The officer tossed down his pen. "You want to handle it, Elliot? Go ahead. I've already had a long day." He held up his hands on either side of his head and wiggled his fingers. "She says she senses fires." He left in disgust.

Grant looked at the woman. She sat quiet and tense. Not the normal attention seeker that came in with information. He wouldn't put it past her, but he wasn't willing to write her off. You never knew where a break would come from. He'd heard of psychics helping police. If she were a fraud maybe she might slip up and give them something. They certainly needed it.

He sat behind the desk and offered her a reassuring smile. "Don't worry about him, he doesn't believe you."

She boldly met his gaze. "Neither do you."

He leaned back and raised a brow aware he'd underestimated her. She had a nice voice. "No, but I like to be more civil about being closed minded."

She rewarded him with a small smile.

Pretty too. He adjusted his tie. "What's your name?"

"Victoria Spenser."

He started to scribble out her name, but the pen ran out of ink. He began to swear then glanced at her and thought better of it. He tossed the pen away and grabbed another that leaked. This time he did swear and threw it in the direction of the trash can. It missed.

She held out a pen.

Grant took it and grinned. "Bet you knew I would need it."

Victoria couldn't help but return his grin. "No, I don't have premonitions. I just see arson as it happens. Like an element guide. I can't explain." She felt foolish. How could he understand when she barely did herself?

"You're like an empath, right?"

"A what?"

"You can experience empathy for others or inanimate objects and stuff."

"It has a name?"

"Yea, I read up on it when I was trying to impress this girl—" He cleared his throat. "Forget it. Anyway you don't have to explain. Just tell me what you saw."

Victoria became still, allowing herself to surrender to the memory. "The night was perfect for it. Everything was planned. I think there are three men. One is the leader; he watched the fire burn. The other man inside he radioed the lookout that he was safe inside. It's dark and it's cramped inside and smells like plastic."

"A container?"

"Maybe."

"I feel heat then pain. The blast was bigger than expected and he's hurt. He's glad."

Grant shook his head. "Who's hurt? Who's glad?"

She furrowed her brows. "I'm not sure. I think it's the firestarter inside and one of the others is glad. The one who's watching I think."

Grant looked at her a moment then finally said, "Okay thank you. We'll be in touch. What's your name again?"

"Victoria Spenser."

"And where do you live?"

She supplied the address.

He gave a low whistle. "Nice neighborhood."

"I'm a housekeeper."

"Who is your employer?"

"Mr. Robert Braxton. I work on his estate."

Grant paused. His pen hovered over the paper. He felt certain he'd misheard. "Who?"

"Mr. Robert Braxton or sometimes Dr. Braxton my aunt tells me."

He glanced up and rubbed his nose. "Robert Braxton. You're the housekeeper of Robert Braxton?"

She frowned uncertain why he felt the need to repeat the name. "Yes."

Grant set the pen down and leaned back, grinning. "Are you putting me on?"

"No."

He laughed. "I get it. This is a joke because I picked up that tabloid, right? Very funny." He pointed at her. "Well, you can tell Mr. Braxton that I'm not going to fall for any little game he's trying to pull. And you can…." His words trailed off when she continued to look at him confused. His smile dropped; he fell forward shocked. "You're *serious?* You're Braxton's housekeeper?"

"Yes."

"And you see visions?"

Victoria nodded. "Yes." She tilted her head and stared at him a little worried. "I don't see where you're confused."

He clasped his hands behind his head amazed. "Does he know you're here?"

"No."

The corner of his mouth twitched. "This is interesting." *Very interesting.* He stood and held out his hand. "Again thank you for coming. I appreciate the information." She nodded then left. Grant watched her leave then fell back in his chair.

The other officer came in and patted him on the shoulder. "Did she read your fortune?"

Grant quickly covered his notes. Braxton had a reputation to consider. If anyone found out about his housekeeper it would cause trouble they didn't need. "Maybe next time," he joked, but didn't feel like laughing anymore. Victoria had made some good observations. She talked about the radio, which tied in with the walkie-talkie they found. So two people were involved.

She mentioned three. The third man didn't make sense to him so he'd start with the two that did: the fire-starter and his lookout. She mentioned a man was injured. That could help them. He called up Braxton.

"We need to check the hospitals," he said.

"I was thinking the same thing," Robert said impressed. "Because of the explosion it's likely the fire-starter was injured or could be dead. My guess is the starter is seriously injured."

"Yea. We need to call hospitals and find out about any fire-injured patients."

Robert paused. "You sound certain. What tipped you off?"

Grant smoothed down his tie and cleared his throat. "Just a hunch."

* * *

Emergency department room nurse, Andrea Lederer, had had a hellish day the night of the fire. She'd worked until nearly midnight the previous evening covering for a geriatrics nurse who had food poisoning. When she got home she discovered her roommate had stripped the apartment bare and eloped with her boyfriend. That night she'd hardly slept then dragged herself out of bed for the afternoon shift only to find her car wouldn't start. She ended up taking the bus.

Today felt like half the city had shown up in the emergency room. When the phone rang, she grabbed it eager for the brief escape from demanding patients. A man came on the line when she answered.

"Hello this is detective Grant Elliot an arson investigator with the police department. How are you doing today?"

He had a nice voice, but she wasn't in the mood to care. "Don't ask."

"I'm sorry. I've had days like that myself."

Really? Then you'd know I don't feel like talking. "How can I help you?"

"We need to know if you've had anyone show up there either last night or early this morning with a fire injury."

Andrea rubbed her tired eyes and heaved a heavy sigh. "Hold on a sec."

She ran a finger down the clipboard log of admissions. Gun wound, eye pain, unexplained bleeding... "Sorry we don't have any burn victims. Either last night or today."

"Thank you," he said, but sounded let down.

She fought back a yawn. "No problem."

* * *

Grant hung up the phone. He stared at Robert who'd finished his calls earlier and had come up empty. "Nothing," he said.

Robert shrugged. "You look disappointed."

"She sounded so sure."

His gaze sharpened. "Who? You found a witness?"

Grant shifted in his chair. "Uh, not quite."

"What do you mean, not quite?"

"Don't take this the wrong way, but I met your new employee and it seems she thinks she has a special gift."

Robert's eyes darkened. "Tell me what happened."

At the hospital Andrea wiped her eyes and pushed the clipboard aside unaware of the information on the second page of the admissions list. A third way down was the name of a man brought into the hospital shortly after dawn suffering from second and third degree burns. A man who'd received emergency treatment then left refusing to be admitted. A man some would say looked like the walking dead, and others would say was.

CHAPTER SEVEN

Victoria polished the wooden railing with extra vigor, chastising herself. She shouldn't have gone to the police. She should have known better. The man she'd spoken to seemed nice, but she felt the atmosphere changed when she mentioned Mr. Braxton's name. Perhaps they'd investigated together once. Aunt Janet had never been specific what Mr. Braxton investigated. She heard the front door close then his heavy footsteps. She was getting used to the sound, almost surprised the earth didn't tremble when he walked.

"Ms. Spenser."

She glanced up. Blood drained from her face. Stark fury blazed in his eyes as he stood at the bottom of the stairs. She kept her voice level. "Yes, Mr. Braxton?"

"In my study. Now." He spun on his heel and left. She walked down the stairs, followed him down the hall then stopped. She didn't know where his study was. She'd been kept on the east section of the house and had yet to get a full tour. She stared at the row of

doors and began to open them. One was a library,
another a gallery. She was about to enter a third when
Robert stuck his head out.

"What are you doing?" he asked.

"Looking for your study."

He stared at her a long moment then sighed. "It's
here."

Inside the study she saw a worn shovel in the corner,
newspaper clippings, maps and lots of books. He sat
behind the desk making no attempt to hide his anger,
but he kept his feelings controlled. He didn't drum his
fingers or fidget. He just sat completely still and watched
her like dark creatures who liked to hide in the shadows.
He then clasped two fingers like a steeple and tapped
them against his mouth, his eyes never leaving her face.

After a few moments of this, Victoria lost her patience.
"It's better to burst than to boil."

His hands fell to the desk. "What?"

"Speak your anger don't suppress it."

He leaned back and twirled a pen on the desk. He
lowered his gaze as though the sight of her hurt his eyes.
"My dear woman," he said quietly. "The level of anger I
feel at this moment could not be expressed."

She folded her arms. "What have I done?"

"I've convinced myself that you're new to this country
and perhaps financially strapped. Therefore, you wanted
to make some income and decided to—"

"If you are accusing me of something speak plainly."

His expression darkened. "I don't think you would
want that."

"I would like nothing better."

He pressed his palms together. "I think you're a fraud."

Victoria straightened. "No, I am not."

"Didn't you go to the police and tell them about your dream of the warehouse fire?"

"It wasn't a dream. It was a vision."

He raised his brows surprised. "So you don't deny it?"

"I have nothing to deny."

"Naturally. You no doubt believe your own delusion or you're a very good liar."

"I didn't lie."

"You didn't?"

"No."

Robert pinched the bridge of his nose. "Okay let's see if we can understand each other."

She nodded. "Yes, let's."

He paused surprised by her challenge, determined not to let anger rule him. "You don't deny that you went to the police station with information about the warehouse fire?"

"Yes."

"Yes, you do deny it?"

"No, I don't deny it."

He nodded. "You also don't deny confessing that you saw the fire in a dream, excuse me, vision?"

"Yes, I don't deny it."

"You also don't deny hoping for a monetary reward for your services?"

Victoria folded her arms.

He grinned triumphant. "Ah, so you have nothing to say to that."

She lifted her chin. "My mother told me that silence is the best answer for a fool."

His grin fell. "And Emerson said that pride is the never-failing vice of fools."

She met his accusation without flinching. "Pride is not a vice."

"It is certainly not a virtue."

She smoothed out her collar. "Pride in a woman scares most weak men."

"Don't confuse pride with confidence."

"What's the difference?"

"Pride is merely a form of conceit."

"To some, but if no one is proud of you, what else can you have but pride in yourself?"

A muscle in his jaw twitched. "Pride can be a barrier to other feelings."

"Such as?"

"Compassion."

"I do have compassion for others."

"That's why you create a false idea that makes you believe you're special in some way?"

"I didn't create anything. I spoke truthfully but will not waste my breath trying to convince you."

He smiled faintly. "We've gone off the subject."

"The subject, if you've forgotten, is your belief that I am an liar. I happen to disagree."

"So you're determined to stick to this charade?"

"It's not a charade."

He turned away in disgust. "You're all the same. Con artists and thieves. You don't care who you hurt." He looked at her again and bit his bottom lip. "However, you surprise me. Your type usually likes to get paid first."

"I spoke the truth."

Robert stared at her in wonder. "I gave you a job and you still lie to me. Very convincingly I might add."

"I'm not lying. I saw the fire."

He pounded the desk with his fist, rattling the pens. "Then why was your vision wrong?"

She stared at him startled. "What?"

"There were no reported fire injuries. We called all the hospitals and came up with nothing."

"There was a mistake."

He pointed at her. "You either knew we'd not find anything because you're a fraud or you know something and you're pretending to use this supposed gift to cover yourself or someone else."

"No."

"Don't you realize how cruel it is to build up people's hopes just to make yourself feel important?"

"I went to the police because I wanted to help. The vision was real. I wanted to help before someone got killed."

"Where were you the night of the fire?"

Her eyes widened. "Now I'm a suspect?"

"Where were you the night of the fire?" he repeated in a harsh tone.

"At the house with my aunt. We went out that evening to go to church."

"Which church?"

She gave the name. "Don't worry. They'll remember me."

"Of course they will."

She folded her arms tighter.

"Why didn't you come to me first?"

"Because the psychic on the TV went to the police."

Robert rested his chin in his hand glad he was getting somewhere. "So you got this idea from the TV?"

Victoria lowered her eyes.

"Then next time you have a supposed vision, you come to me first."

"I prefer to go to someone who believes me," she said in a quiet voice.

"You think people at the station believed you?"

"One man seemed to."

Robert shook his head amazed by her act. "He was humoring you, darling. It's what you do with crazy people."

"Don't call me *darling*." She glanced up. "And I'm not crazy."

"No, you're not. You've just convinced yourself of this special power. You're under the delusion that the nightmare you had last night was in direct correlation with the warehouse fire."

"No."

He took a deep breath. "I don't think you heard me correctly. So listen carefully." He leaned forward and enunciated every word. "Your...vision...was...wrong."

She shook her head. "No, it wasn't. Someone made a mistake."

"Yes." He tapped his chest. "I did." He opened his drawer. " I'll give you two weeks pay so you can look for another job."

A quick look of panic flashed in her eyes. "You want to get rid of me because of this? I'm speaking the truth."

"Ms. Spenser—"

"I was with my aunt. You can ask her."

Robert hesitated, then closed the drawer. "If I were to let you stay, I don't want to hear anything more about this vision thing."

"Okay."

"Good."

"Except—"

He buried his face in his hands a moment then looked at her. "Except what?"

"You're going to investigate the site, correct?"

"Yes."

"Please. Please check the north center of the building."

"The north center?"

"Yes."

"You think I'll find something?"

Victoria nodded.

Robert sighed. A part of him felt sorry for her another part wanted to wring her neck for succeeding at such a convincing act. "Okay, if I discover something, I'll consider what you believe; if not, you drop this game for good."

She clasped her hands in her lap. "Okay."

He pointed at her his voice firm. "I mean forever. Never mention it again. Are you still confident?"

"Yes."

He sighed. "Or just stubborn?"

She raised a mocking brow.

He reluctantly smiled. "Yes, I know. I'm stubborn too."

* * *

At the burn site, Grant shouted to Robert over the loud roar of the nearby crane operators lifting twisted I-beams and slabs of debris. "Did you talk to her?"

Robert nodded. "Yes."

"What did she say?"

"Nothing interesting."

Grant let the matter drop and turned to what remained of the warehouse. "There were no signs of forced entry."

"Hmm."

"If this is arson, the intruder knew how to get in."

"Key?" Robert guessed.

"Maybe, or he knew of some other way to get in without setting off the alarm. For example hiding himself in a container, like Victoria said."

"She said she smelled plastic and felt it was cramped and dark that could mean anything."

"It means a container."

Robert ignored him. "If he knew the building or had a key…"

"Perhaps a disgruntled employee?" Grant finished.

"Or the owner."

"The owner's a woman. Women rarely set fires."

"She could have hired someone."

"True. Unfortunately, we won't know how successful business was until we get some papers."

Robert stared at the site thoughtful. "The starter probably used a timer so he could escape before the thing blew."

"Either that or he didn't escape."

Robert opened the trunk of his car. "Time to get some questions answered." He put on his gear—heavy turnout boots, fire hat, SCBA (self-contained, breathing apparatus), two-way radio—then entered what was left of the warehouse. The warehouse now resembled a dark, blackened tomb with puddles of water slickened by oil. Smoke still oozed from the ground like a trapped ghost in the gloom. Unidentified black things cluttered the building; Robert stumbled over them because he could hardly see. He flashed his wide lens flashlight to guide his path.

The place felt like an oven. He could feel the heat through his boots, as sweat rolled down his back and trickled down his armpits and legs. A rush of excitement pushed away the discomfort. He felt like a pathologist. Instead of human corpses, he had a cadaver of steel and wood. He knew the warehouse had died of fire, but an investigator went past the *how* to the *why*.

He now had the chance to use his knowledge of the elements in the fire triangle—heat, fire, and oxygen. He knew how they created certain burn patterns. Flame behavior was his specialty and he would let the building tell him the story. He checked the windows for signs. Smoldering fires cracked them like spider webs leaving them with a greasy residue, but fast-burning fires created an explosive rush and blew glass apart before smoke could glaze them. He also looked for fire cones, heat lines, trailer marks, accelerated residue, and char depth.

He radioed Grant. "You could lose the remains of the *Titanic* in here."

He eventually determined that the flashpoint had occurred almost simultaneously at several different locations. He guessed the fire had ignited suddenly, which was an all-but-certain indicator of arson. He hesitated to be certain because there had been cases were multiple points of fire were accidental. He doubted this was the case.

Walking was about as easy as dancing on shifting sand; he kept losing his footing. He made his way to the north center and thought of Victoria. He didn't believe her vision, but he wouldn't mind finding something useful, plus a part of him wanted her to be right, though he didn't know why.

He reached the north center and saw nothing. He walked a few feet then staggered and fell. He landed in a field of five-gallon hard-plastic jugs, his facemask slipped from his face. He quickly replaced it and swept his flashlight across the jugs. He stared in surprise that so many jugs were in tact. A large amount had their caps off.

He read the label. It said the jugs contained kerosene. He doubted it. Kerosene was slow burning. There was no way it would be considered the accelerant that created the explosion and resulting fire, but he couldn't go on hunches. It was the lab's job to find out what it was. He took one of the jugs that had residue inside.

By the time he emerged outside, his eye was swelling shut and his forehead began to burn from whatever his face had touched when he fell.

He saw Grant and held up the jug. "There are dozens of these in there, many with no caps. I think there's something toxic in them and I don't think it's kerosene."

Grant looked at him, as Robert removed his gear. "She led you to the jugs, didn't she?"

"Actually, I fell on them."

"You know, there are people who can see crimes."

"Yes," Robert grumbled. "And there are also some people who can see fairies and little green people."

"Not all psychics are con artists."

"No, some are just mislead. They believe in things that make no logical sense."

Grant nodded. "Right. So how many ladders have you walked under recently?"

Robert tossed his hat in the trunk.

"I believe her."

He turned to Grant appalled. "Why?"

"I just do."

"That's not an answer."

"She could be right about some things. Psychics have solved cases before. We could use some help with this."

"We have the ATF."

Grant frowned. "Real help, not overblown egos."

Robert studied him. "This dislike of the government wouldn't be anything personal, would it?"

He shoved a hand in his trouser pocket. "No. So what do you think?"

"She was wrong about the fire injury."

"Yes, but she was right about this."

"A good guess. Or she's involved. You noticed the owner's sister is Caribbean? She could be—"

Grant swept a hand through the air, cutting him off. "She's not involved and you know it. Look, remember when you first came on board? Your way of doing things initially angered a lot of the good old boys. But I stuck by you even though you challenged some of my beliefs on fire investigation."

"I just know—"

"Just as I was flexible to learning something new, I'm asking you to do the same."

Robert shook his head surprised by the request. "I have staked my reputation on trying to establish arson investigation as a legitimate science. People think it's bunk, because of its oral traditions and guesswork. Now you want me to throw that all away and base my investigation on some woman who's sees fires in her dreams?"

"Yes."

"For all we know she could be mentally unstable."

"You know there's not one loose screw there."

Robert sighed fiercely then leaned against his car, resigned. "All right. You may have a point. Check up on her. I'll give you some more information tonight."

"Good."

"Stop smiling. I'm not convinced yet. Did you learn anything from the walkie-talkie?"

He nodded. "Yea."

Robert straightened. "What?"

"That Radio Shack sold a million of the damn things. It seems Victoria Spenser may be our best hope."

Prescott Delaney loved his chili spicy with lots of cheese. Bubba's Diner provided some of the best. He glanced over the table at his colleague Rona, the administrative assistant at the construction company where he worked. A sweet girl most people looked past. He never had that problem. People usually took notice of him.

He knew he was a good-looking guy. Sure, age had taken some of his hair, but he was still in good shape.

He made sure of that with his daily workouts. He wished his dad could see all that he'd achieved. He'd make his old man proud. Construction on the Latviska Dance Studio was almost done, and he already had another job lined up.

The waitress stopped by his table. "Is everything fine?" She was pretty, so he smiled at her. "Yes."

She smiled back. "Let me know if you need anything."

"Sure." He watched her leave. She had a nice body, not much of a backside, but he wasn't much of a butt man. He liked hips.

When he was a skinny, shy kid girls used to make fun of him all the time. Then he learned how to build things. Thanks to his dad. His dad had shown him how things worked. Taking him around town and pointing out the different structures of buildings and carting him around on construction jobs. The hard work helped him bulk up and gave him the confidence he needed. He wasn't the smartest kid in school, but if you need anything built he was the guy.

That's when the girls came running. It seemed they liked a guy who knew how to use his hands, and they let him use his hands all over them. Instead of them laughing at him, he laughed at them. Sweet revenge and they didn't even know it. Women were so predictable. He looked across the table at the mousy woman sitting in front of him. Rona was different. She was always sweet. Unfortunately, she seemed to like going from one bad relationship to another. Her present boyfriend was an idiot. You could never figure out his mood.

That's why he did without relationships. He liked

to keep things under control, and you couldn't control people. Give him an old building and a bunch of tools any day.

Prescott finished his chili then requested the bill. After he paid, he helped Rona with her coat and walked her to the door. On the way there she tripped. He grabbed her arm before she fell. "Are you okay?" he asked.

"I'm fine. Just clumsy."

He glanced down and saw that a tile had shifted. He called the manager. "The tile is loose. You should get it fixed."

The man used the tip of his shoe to push the tile back in place. "There it's fixed. No big deal."

Prescott stared at the other man. His right temple began to pound. He was laughing at them. Being disrespectful. He'd had to deal with that most of his life. Though he never went around thinking he was better than others, others thought they were better than him. They'd disrespected his father too just 'cause he didn't finish high school. He felt Rona's cool fingers on his arm. "Come on Prescott, time to get back to work."

He held the door open for her as he studied the building structure. "They should have apologized," he muttered as they walked to his car.

"It's okay I wasn't hurt."

She was always so forgiving. That's why people treated her like crap and she didn't even notice. He wouldn't come back here. They wouldn't get another cent of his money. He got into his car and pulled onto the main street. He glanced at the building through his rearview mirror. Bubba's Diner had been around for a while and they weren't keeping it up. The neon sign needed fixing, they needed a new roof, and there were cracks in the structure.

The building was dangerous. It deserved to burn.

CHAPTER EIGHT

He hadn't come home yet. Victoria twisted the buttons on her cardigan. Had he found anything? Would he accuse her of lying again? She looked at her aunt reading and wished she had the patience to do the same. She lacked the gift of patience. She felt energy whirling inside her. She had to get out. Dusk painted the land, while a calming darkness scuttled away the memories of the day.

She closed her eyes to calm herself and saw a flame—a tiny flicker of light. Her skin grew prickly with mounting unease. Oh no. Not again. Not tonight. But somehow she wasn't surprised. She'd been prepared. She knew he would start again.

Janet glanced up from her book. "You're restless. What's wrong?"

She must act normal. Nothing was wrong. Nothing. "Headache."

Janet raised her brows.

"I've been trying to memorize the layout of the house.

So I won't get lost." She laughed—the sound felt false, but her aunt didn't take notice.

Janet jumped to her feet and grabbed Victoria's arms. She shook her. "Another one?"

"It's tiny. Nothing to worry about."

Her grip tightened. "You must not let this control you. Be strong."

"I am strong."

"Whether it is a gift or a curse you must not let it overwhelm you. Do you hear me?"

Sweat began to gather on her skin. "Yes." She could feel the flame growing. She jumped to her feet. "I'm going for a walk."

Victoria escaped outside, drinking in the sweet, cool scent of evening. Her shoes swished through the giving grass as she rushed in the direction of the greenhouse. Flowers always calmed her, their scent pushing away the smell of burning. *I will fight you. I am strong.* She pushed through the attack of emotions, as her legs grew heavy. She must get there. Nothing must stop her.

She needed a destination to focus on. The greenhouse was a lighted beacon in the coming evening and she was a ship being led towards it. But the vision grew. She saw cracked black and white tile flooring, peach cushioned booths, metal stools, and family photos crumbling to black ash. A restaurant owned by a family for generations. Someone's life work slowly eaten. She held her head and briefly shut her eyes, a wave of all the sensations washing over her.

She grabbed the latch to the greenhouse. It opened easily and she stumbled inside vaguely aware of the intense warmth that clung to her. She took a deep breath. Flowers meant safety. They were so innocent, so lovely, so pure. She felt like a child stepping into an enchanted forest where lilies danced and Cheshire cats smiled without faces.

Tall trees climbed all around, foliage crouched in the shade, moss crawled across stone and various flowers began to stretch from pots, whereas others had yet to push their heads above the soil. The dreamlike space, however, could not erase her nightmare of destruction. The flames continued to devour and he was laughing. Triumphant. She grabbed a table to steady herself. Her elbow hit a little pot. It fell to the ground and shattered.

"What are you doing in here?" a voice demanded.

It took all her strength to respond. "I just wanted to see the flowers."

"Why?"

"I don't know."

Robert came from behind a tall palm ready to give a sharp retort then he saw her face. His voice filled with concern. "What's wrong with you?"

"It's so hot." She crumpled to the ground.

He rushed to her side and knelt beside her. He half-sat her against his thigh, rubbing her hand then touched her cheek, surprise by how clammy her skin felt. She needed medical attention. He began to pick her up.

Victoria seized his sleeve and shook her head. "No."

"You need a doctor," he said.

"No," she gasped. "Please. I need a moment…to… breathe."

"But—"

"Please."

Robert muttered something, but did as she asked, watching her labored breathing until color came back into her face. She licked her dry lips. "It's too late now. It's over." She struggled to stand.

He stopped her. "Be still. You need to rest." He paused. "It's too late for what? What's over?"

She briefly closed her eyes. "It's just too late."

He continued to rub her hand. "You probably worked yourself too hard today. You should take better care of yourself."

A bitter smile touched her lips. "You think I'm crazy."

He sighed resigned. "To be honest I don't know what I think of you." But he knew what he wanted. He wanted to touch the curve of her neck, her cheek, her hair, every inch of her body. His body grew harder with every rise and fall of her chest. For the first time in his life he didn't want to think at all. He watched her draw in her knees and rest her chin on them.

She smelled good too. Like a fresh breeze. "Do you want to talk about it?"

Victoria shook her head.

"Sometimes it just helps to talk, even if…"

"Someone doesn't believe you?" she said dryly. "No. You're wrong. I've spent my entire life with people thinking things about me that aren't true. Talking doesn't help."

"But you don't know if—"

"What's the point of speaking when nothing you say is useful?"

Robert fell silent, hearing the hurt in her voice. He ran

a hand over his face then said, "I did find something in the north center."

She turned and looked at him with hope in her eyes. "So you believe me?"

His eyes slid away, he did not want to encourage that hope. "There are still so many factors that need to be considered."

"Such as the possibility that I'm involved in some way?"

"I'm not accusing you of anything."

"Doesn't matter." She frowned, looking at him closely. "What happened to your face?"

"I fell."

She touched his forehead. "Does it hurt?"

He jerked away. "Ow! Yes. You're supposed to ask that before you touch it."

She yanked her hand back, trying not to smile. "Sorry."

"It's okay."

"You should—"

"I took care of it." He cleared his throat. "Thanks anyway."

"Okay." Victoria turned away wanting to create distance between them. She scooped up the plant and placed it in an empty pot. She stood then set it on the table.

Robert watched her. That seemed to be all he did lately. He liked how she moved with such purpose. He also liked how her rear looked from this angle—like buns straight from the oven. He suddenly became very hungry for something he couldn't eat. He rubbed his hands together desperate to think of something else. "You couldn't resist coming in here, could you?"

She looked down at him. "No, I couldn't."

He stood beside her. "Believe it or not, I know the feeling." He fingered the petals of an orchid.

"The feeling of being unable to resist?" Victoria watched his fingers caress the petals. He had nice hands, nice gentle fingers.

"Yes." His dark eyes split the distance between them. It wasn't the color, but the remoteness that held her, that caused a rush of heat to fill her body. His voice, however, remained neutral. "I have help." A little grimace marred his face. "I always have help. But I like to tend to them myself sometimes."

"Nothing compares to the feel of soil slipping through your fingers."

His fingers stroked the orchid stem. "No. My grandfather was an avid gardener. He started after my grandmother died. He said he created the garden so that he could have fresh flowers to lay on her grave, which he visited three times a year."

She swallowed, watching as he pushed one finger deep into the soil. She could feel her body tighten the deeper he went; could feel moisture gather between her legs.

"My grandfather said when I was five I would pick flowers then try to replant them so he encouraged my interest. He always said there were so many horrible things in this world and that everyone should make their little corner beautiful."

She could barely concentrate as his finger moved around in the soil. Her breathing grew shallow, a trail of perspiration slid down her back. "Sounds wise."

"He was." Robert removed his finger with such sped that she gasped. "Are you okay?" he asked.

She laughed weakly. "I'm fine. Interesting story."

"Hmm." He stared at her a moment then turned away.

Victoria took a deep breath and relaxed. "I saw a picture of him in the carriage house. He was a handsome man."

"It's a family trait of course."

"As well as humility?"

He thought for a moment then shook his head. "No, I don't think that's a trait of ours. What are Spensers known for?"

"I think you already know."

"Pride."

"Perhaps a little too much." She turned towards the windows where an old sun rested its weary head against the hills allowing darkness to cover the lawn. She felt him close. He could never enter a room without her knowing he was there. She felt as though there was a strange invisible bond between them.

"Is this why Natalie left?" she asked desperate to break the strange spell and build a wall. "Because of moments like these?"

"Who?"

She smiled a little sad. "You don't even remember their names, do you?" She shook her head, keeping her back toward him. It was her best defense against her pull to him. "I will only clean your house, nothing more, although you may expect more."

"I don't know what you're talking about."

"I'm talking about you and Natalie."

"Natalie left because she was unhappy."

She turned to him and studied his face. "You honestly believe that. Ah, yes, I can see you do. You didn't know how much she loved you."

His brows drew together. "Natalie was young and impressionable, that's all. Merely a housekeeper who did her job well." He folded his arms. "Why would I pay special attention to her?" Once he said the words, he regretted them.

"Yes, why?" she taunted. "Perhaps for the same reason you would pay attention to me. Because I'm here. Don't worry you wouldn't be the first to have such thoughts."

He let his hands fall. "I didn't mean that," he said gently. "I meant—"

She held up her hands, fending off any explanations. "Don't say anything."

He looked at her his expression guarded. "I will not apologize for something you don't understand."

"I bet you've never had to apologize for anything."

"You're wrong. People expect me to apologize for a lot of things. I refuse. Is it my responsibility to care for the feelings of every young woman who hopes that I will make her dreams come true? To provide the job for every man without one? To do nothing just because I was born into wealth?"

"And am I suppose to apologize for being poor? For feeling and seeing things others can't see? Should I apologize for all the things others don't understand?"

"Would 'others' be me?"

She took a step sideways. "I should go."

He moved in front of her. "Did you see a fire?"

"Yes." She took a step around him.

He blocked her path again. "Big or small?"

She looked at him frustrated. "They're always big. Please move."

"Not yet. What was it?"

"You don't even—"

"I know, but I'm curious. What was it?"

"It was a restaurant shaped like a block."

He thought a moment then asked, "Where did it start?"

"In the kitchen, an electrical spark."

"So it was an accident?"

"That's how it's suppose to look," she said then raced past him.

Robert sat in his bedroom. Another fire. So she says. Unfortunately, Victoria said a lot of things that seemed to echo in his head. Her comments about Natalie bothered him. He didn't like the picture painted of him as a cold employer who had taken advantage of the affections of a young girl. What disturbed him most was how close to the truth she was. He'd known Natalie'd had some silly crush on him, but he hadn't paid much notice. He couldn't even remember what she looked like or recall the words of her tearful goodbye when she had left.

He'd just given her the rest of her salary, wished her luck, and returned to the current issue of *Scientific America* he'd been reading. He had been cold and unfeeling. I had become a habit. It had been the only way to survive his marriage to a woman whose sunny smiles and laughing eyes hid a heart of coal. At the beginning of hi marriage he'd craved her warmth, but in the proces she'd frozen his heart. He didn't remember becoming as hard as her.

He sighed. He should have handled Natalie better. He could have asked her why she had to leave so suddenly, but he'd been too bitter to care…too insulated in his own guilt about his marriage to have compassion for others on a level deeper than pure intellect. Strangely enough, he wasn't bitter now and he didn't feel guilty, but something still haunted him. He wasn't sure what it was. He hated the ambiguity of such emotions.

He definitely hated the ambiguity of what he felt toward Victoria. He didn't understand her. Didn't trust her. There was something about her, however, and he couldn't get her out of his mind.

He pressed a fist against the flat of his hand and swore. He was too grown to be ruled by curiosity. He liked the order of his life. The darkness in him was a comfort, a feeling he could trust. How could he let her close when the darkness in him cringed at the light that surrounded her?

He turned on the TV needing some noise. Susannah Rhodes came on the screen. He lifted his remote to switch channels when she said, "Bubba's Diner now lays in ashes.…"

CHAPTER NINE

Robert stripped off his gear after investigating the burned restaurant, his spirits low. Bubba's Diner had been a part of the landscape for generations. One night had changed all that. Two fires in one week. Perhaps they were connected. He doubted it. Restaurant fires started by arson were usually quickly solved. Either the owner did it for insurance or an employee wanted revenge.

"So we meet again, Braxton," Caprican said.

Robert closed his trunk.

"Where's your buddy? Or do you think you're the only competent investigator around?"

Robert sighed, not in the mood to argue. "We used to be in the same business."

"Yes, before you stabbed me in the back at the Tract's trial."

"I stated what I knew."

"Which was nothing. I stand by what I said then. And Tracts killed his wife. He burned her alive for the insurance money. The evidence was all there, and just becaus you were able to confuse the jury and put doubt in their minds doesn't mean he was innocent."

Robert rested a hand against the hood of his car, trying to keep calm. "Multiple points of fire do not always equal arson. Plus, the laboratory used by the department didn't comply with the standards of ASTM." The American Society for Training and Materials was important in his field. "That left doubt about the accuracy of the results. The trial was about a man's life and maintaining our reputation as protectors of the innocent."

"He was guilty. You can't convince me otherwise. I've been in this field over twenty years. I've learned—"

"A lot of myths that have put some innocent people away. You're still doing it."

"And you're letting killers walk free."

"The point is that the insurance company didn't want to pay."

"They shouldn't have to pay a murderer. We were right, Braxton. The proof lay in the pour patterns and how the body was found. Years of investigative techniques can't be wrong."

"But they were."

"Why don't you go home and write another book about it? I'll go and do my job. Unlike some, I need the money."

Robert got in his car and slammed the door. He took a deep breath. He wouldn't let Caprican get to him. He knew the trial ended the way it should have. Evidence was key. Except in this case. Despite Victoria's vision all the evidence pointed to an electrical fire with no sign of arson. He'd send samples to the lab and see what they found.

He tapped his steering wheel. How had she known about the fire if she hadn't been there?

The phone rang just as he stepped into his office.

"This is Susannah Rhodes from—"

Robert interrupted her. "Yes, I know where you're from."

"Could you say a few words about the Bubba's Diner fire?"

"I'll give you the number to—"

"I already have it," she said. "They say it's likely an electrical fire."

"Yes."

"Have there been any new developments regarding the warehouse blaze?"

"No."

"Could there be a possible connection?"

"Let me switch you." He pressed the button before she could protest. He leaned back and stared at the ceiling trying to sort his thoughts. If the warehouse fire and the restaurant fire were connected, they were in deep trouble.

Grant came into the room a few minutes later. "You're not going to like this."

Robert sat forward. "Probably not. Bubba's Diner burned."

"Yea, I know and an apartment caught fire because o a waffle iron in DC." He paused. "Why did you mention the restaurant?"

"No reason." There wasn't a connection. Things wer always burning somewhere.

Grant waved a file. "I have bad news."

"What?"

He tossed the file on the desk. "Your little maid has a fascinating legacy."

Robert drew the file toward him. "What do you mean?"

"Open it."

A sense of dread spread through him. She was probably part of a long line of phony psychics charged with petty misdemeanors and fraud. Robert opened the folder and began to read. A sudden anger gripped him as he gazed at the truth. He struggled to control his emotions determined not to overreact.

"Are you okay?"

"I'm fine," he snapped. " So her father is Vernon Taylor?"

"Yep."

"Vernon Taylor," he repeated though the name had been seared into his memory. Vernon Taylor was one of the most notorious firestarters in New York history.

"Yep."

Robert felt his gut clench and steeled himself, pushing his anger down. He closed the file and tapped it. "How hard was it for you to find this out?"

"Not too hard."

"How easy do you think it would be for someone else to find out?"

"They'd have to really want to know. I don't think they'd make the connection. Why?"

"Because she's working in my house."

"Scared?"

He shook his head. "No, but the public would have a circus with this. I'm an arson investigator."

"I still think we should use her."

"Even after knowing this?"

"Especially knowing this." Grant rested his elbows on his knees. "He could have taught her stuff. She knows fires. Maybe that's what makes her sensitive to them. He was a pyro she could pick up on his energy or something. As an empath she may be sensitive to that pull."

Robert stared at him confused. "As a what?"

"An empath."

He scribbled the word down then jumped to his feet.

Grant watched him grab his things and open the door. "Where are you going?"

"To the library. I need to understand what the hell you're talking about."

Three hours later, Robert stared amazed at the books and papers piled in front of him. There really was such a thing. Such a person. He'd been skeptical when he'd quickly found information about empaths online. Any nut could put up a website. But the books amazed him. People, respected doctors, truly believed in this phenomenon. ESP he'd heard of, reincarnation...yes. But empathy

One book hooked him from the start. Writings by Dr. Michael Kent of the Everette Institute in Washington DC. They'd conducted a study with Victoria as a participant. He glanced at his watch. He'd make it there in good time if he left now. An hour later he stepped inside the clinical walls of the institute surprised by its modern design. He'd expected crystals hanging from the ceiling and people wearing sandals and discussing the benefits of wheat germ.

Robert approached the front desk. "Hello, I'd like to speak to Dr. Kent."

The receptionist smiled at him through her curtain of black hair. "Who should I say wants to gift him with their presence?"

Did she just speak English? "Dr. Braxton."

"Okay Dr. Braxton please have a seat."

He did, sinking in a chair so low his knees nearly reached his forehead. A few minutes later a little man with shaggy gray hair came up to him, smiling wide. "Dr. Robert Braxton it's a pleasure to meet you. I read your dissertation on addictive personalities and was very impressed. Please follow me." Once in his office he asked, "How can I help you?"

"I'm interested in discussing a participant in one of your studies. Victoria Spenser."

"I'm afraid the information about our participants is confidential."

"But you wrote all about her in your book, *The Levels of Empathic Abilities*."

Dr. Kent hesitated. "I can assure you that I used false names."

"She was case thirty-two."

Dr. Kent took the book down and flipped through it. He read a few passages then glanced at Robert. "Amazing."

Robert straightened satisfied. "I told you she was there."

"No, it's amazing that you could decipher who this young girl was out of all the participants. Has she not changed much?"

"I don't know. I don't know her very well."

He sent Robert a strange look.

Robert shifted uncomfortable. "But I know enough about her to make a basic deduction based on certain factors." When Dr. Kent didn't reply, Robert said, "I want to know the likelihood of an empath causing fires."

"They are usually more destructive to themselves than others." He paused, remembering back. "She was a special case. A colleague of mine was on vacation in Jamaica when she saw her wandering alone. My colleague also heard about the stories the people shared about her. With no objections from her family we brought her to the Stevenson Center."

"An asylum?"

"I don't like that term. I prefer—"

"Doesn't matter. How long was she there?"

"A couple of years. We helped her emerge from the wall she'd built around herself and discovered she had a great sensitivity to heat and fire. An uncle eventually came and claimed her. I believe they thought she was cured."

"So empaths can predict things?"

"They can see things. Current events. Depending on the level, some can't give you precise data, but enough clues for a lead. Emapths have been known to help police in their work."

"Have they been known to make mistakes?"

Dr. Kent spoke with caution. "They are human."

"So that's a *yes*?"

"It's rare."

He tapped a beat against his knee. "I see. So it wouldn' be intentional?"

"If an empath shares information, they're taking the big risk of not being believed. If one comes to you with information, it's out of a willingness to help, not harm."

Victoria twisted her hair back, trying to fight a yawn. She hadn't slept well last night, but she was used to that. She rarely slept well. She walked to the house bundled in two cardigans to protect her from the brisk morning. She knew she looked like an Arctic traveler, but was too warm to care, and no one said anything. Toward evening she headed into the dining room to polish the table.

She loved the dining room, with its high ceiling and mahogany table with carved legs and wood inlay. This evening the sun seeped through the windows, casting a bright sheen on the wood.

"Did you rob a flock of sheep?" Robert asked in disbelief staring at the layers of clothes.

She turned and saw him standing in the doorway, large and arrogant and every much lord of the manor in gray trousers, dark blue shirt, and sweater. She fought her response to him. Every time she saw him, she felt as though the air had been knocked out of her.

"What did you say?"

Robert came into the room and stood across from her. "You're wearing enough wool for twenty sheep." He took off his sweater. "Here, wear this instead."

She glanced at the object as it waved its promise of warmth. Unfortunately, it had one major defect. It was his. "No thank you, Mr. Braxton."

He continued to hold the sweater out to her.

She refolded her rag and began wiping the table again.

He draped the sweater over his shoulder. "You can't be comfortable in all those clothes." He quickly examined her. "You don't need the extra padding."

"I'm aware of that."

"It was a compliment."

She rubbed the table with extra vigor. "You also could do with a little less padding yourself."

"I'm in excellent shape."

She stopped and stared at him. "I was referring to your ego."

"I see your tongue has been sharpened today."

"Purely for your amusement, Mr. Braxton. I know how you like to be entertained."

He came around the table and narrowed his eyes. "Is your goal to entertain or provoke?"

"I'm just a housekeeper, Mr. Braxton. I'm not significant enough to provoke you."

He stopped next to her as she pushed a chair in, trying to ignore the aching desire to touch her. "Careful butterfly," he warned quietly. "Laughing at the eagle may get you eaten."

Victoria rested against a chair and quirked a brow at him. "Are you hungry?"

"You do like taking risks, but the question is: Are you merely clever or just reckless?"

"Perhaps I'm just bored and find you an easy target."

His voice deepened. "An easy target and a woman that likes to aim. That makes for a dangerous combination."

She met his stare though she shivered inside. "Tha shouldn't mix."

"Or can't resist," he countered.

Her eyes fell.

"Wear the sweater," he said. "I don't like my employees looking ridiculous." When she began to protest, he placed a finger over her lips. "Your tongue or your job."

She took the sweater, managing a thin smile. "Thank you, Mr. Braxton."

"See how easy that was?"

She maintained her brittle smile. "I'm sure a rash will form later."

He tapped a beat on the back of a chair. "I found out some interesting information today."

She stopped, goose bumps forming on her arms. "About the fire?"

"About your father."

Victoria gripped the rag and began wiping the top of a chair prepared for the storm of accusations expected to come. She kept her voice cool. "I see."

"He had quite a reputation. He started fires for profit and made a good living until one day he got crazy and set fire to a motel and cooked 80 people in their sleep."

"He was sent to prison for that."

"Yes, and he escaped after fifteen years. No one has seen him since."

She began to wipe with extra vigor. "I haven't seen him if that's what you're wondering."

"That's not what I'm wondering." He seized her wrist and took the rag from her. "I know you spent time in an asylum because of an unhealthy preoccupation with fire."

She struggled to release herself. "So now you have your proof that I'm crazy."

"No, I just wanted to find out more about you and I did." He let her go.

She rubbed her wrist though his grip hadn't hurt. "And I suppose you also found out that I was born in New York. That I lived there with my mother and father for a while. That I grew up with the smell of gasoline, kerosene, and smoke. That the clothes on my back, the food I ate, the house I lived in all came from the destruction of someone else's life." She rested a hand on her hips. "If you had money trouble, or you had a grudge you came to Vernon Taylor. He would make all your troubles turn to ash. I've seen plenty of troubles burn—houses, shops, cars, bodies. Mum eventually left him and returned to Jamaica. When she died, I moved in with relatives. And I frightened every relative I lived with. So are you afraid too? Afraid that your home may go up in flames?"

"No."

Victoria folded her arms still stinging from the pain of her past. "You don't know what it's like to be your father's child. To be a constant outsider no matter how hard you try."

Robert scratched his chin and laughed without humor. "As a matter of fact I do. My grandfather was a rich man. I can't seem to escape it. I'm worth a lot of money I didn't earn, and there are plenty of people who like to remind me of that." He hesitated. "Are you afraid he'll contact you?"

"No."

He set the rag down, averting his eyes. "A restaurant burned last night."

Her hands fell to her hips. "And you think I'm involved?"

He sent her a sideward glance. "No, it was accidental."

She shook her head. "It wasn't accidental."

"We'll see what the evidence points to, but there was no trace of an accelerant."

Victoria fell into a chair and stared up at him in disbelief. "But—"

His face softened. "I know you have good intentions, but the science doesn't prove your claim. I have to go based on what I know."

"Not what I see," she said defeated. She hung her head.

"Exactly. Now I—"

Katherine came into the room. "Ms. Spenser, I need to speak to you about the—"

"She's busy at the moment, Ms. Anderson," Robert said annoyed by the interruption. "You'll have to attend to the matter yourself or wait until later."

Katherine looked taken aback then calmly said, "Yes, Mr. Braxton." She shot Victoria a glance then left.

Victoria stood. "Maybe I should see what she wants."

Robert gently pulled her arm, forcing her to sit. "Ms. Spenser, this is my house not hers. You only answer to me." He drew out a chair and sat. "So what can you tell me about it?"

She became still letting the sensations come back to her. "It was the same man from the warehouse. The third man.

He's good. He knows buildings. He won't make mistakes." She paused. "He reminds me of my father."

"Do you think it's him?"

"No. I don't think so."

"Do you think the building burned for profit?"

"No, the first one started that way, but both are about revenge. He thought the restaurant was poorly made. So he burned it."

Robert rose to his feet. "We'll see what the lab comes up with."

"You won't catch him easily. He'll—"

"Thanks for your help." He looked at the table. "You're a good worker."

"I'm happy to be here."

"I'm glad you're…" He bit his lip then made a show of looking at his watch. "I have a call to make." He patted her on the hand, indulgent. "Keep up the good work." He left.

Victoria stared at her hand irritated. He'd patted her as though she were a pouting child that needed reassurance. She knew what she'd seen, but why didn't anything make sense? If they didn't stop him, he'd grow more careless. Would he snap as her father had? She stared at Braxton's sweater then stripped off her layers and put it on. His body heat had made it almost indecently warm and his cologne clung to the cashmere wool mix. She shook her head to stop any other distracting thoughts and went into the kitchen.

"Whose sweater is that?" Dana asked as Victoria opened the closet.

"My uncle's," she lied.

Dana stared at her, tapping her chin. "I could have sworn that Mr. Braxton has a sweater just like that."

Victoria closed the closet and flashed a bright smile. "Amazing."

She didn't return his sweater simply because she didn't want to. If he wanted it back he could ask her for it. She wore it the next day letting it warm her through the cold morning until the sun offered enough heat so that she could wrap it around her waist. It was like having him near. She liked the feeling, though felt ashamed to admit it.

The sweater gave Robert just as much trouble. He liked how she looked in it. As if she belonged to him. He liked seeing how the sleeves swallowed up her arms, how it seemed to claim her like a high schooler wearing her boy-friend's lettered jacket.

It filled him with possessive thoughts dangerous enough to tempt him to risk her temper. His body re-sponded at the thought of how she'd be in bed. He wondered what kind of fire she would be. A quick flame or an inferno? Unfortunately, a sweater wasn't a big enough net to capture this butterfly. He leaned back in his chair, trying to ease the strain of his erection and glanced around his book filled office.

No, he was wrong. He didn't want to capture her at all. No matter how intriguing she was. No matter how she challenged him to analyze and classify his unwanted feelings for her, he would not act on them. She had her place in his home and he had his. Chaos came when order was ignored. He didn't want to risk that.

Besides, they argued about everything except one thing. If there were a firestarter involved in these two fires, he would burn again.

Grant toyed with the change in his pockets as he listened to ATF agent Melinda Brenner talk to Braxton. The wind had loosened her hair from its ponytail and he had a strange urge to fix it. She was usually so together that the wayward strand irked him. It softened her hard edge look of ball crushing ambition. She almost looked human.

He understood her drive though. As the first of his family to make it through college he knew where focused energy could take you. He just didn't feel the need to go around thinking he had something to prove. Perhaps it was different for women in high positions.

He sighed. They still hadn't gotten a hold of the elusive Ms. Warren. She hadn't returned yet. So there were no inventory records, bills, or other papers to send to the auditors to find out what this pile of rumble had been all about. The lab concluded that an accelerate had been used. Too bad they hadn't found remains of a timer or detonator starting in the north center section where the jugs were discovered. So how did firestarter get the 300 jugs into the warehouse to get the fire started?

"Who manufactured the kerosene jugs?" he asked when there was a pause in the conversation.

"A company called CHC," Melinda said absently as though he'd interrupted a more important discussion.

He didn't care. "What do you know about them?"

"We didn't come up with anything. The company doesn't exist in the U.S."

"Great, an invisible foreign company. Just what we needed."

"The lab identified the CHC residue as acetone."

Robert shook his head. "Nasty stuff."

Grant grinned. "Not if you want to start a bonfire."

Melinda walked past him and turned to Robert. "Let's go inside."

An hour later, Melinda flashed her light through the murky darkness, gloom, and drifting ash to the point of the fire's origin. Robert stood next to her—patient and alert. They both knew the answers were here waiting for them to find them.

"Who stored things here?" Robert asked.

"We won't know until we get papers from the owner, and no one has made an insurance claim yet."

She moved her flashlight and let it bounce off the charred remains of a cabinet. "Things are getting cold fast."

"I know." That was always bad news. The colder the trail, the less likely they'd be able to capture the culprit.

Sunlight slipped through like a beam of swirling dust from an opening in the roof. It illuminated a single large square where the CHC containers had been concentrated.

"The acetone is the key," Melinda said. "Acetone is a controlled substance. You can't legally buy it in large quantities without the seller's keeping records on who buys it and where it goes."

"What do you think that means?"

She chewed her lip. "I don't know exactly how it's use legally, but I know one thing."

"What?"

"Dope smugglers process cocaine with it."

Robert understood where she was leading. "Whic means big money." And if business was too goo someone may have wanted revenge.

CHAPTER TEN

Victoria walked in the direction of the carriage house, but stopped when Katherine approached her. "Do you know where Amanda is?" she asked.

"No."

The corners of her mouth turned down in disapproval. "She has a habit of disappearing."

"She is a child having fun," Victoria said. "It's spring. She can't help it."

"She can learn to help it. Having fun has its place." She measured Victoria with one significant glance. "Everything has its place. Always remember that." She walked past.

Victoria resisted the urge to say something rude then continued walking. She stopped when she saw the same dog from the first day, resting under a willow tree. It didn't look at the cardinal whizzing past or notice a squirrel racing up the trunk. It just continued to rest his head on his front paws the breeze blowing his golden coat. Victoria approached the dog; it growled low in its throat.

She knelt in front of it and held out her hand. It raised its head and sniffed her hand then growled again in greeting. She rubbed its ear.

"Why are you so sad?"

"Because Bailey's gone," a young voice replied from above her.

Victoria peered between the branches and saw Amanda stretched out on a limb. Bark and dirt spotted her white stockings, while her shoelaces hung undone.

"Who's Bailey?"

"The other dog. A black Lab. He was old. I miss him too." She sighed. "He was the best dog in the world. Everybody thought so, even Uncle Robert, though he'll never say so. Great-granddad gave Bailey to him as a puppy when he was fifteen after his dad had died. He was really sad and Great-granddad was worried. Mom said that when Uncle got Bailey he was never sad again. They were the best of friends and he would even take him on his trips.

"When he didn't, the house always knew when he was coming back because Bailey would stay by the window all day until he arrived. Uncle didn't really want Benjamin." She stared down at the sad dog below her. "But one day he saw Bailey playing with him and another time saw him wandering around the property, so he adopted him. They all got on real well. When I came to stay, Ms. Dana and I would call Uncle and the two dogs The Three Stooges. But then Bailey got sick." Her eyes filled with tears. "I didn't get to say goodbye. Uncle just took him away and buried him."

"Where?"

She pointed. Bitterness entered her tone. "He's out there."

Victoria squinted at the great expanse of green that seemed to stretch and only touch sky. In the distance, she saw a lonely twig sticking out of the ground.

"It must have been hard for him. That's why he didn't tell you."

"He just ignores poor Ben as if he doesn't exist." She rubbed her eyes. "I wish he'd given me the chance to say goodbye."

"You still can." She chewed her lip thoughtful. "Everyone needs a chance to say goodbye." She thought of the kiss her mother had given her before she drove into town and out of her life. "Every spirit deserves a proper burial."

Anticipation replaced her bitter tone. "Do you think we could have a funeral for him?"

She looked at the dog and considered the question. She'd never done a funeral for a dog, but didn't see a problem with doing something. "I don't see why not."

"We could have it on Saturday after breakfast. We'll have to bring flowers and wear black." Amanda sat up and swung her legs. "I'll wear the same dress I wore to Granddad's funeral and get a black bandana for Benjamin to wear."

"That sounds fine. Now, next question. What are you doing up there?"

She groaned and lay back on the limb. "Nicholas and Patrice are coming," she said gloomily.

"Yes, I know. Who are they?"

"My cousins," she grumbled. "I hate them more than my flute lessons."

"Why?"

"Because they're stupid."

"Are they your age?" she asked, wondering if that w
why she didn't like them.

She shook her head. "No way. They're old like twen
two or something."

Victoria did not feel the need to explain that twen
two was not old. "Okay, so you don't like them. That st
doesn't explain why you're in a tree."

"I'm on the lookout. I can see people drive u
from here. It's a great place to hide from people ar
see everything that's going on. Do you want to con
up and see?"

Victoria stroked the trunk of the tree, trying
remember the last time she'd climbed one. "Not th
time. I have to find the gardener."

Amanda looked around then pointed. "He's starte
planting flowers near the side of the house."

She turned and saw a group of men hauling mulch.

"You can't miss him. He'll be singing to himself. O
key."

Victoria went to the side of the house and let her han
sink discreetly in the soft earth. The sight, feel, and sme
of new soil always gave her a special thrill. She picked u
a handful and let it paint her palms with its richness. Th
sky was still and the clouds hung like suspended smok
At home she would have finished the washing, then mak
sure Chassie was fed and wait while dukunu boiled on th
stove, its aroma already seeping through an open windo
like a beckoning finger.

A deep voice, occupied in song, broke through her thoughts. She turned and saw the same man from before—Foster, Mr. Braxton's assistant. He wore an old T-shirt displaying muscle as defined as rocks on a waterfall, his sandy brown hair plastered with sweat.

"You can't be the gardener," she said.

He turned to her and smiled. "Well I am. I took up the job recently."

"Why?"

"I like it." He began to sing again.

"That song belongs in a pub," she said, listening to the bawdy lyrics.

He didn't spare her a glance as he expertly worked the ground. "Hmm, too bad. Pubs don't agree with me. So I'll just have to sing here."

She tilted her head to one side. "Is it the pub or the liquor that doesn't agree?"

"What do you think?"

"How long have you been away from it?"

"Two years."

She knelt beside him, curious. "Were you a mean drunk?"

"I'd like to think not. I'm sure others may have a different opinion."

"So you haven't worked here long then?"

"I have."

She furrowed her brows. "Even when—"

"When I was drinking? Yes. I never let it affect my work." His voice fell. "I just let it destroy everything else."

She felt his sadness and thought of the man who'd

burned down her aunt's flower shop. She wondered if he regretted what he'd done, if he even remembered it.

"Braxton was good to let me work for him."

"I'd like to work for you."

He scratched his head. "Work for me?"

"Yes. I'd like to be your assistant."

"Why?" His eyes twinkled. "You have trouble with the bottle too?"

"No, I just want to help. I'm a good worker."

He looked her up and down. "You're certainly built for it."

"I'm built for a lot of things."

He ran a hand through his hair. "Too bad I'm too old to find out what other things."

"You're never too old."

He pressed a hand against his chest and bowed. "Flattery is the key to everything, my dear."

She picked up a bag of mulch and dropped it next to him. "I know a lot about planting and I'm full of knowledge and you could—."

He held up his hand. "I don't need a resume. As long as it's all right with the boss it's all right with me."

"Mr. Braxton has no complaints."

She passed the afternoon with Foster, listening to his singing as she followed his pattern of planting, digging holes, and then tucking new plants into the ground. They discussed the structure, and which plants would fit where. He showed her several garden diagrams and talked of the upcoming contest, sure they would win. Although pleasure filled her time in the garden, however, she sensed something was wrong. Because she couldn't identify the cause of her uneasiness, she dismissed her concerns and worked into the evening.

Prescott glanced at the newspaper article and laughed. Accidental fire. Perfect. He knew starting it in the kitchen was the best. Yep that pile of crap needed to be burned, and it had burned beautifully. He'd done the owner a favor. At least the owner would get his insurance claim and perhaps he'd learn to build a better structure next time.

Prescott pulled his eyebrow thoughtful. Perhaps he could call and offer to help. Wouldn't that be a nice turn of events? A contract like that would be great. There was always the upside to destruction. Something needed to be rebuilt.

"I didn't call you over here to read," a raspy voice said. "What do you think?"

Prescott turned his attention back to the window he'd measured. The old woman beside him wanted a built-in window seat. "I think it's definitely doable."

"How much?" When he told her the estimate she scoffed. She turned her wrinkled face to him and narrowed her eyes. "That's a damn rip off. You're all crooks."

He calmly listened to her tirade. She was old and frightened. She lived alone with no family, except a little dog, and probably couldn't afford him. She probably lived on a government check every month. Maybe she even invited contractors over just to have some company. Sad how society threw old people away. Either shuttling them into nursing homes or leaving them in crumbling old buildings like this.

Her house needed a lot of work, work she couldn't afford. She shouldn't suffer because of that. He'd do her a favor and make it all go away.

Grant tapped the carton of cigarettes inside his jacket pocket with relief as he stood near the interview room at the ATF office. Ms. Warren had finally decided to come out of hiding or grace them with her presence whatever was right. He watched her as someone handed her coffee. An older good-looking woman who carried her age well, she had her sister's blonde looks, but with a more sophisticated air.

He glanced at Melinda and could see she didn't trust the woman. He didn't care about trust; he just wanted some answers. It was his turn to go into action. She and Robert were good at investigation, but interrogation was his territory.

"Try not to drool," Melinda said.

He winked and tugged on the lapels of his jacket. "Don't be jealous." He shut the door in her face then sat down. He studied the elegant way Ms. Warren sipped her coffee as though it was in fine china instead of a plastic cup. He nodded toward the cup. "It's certainly not Blue Mountain, is it?"

She merely stared at him.

He sighed. She wasn't going to be easy to charm. "Thank you for coming."

"Did I have a choice?"

"You always have a choice. It's the consequences you

can't control." She looked at him with such condescension he wondered if he'd done something offensive. Perhaps he hadn't shaved close enough this morning. Then he remembered he was a cop and that usually offended a lot of people. "Do you have insurance for the level of loss you've incurred?"

"No. I'm insured of course, but I never anticipated something like this. I know that most of my customers have insurance, but I am responsible for those who don't."

"What do you store?"

She took a sip of her coffee. At the rate she was going, the coffee would last for days. He didn't blame her, the stuff was awful. "Many of my clients store excess merchandise. Or cargo waiting inspection by U.S. customs."

"You're custom bonded?"

She nodded, setting her cup down. "Yes, I have about twenty to thirty clients."

"Did any of your clients claim extravagant loss?"

"If you are suggesting someone burned down the warehouse for insurance purposes I think you're mistaken."

He shrugged. "It's possible."

"All my clients make their income through legitimate routes."

"What about employees?"

She crossed her legs and rested a hand on the table. "What about them? I have loyal, hardworking employees. They are family and friends of long standing. I select the best."

"So you haven't fired anyone recently?"

"No. I did my own questioning and no one saw

anything suspicious that night. There was the regular activity of transferring merchandise in and out, nothing more."

"We'd still like to get a list of people working there."

She paused a beat then said, "Fine."

"You're very successful in your business. Especially for—"

She raised a perfectly arched eyebrow. "A woman?"

"No, the kind of business you do. I didn't realize it was so lucrative."

"It can be if you run it well, and I'm good at business."

"Perhaps there is someone who could be jealous of your success?"

"No, I am well liked."

He wondered about that. Perhaps elsewhere she pretended to have a pulse. "Do any of your employees use two way radios?"

"No."

"Do you warehouse hazardous material?"

"Maybe a few drums of insecticide."

"Chemicals, oil, gasoline…" he suggested.

"No."

"Fertilizer, kerosene…"

"No."

"You're positive?"

Her eyes flashed with annoyance. "Is the word *no* a foreign term to you?"

He grinned. "Only when it sounds like a *yes*. So you know everything that is stored in the warehouse?"

"It is my business to know."

"Do you know how acetone is used?"

"No."

"So you're not aware that it could be used to process cocaine?"

Her face lit up with interest. "How?"

Grant left the interrogation room soon after. Melinda and Robert looked at him expectantly. Melinda spoke first. "Find out anything?"

"Yes, I thought island women were supposed to be hot. That woman could freeze a man's dick off."

"Anything about the *case*?" Melinda asked exasperated.

"Her eyes lit up when I said you could use acetone to process cocaine. She's either clever or naïve. She said she didn't know anything about hazardous materials."

"But there were jugs full in her warehouse," Robert said.

"I think she's lying," Melinda said.

Grant shoved his hands in his pockets. "I don't."

Robert folded his arms. "If she's not lying that means she didn't know."

"Right, so then the question is, who benefited?"

CHAPTER ELEVEN

Victoria sat in the kitchen with Dana, Janet, and Robert holding her week's salary in amazement.

"You can hold it to the light to make sure it's real," Robert said.

She ignored him, counting the money again.

"What are you planning to buy?" he asked her.

She glanced up at him. "I want to buy a headstone."

The corner of his mouth quirked up. "You're thinking of killing someone?"

She kept her gaze steady. "Only in passing. I need to buy a little headstone for a dog."

"You've been talking to Amanda about Bailey. His personal publicist. I'm surprised she hasn't created T-shirts with his photograph on it." He rested back and clasped his hands behind his head. "Has she drowned you with tales about that beloved dog?"

"She told me that he was your favorite," she said carefully.

"And so he was," he said nonchalant. "But now he's dead."

"Right, and you have Benjamin, but you ignore him."

He let his hands fall and briefly looked away uncomfortable with where the conversation was heading. "I'm a busy man."

"Too bad dogs don't understand such excuses. Unless of course you sat him down and told him about your life and work. He just thinks you don't care."

He met her eyes. "He has everything he needs."

"Except his best friend."

His jaw tightened. "His best friend is dead."

"I was talking about you," she said softly.

"I told you, I'm busy."

"You weren't too busy for Bailey. You scheduled to take him on trips and had him in your study. He was your constant companion."

Robert stared down at the counter. "And he's dead," he said in a rough voice.

"But Benjamin's alive. Don't punish him because you had to put Bailey to sleep. You're being cruel and cold, although that is not unusual, that won't bring Bailey back."

He pounded his fist on the counter and glared at her with such vehemence her throat closed. "You don't know anything about Bailey or me." He stormed out.

"Why must you push him so?" Janet asked, watching the kitchen door swing in and out. "You are going above your station."

"But I'm right," she said. Her words, though, sounded hallow and mean. She hadn't meant to push him. He had looked at her with those intense unreadable eyes and she'd assumed he'd felt nothing. He was an easy target almost daring her to fling an arrow at him and hit the bull's eye. He had every right to fire her and most likely would. Who was she to tell him how to live his life? Who was she to casually bring up old wounds and tell him how to heal them? Why had she felt the need to bring him to anger? She had always used her words as a shield or a weapon, but for the first time they brought her shame.

"I didn't mean to push him," she said.

"You'd better save that money," Dana said. "I won't be surprised if he gives you the ax."

Victoria wasn't quite sure of the words, but understood their meaning.

"I'm sure if she apologizes everything will be fine," Janet said.

"I only thought he should give Benjamin away if he doesn't want him."

"That's the problem with you. You have too many thoughts and have a terrible habit of sharing them. You must learn not to."

"Men don't like women with too many opinions anyway," Dana added.

"You mustn't—"

The three women grew quiet when Robert returned to the kitchen.

He walked up to Victoria and handed her a picture. "That's Benjamin when he first arrived."

She stared down at a picture of a pathetic dog that probably hadn't had a good meal in weeks, his ribs were showing, and his coat was dull and probably infested with fleas. She looked up at him. His eyes were filled with hurt more than anger.

"I took care of him," he said. "He was sick and I made sure that he received the best care. I have the bills to prove it. I bought whatever medications he needed, made sure he was well looked after until he became healthy. And all the while Bailey was getting sicker and sicker and there was nothing I could do." He took the picture and stuck it in his shirt pocket. "As you can see, Ben's still healthy and I continue to make sure that he's taken care of. He has toys to play with and plenty of space to run. So no matter how disappointing it is to you, I'm not a complete monster."

Shame made her eyes moist. "I know. I'm sorry."

"Good." He sighed as if a giant burden had been lifted. "We will leave in ten minutes."

"We?"

"Yes. I'll help you find this little headstone of yours."

She touched his sleeve before he could turn. "If you are going to fire me, do it here. You don't need to take me away and say it."

"I am not going to fire you." He shoved his hands in his pocket and offered the shadow of a smile. "I've been forewarned about Spenser pride. Fortunately, it's tempered by sympathy."

She bit her lower lip and let her lids slip over her eyes. "Then why do you want to take me into town?"

"Braxton vanity. I want to make sure you don't create a monument on my land."

"You really don't have to go through the trouble," Janet said. "I could take her later."

"It's no trouble," he said in a manner that closed the issue from discussion. "Go and get changed and I'll pick you up at your house." He turned and left.

The women stood silent.

Dana was the first to speak. "It's getting really eerie the way he hangs around in the kitchen."

"It's his kitchen," Janet said.

Dana turned to Victoria who was chewing her lower lip. "Are you really going to have a burial for Bailey?"

"Yes, Saturday morning," she said absently, still remembering the hurt in his eyes and the forgiveness that later replaced it. " It was Amanda's idea."

"It would be," Janet muttered.

"Bailey deserves it," Dana said. "He was a good dog. Perhaps I could make something special."

"Nothing fancy. It's just a dog."

"Anytime is a good time to celebrate with food," Victoria said.

She frowned at her. "Why are you still hanging round here? Shouldn't you be getting ready?"

Victoria reluctantly walked to the door. "I wish you could take me."

"Wishing is for wells. Get moving."

She raced to the carriage house, jumped into a pair of jeans and changed into three different tops then remembered it was just Mr. Braxton and chose a purple blouse. She was down the stairs by the time the doorbell rang.

Robert blinked at her when she answered the door. "That was fast. I expected to wait. Did you fly here?"

She closed the door behind her. "A woman has a right to her secrets."

"True."

She followed him to his car then stopped. "What kind of thing is that?" She knew he owned three cars, but never expected one to look like this.

"That's an SUV," he said, insulted.

No, it was a black metal monster with huge tires, chrome trim and massive doors.

"Good Lord," she whispered when he opened the door. She looked up into the gray interior and deep leather seats. She glanced around to find something to stand on so that she could get in without looking silly. When she didn't find anything, she grabbed the door and tried to push herself off the sideboard. She wouldn't have made it if Robert hadn't grabbed her waist and given her the extra boost. She sat down hard on the seat and shook her head. "Big garden, big house, big car. You like everything big, don't you?"

"I'm beginning to." He winked and closed the door.

The drive into town was shorter than she'd expected. The town of Maron was peppered with family named restaurants, boutiques and assorted specialty shops. Robert drove into Harlans' nursery.

"Need help getting out?" he asked after he had parked.

"No." She pushed open the heavy door and jumped down from her seat. She stared at the overflowing variation of garden ware and plants.

Robert began to go inside when a woman dressed in Harlan apron blocked their path. She sported a toothy grin and dyed hair as yellow as a hot butter. "Well, Robert, we haven't seen you here in a while." She looked at Victoria. " And who's this? Aren't we pretty?" She looked up at the sky. "Wow! It's a great day for planting, isn't it? So what are you planning to do? Do you have a special project? Is there anything I can help you with?"

He took Victoria's arm and led her away. "No, I'm just looking, thanks."

"Why didn't you tell her what we were looking for?" Victoria asked, trying to keep up with his quick pace.

"Because starting a conversation with that woman is always a mistake if you plan on leaving before tomorrow."

"She seemed nice enough. Very interesting."

"It wears off after a couple hours, trust me."

He led her to the garden statues where there was a large selection of gnomes, posing cupids, and dolphins in flight. Victoria saw him heading towards a troll.

"Don't even smell it," she warned.

Robert raised a brow but turned away. He picked up a stone instead. "Here we are."

She folded her arms. "What is that?"

"What does it look like?"

"It looks like a rock. I can't go from a twig to a rock."

"We can put his name on it and it becomes a head-stone. Notice the word *stone.*" He waved the object.

"It doesn't look dignified."

"What are you looking for?" he asked dryly. "A marble slab with gold etchings?"

"No." She glanced around and found a long slab with a glazed surface. She pointed. "Something like this."

He shook his head incredulous. "You're willing to spend your entire salary on a dog?"

"No, of course not."

He covered his mouth to hide a grin. "Look at the price."

"I'm sure it can't be that much." She looked at the price and cringed. "Oh."

"Exactly." She looked so disheartened; he softened. "Okay, we'll split the cost." At her horrified expression he hastily added, " I mean you'll pay one third."

Even one third would be more than she'd be able to spend. "It was a silly idea. We'll go with your rock."

He put the stone down and picked up the slab. "It was a nice idea. Since Bailey was my dog I should pay for it."

"But—"

He rested a brotherly arm around her shoulders. "Let's argue after I've paid for it, all right?"

"I know I'll win," she said, debating whether to pull away or move closer.

Robert gave the slab to an etchist on the premises. The man sat in a little booth with samples of his work surrounding him.

"What would you like it to say?" the man asked, blinking at them through large glasses that magnified his hazel eyes.

Robert looked at Victoria. "You're the funeral director."

"Don't be facety." She looked at the etchist. "Bailey Braxton." She frowned at Robert. "What were his years?"

"1985–2003."

"Put that, too."

"Is this for a dog?"

Robert folded his arms. "No, it's for a goldfish that live very long."

Victoria kicked him. "Yes, it's for a dog."

The man gave a low whistle. "Wow he lived a long time Probably about half the time you were married, right Who owned him first?"

"We're not—"

Robert covered her mouth. "I did. Bailey was my dog.

"I'm sorry for your loss. It will take me about an hou to finish."

Victoria moved his hand from her mouth. "Bu we're not—"

He covered it again and ushered her away. "Okay, we' come back," he said over his shoulder.

Victoria nudged him and he released her. "Why di you make him think we were married?" she asked onc the man was out of hearing.

"Because being engaged didn't sound as exciting."

She opened her mouth to respond, then decide there was no reply to such logic. She roamed aroun the shop instead.

She saw a row of red pansies. "Those would be lovel towards the east of the house next to the daylilies."

"Speaking of gardens…"

She knelt down and picked up a pot. "Were we?"

"Yes. I've heard you've been helping Foster witl the garden."

She glanced up guilty. "I hope you don't mind."

"Which is why you asked me first," he said sarcasticall "You were so eager to hear my opinion on the issue."

"Mr. Braxton, I—"

"Forget it. If I had minded you would have known by now. Besides, Foster could use your help. I want to win the garden contest not only because I hate losing, but if we win, it will be great exposure."

She stood. "Exposure for what?"

"Many of my garden workers have had to deal with various addictions and it is my personal theory that gardening heals the spirit. Winning a national competition will give credit to this theory and would be fantastic for me and for them. Especially Foster. It would do him good to receive acknowledgment for his achievements."

"But the garden looks lovely as it is."

"Ah, but nothing speaks like success."

"He has a lot of great ideas."

"Yes." Robert suddenly turned. "Let's go to lunch, I'm hungry."

Victoria looked at the SUV with a dubious expression.

He looked over his shoulder and grinned. "Don't worry. We can walk there."

They stopped at a little restaurant called Tina's Big Grill, walking into the subdueed murmur of voices and clink of silverware. They sat in a booth covered in pink vinyl located against the wall.

"The desserts here are great," Robert said, pushing away the menu. "Would you like a banana split?"

"No, I like mine whole."

He laughed. "No, not a real banana. I mean it is a real banana cut in half but...never mind let me order it for you. You'll be in for a treat."

When the dessert arrived, Victoria stared stunned by

the sheer size of it. Scoops of chocolate, vanilla and straw-
berry ice cream sandwiched between a banana that had
been halved, piled high with whipped cream, nuts and
cherries. She stared at it for so long, the ice cream began
to melt and drip onto the table.

Robert reached over and shook her shoulder. "You're
supposed to eat it."

"It's so beautiful."

He picked up her spoon. "It also tastes good."

"Could you eat all this?"

"Sure." He dragged the bowl towards him. "Want me
to show you?"

She pulled the bowl back. "No." She took a
spoonful and shut her eyes in ecstasy as the sweet
tastes engaged her senses. No Jamaican snow cone
could compare with this.

"Is it good?" he asked, reaching for a taste.

She slapped his hand away.

He rubbed it, feigning hurt. "I'll take that as a *yes.*"

After a few more spoonfuls, she allowed him a taste and
he gave her a sip of his milkshake. Then they fell into a
conversation about the desserts they've had and those
they would like to try.

"Robert, it's been a long time." An attractive woman in
a soft gray linen suit approached the table.

Robert glanced up and held out his hand. "Lilah."

She slid into the seat next to him, wearing such a
strong perfume that Victoria sneezed. Robert blinked
to keep his eyes from watering. "I read your latest book
and thought it was fabulous. I totally agree with you

crusade to change the view of arson investigation. I recently attended…"

"This is Victoria Spenser," he interrupted, gesturing to her.

The woman glanced at her and shook the tips of her fingers. "A pleasure." She turned back to Robert. Her dismissal subtle, but poignant.

They began a conversation while Victoria finished her banana split, which suddenly didn't taste as heavenly. She struggled not to let her spirits fall. She had no idea what they were talking about and hated the feeling of not belonging that stole her joy. She watched Braxton as he tried to explain his opinion in large foreign terms and remembered that she just cleaned his house and worked in his garden. The few hours she had spent with him had caused her to forget that. They had made her forget that they weren't equals.

"Thank God," she heard Robert mutter. She looked up and realized the woman was gone.

She glanced around the restaurant then at him. "Where did she go? What happened?"

He stirred his milkshake. "A miracle apparently. She received a phone call and had to leave." He shook his head in wonder. "Every time I meet that woman I'm convinced that she's an imbecile and she always confirms my theory."

Victoria swallowed a spoonful of ice cream to keep from smiling. "She sounded intelligent to me."

"Probably because you couldn't understand a word he said. Unfortunately, I could and found nothing of importance to salvage. The only thing that saves her from being a social outcast is that she's pleasant to look at."

Victoria rested her elbows on the table. "So you wouldn't give an ugly woman the time of day?"

"No."

She stared at him appalled. "That's dreadful."

He shrugged, scooping up some of her ice cream. "It's a compliment to you."

"I'm not sure I trust your compliments."

"Be honest. Appearances count."

She frowned unconvinced. "No they don't. It's the inside."

"One of our long-lasting myths. Yes, on other deeper levels it's the inside that counts, but most people aren't deep. Would you rather take medicine from a spoon or a dirty palm?"

"It's not the same. You can't compare people to medicine."

"Sure I can. People are pretty much like it, something you endure."

She licked some ice cream off her spoon. "You don't like people very much."

"Does it show?" He gave a world-weary sigh. "And I've tried so hard to hide it."

"Strange profession you chose then for someone who doesn't like people."

"Yes, I know."

She rested her chin in her hand. "Why did you choose arson investigation?"

He thought for a moment then began to smile. "You won't believe me."

"Try me."

He lowered his voice as if sharing a secret. "Because I want to know the answers to things that at the surface seems unexplainable. My major originally was psychology."

"Why?"

"I needed answers."

She leaned forward. "To what?"

"To why we are the way we are. Why certain systems never change. Why we continue on a path of destruction though we have the answers to avoid it."

"Did you ever find the answers?"

He shook his head. "No."

She let her hand fall. "No one can know everything anyway."

"I can try."

"And fail."

"Not necessarily."

She let the subject drop and they finished their desserts. Later they picked up the headstone and returned to the house. Victoria saw Foster staring at the garden with hollow eyes. She ran up to him; Robert followed.

"What's wrong?" he asked.

Foster covered his eyes and shook his head. Behind him the answer was obvious.

The garden was dying.

CHAPTER TWELVE

The once flourishing garden bed looked like a tiny war zone—skeletonized leaves, wilting branches, and flowers losing petals but still persevering, like a smile with missing teeth. Other flowers lay prostrate on the ground like stricken soldiers.

"It's an infestation of some sort," Foster said gravely. He stared at the garden and continued to shake his head. "But I can't figure it out. I was sure I did everything right."

Robert gave him a reassuring pat on the shoulder. "I'm sure you did, but Mother Nature, being a typical woman, is hard to figure out."

Victoria spoke up. "She's not that difficult. I think—"

Foster hung his head. "It's awful. All our beautiful babies, dead."

"Don't take it so hard. There's still plenty of time before the contest. We can dig up the most diseased plants and treat the others."

Victoria tried again. "I don't think—"

"That will be costly, won't it?" Foster chewed his li

anxious. "To get a whole new batch? My ideas were kinda big. I knew I shouldn't have made it so big."

"Cost is not a factor. You know that I am pleased with the design. You did careful planning. Remember the herb garden for the Sunshine Nursing Center? The residents there were thrilled."

"I was a man," he scoffed. "Those old biddies were just happy for the attention."

"I'm sure they enjoyed the garden as well. Your ideas are not the issue. What's killing the plants are."

Victoria cleared her throat. "I think—"

Robert squatted and stared at the damage. " I'll take a sample to get analyzed and figure out what the problem is. Once we figure that out we can go from there." He stood. "Don't worry, we haven't been beaten yet."

"I think I know what you have," Victoria said in a loud voice.

Robert frowned at her. "Why are you shouting?"

She lowered her voice. "I'm not shouting."

"Sounded like you were shouting," Foster said.

She rested her hands on her hips. "I wasn't shouting."

"You're shouting now," Robert said.

Foster sighed. "She's probably upset about the garden."

"Sure she is, but that doesn't explain why she was shout-
ng." He looked at her concerned. "What's wrong?"

She threw up her hands. "You two are impossible.
m trying—"

"Impossible? I've been called a lot of things, but
at's the first. I've always thought we were pretty easy-
ing guys. And considering our entrance into the

competition is dying and I'm not pulling out my hair is a good sign. I don't…"

And from there he began to speculate what was wrong with the garden. Foster added his gloomy predictions and they both ignored her. Victoria watched them then decided to do something to get their attention.

"Braxton, I really do feel bad about…" Foster's words trailed off as he stared at Victoria. Robert turned to see what had diverted his attention and nearly choked.

"What are you doing?" he said.

Victoria quickly buttoned up her blouse. "Now that I have your attention, I think you have a plant eating insect."

"What?" Robert asked a bit dazed, his mind still on what he might have seen if she'd completely unbuttoned her blouse. He wished he hadn't stopped her.

"I saw a garden that looked like this in Jamaica and my aunt said it was something, but I forgot the name. But it's this nasty little insect that feasts on anything. We'll have to get rid of the completely dead plants, bathe the leaves of the ones left, and use a special treatment for the soil. It is a clever insect."

"I've never heard of something like that. Have you?"

Foster shook his head.

"Besides, the bugs in Jamaica are not similar here. I'm sure once I have one of the plants analyzed I'll find a way to treat them."

"But I—"

"Thank you, Victoria." He handed her the headstone. "If you want to finish your striptease act I'll be happy to watch, but I've finished listening."

She snatched the headstone. "Fine."

He shoved his hands in his pocket and walked away.

Victoria glared at his back, wishing she could burn a hole through his shirt. "I could like that man if he wasn't so arrogant."

"He knows what he's about," Foster said, rubbing the back of his neck. "What's that you're holding?"

She glanced down at the headstone and held it out for him to see." It's for Bailey's funeral."

"I didn't know he was going to have one. He's been dead a long time."

"Amanda and I are putting it together. We're having one Saturday morning after breakfast."

"Oh." He bent down and lifted one plant, tearing out its roots. "I'm surprised Braxton is going along with it. He didn't want any fuss when Bailey died."

"He doesn't have much say in the matter. I doubt he's coming."

He twirled the plant in front of him then tossed it away. "He was a good dog. Benjamin misses him."

"You're welcome to come, if you want."

Foster lifted the head of a plant with the toe of his boot and nodded his head. "Thanks, perhaps I can bury my hopes as well."

Victoria went inside the kitchen to show Dana what she'd purchase, but saw Katherine instead.

"You look bright today," Katherine said with a light smile.

Encouraged by the smile, Victoria felt free to share. "I

had the most wonderful dessert I've ever had. I had a banana split. I've never had anything like it in Jamaica."

She sent her a cool look though her slight smile remained. "That's because you were poor, not because you're Jamaican. I think it best that you rid yourself of this childlike naiveté. Though American's will find it enduring, it gives a false impression. People will use your experience and apply it to others. You must see yourself as an ambassador and only show your strengths. I am careful to do the same myself for Barbados. Though most people hear a Caribbean accent and think Jamaica since your sort are everywhere." She glanced at her watch. "I'd better go. Good day."

"It was," Victoria muttered, hearing Katherine's heels click down the hall.

Clouds the color of dirty cotton stretched across the sky the morning of Bailey's funeral while a heavy fog settled over the lawn. Victoria wanted to be suitably somber so she pulled back her hair in a tight bun and dressed in a simple black cotton dress.

"This is nonsense," Janet mumbled to her reflection in the hallway mirror as she pinned on a hat.

"You don't have to come."

"I know that," she snapped. "You don't have fi tell me what I already know. Where's your shawl? It's chilly."

She fetched her shawl and the headstone then they left. They met Amanda at the willow tree. She wore a black lace dress and had two black ribbons on her pigtails. Ben sat beside her with a black bandana around his neck.

"Where are the flowers?" she asked.

"I bought a headstone," Victoria said.

"But we should have flowers. You're suppose to put flowers on a grave."

"We'll do that later." Victoria held out her hand and took Benjamin's leash. "Come on. Let's go."

The walk to the twig that marked Bailey's grave had the same disoriented feeling as a dream. Fog covered everything causing the house to disappear into nothing and surround them in gossamer gray. Slowly dark shapes formed in the distance like shadow puppets. As the fog cleared they saw: Foster, Dana, and Dana's assistant Trish all standing around the spot.

"You all came!" Amanda cried jumping up and down. "This is great." She saw Foster with a bunch of daffodils. "And you brought flowers." She gave a happy sigh. "Now everything is perfect."

"I brought muffins for after," Dana whispered, as if they were in a cemetery.

"We'll go to my place afterwards and have tea," Janet said. "Now let's get started."

Victoria was a bit vexed that her aunt was taking charge of something she and Amanda had thought of; however, she decided not to make an issue of it and allowed her to continue.

"I'm glad you could all come and give our friend Bailey a proper send off. He was in pain towards the end and knows that his forced sleep, though sad, was a blessing. Now would anyone like to say a few words?"

One by one they all said a quick word about the beloved dog that had roamed the property and had been a companion to each of them for over seventeen years. In closing, Foster replaced the twig with the headstone, and then there was a moment of silence. Amanda ended the gathering with a poem she had written for Bailey, then they all said their final goodbyes.

"It was a nice funeral," she sniffed. "I wish Uncle had come. He would have liked it."

"It might have made him sad."

Her brows fell together in a frown. "I never thought of him being sad. He didn't even care when Bailey died."

"Of course he cared. Everyone shows sadness in different ways."

"Then why—"

"Enough questions," Janet said, taking Amanda's hand. "We're going to the house to eat and give your mouth something else to do."

Victoria began to follow the group, but Benjamin wouldn't move. She tugged on his collar; he refused to budge.

"I'll be there in a minute," Victoria shouted into the fog where everyone had disappeared. She knelt next to the dog and hugged him. "Poor boy." She kissed him on the head. "You know what this is, don't you? But you mustn't be sad, Bailey didn't desert you, and hopefully soon your father will come around to know how special you are. Because you are special and we love you just as much." She felt the dog stiffen as if it wanted to run, but was stopping itself.

She looked up and saw a silhouette pushing through the heavy mist.

"Aunty. I said I'd be right there..." Her words faded as

the silhouette became more distinct. It was clearly too large to be her aunt.

Robert appeared through the fog dressed in a dark suit with a black hat. He took it off when he saw the headstone. He began to kneel next to it, but halted when he noticed her.

"I thought everyone had returned to the house," he stammered, straightening.

"They did, but I stayed here with Ben. He didn't want to leave."

"Oh." He toyed with the rim of his hat. "I just wanted to see what the headstone looked like."

"You saw it before. You were there when it was made remember?"

"I mean, what it looked like in the ground."

She wanted to tease him that he hadn't needed to put on a suit to do so, but he was already embarrassed to see her there so she decided against it.

"I'd better go." She stood.

"You don't have to leave because of me." He put on his hat ready to go.

"I'm not leaving because of you. I thought maybe…" *You'd like time alone,* she silently finished, but it was clear he would balk at such a suggestion. "Why don't we both keep Benjamin company for a while?"

"Okay." He looked down at the dog. "He misses Bailey."

"He misses you even more," she said gently. "Bailey's dead, but Ben's still here. Don't punish him because he wasn't your favorite."

"That's not why I—" He drew his lips in thoughtfully. "Granddad died the day I put Bailey to sleep."

"I'm sorry."

He pushed his hands in his pockets and rocked on his heels. "Yes, well, so am I."

She touched his sleeve. "You did the right thing."

He stared at the ground. "When I came back to the house Benjamin seemed so lost, roaming like a puppy. He'd spend hours waiting in the kitchen, Bailey's favorite spot, as if he expected him to return. And I couldn't explain things to him." He turned away.

"You're thinking too much."

He touched his hat in acknowledgment. "Guilty."

"And you're not telling me the truth."

He spun around startled.

"You're telling me part of it, but not all."

"Is that right?" he asked ironically.

"Yes."

"Stupid me." He slapped his forehead. "I spend all my life trying to find the answers and you have them all."

"I don't have all the answers. I just know what you feel."

Dark, dangerous eyes captured hers. "And what do I feel?"

She tugged on her earring. "You don't want to deal with the pain of burying Benjamin, so you shut your heart to him."

His anger died. "It's foolish to love an animal that much," he said in a rough whisper.

"Why? Bailey loved you more than any other person could. With an unconditional love that humans only have a fleeting understanding. He was with you through every thing. Every success, and every error, and he never judged you. He gave you a kind of loyalty that has no definition

He made you feel okay. I love animals for that. I'm always okay with them. I seem to make people nervous."

"Probably because you see too much. You seem to know everything about me."

"No I don't. I don't understand why you talk more about your grandfather than you do your father."

He shoved a hand in his pocket and stared at the ground. "For the same reason you don't talk about yours."

"You're ashamed?"

He glanced up. "No. It hurts too much."

"I know."

A gentle mist caressed her skin, enveloping her in a dream. In this dream the man before her wasn't her employer, but an ordinary man. And his eyes were no longer remote, but clear and beautiful and she felt the lingering ache in his heart, the memories that haunted him and something else. She felt an attraction that he tried to tame. An attraction that seemed to ebb and flow between them having no place to settle.

His gaze grew intense. She didn't remember him moving, but suddenly he was closer and everything else faded away. His lips brushed hers—light, tender, featherlike. But there was nothing light about the wild jolt that shot through her. When he pulled away, she ran her tongue against her lower lip. It still tingled from his kiss. They stared at each other neither daring to move as they stood at the edge of a bridge they dare not cross again.

Victoria lowered her gaze and took a step back; Robert grabbed her and pulled her to him. He kissed her, sending her inside spinning. Who they were didn't matter. All that mattered was this one delicious moment.

"Victoria!" Janet said. "Are you coming?"

Robert jumped back startled. He swore, Victoria stared at him then began to laugh.

"Victoria!"

She turned to the sound of the voice. "Yes, Aunty. I'm coming." She looked at Robert again her heart racing and covered her mouth to keep from laughing harder.

Robert scowled. "What's so funny?"

"You look as though you want to murder someone."

His voice grew soft, as his eyes raked over her body. "No, not murder."

Victoria abruptly stopped laughing seeing the smoldering desire in his eyes. She took a step back. "I'll leave you two."

He nodded. "Yes, I suggest you do." For a moment they didn't move, then Robert turned his back to her.

She walked away and glanced back only once to see the silhouette of a man kneeling beside his dog. Soon they disappeared into the gray of the morning. She touched her lips still feeling the taste of his. She licked her lips with a bit of unease, as the fog grew denser. She stumbled losing her way. Her chest began to burn as though smoke invaded her lungs, choking her. She felt heat suffocating her and held her hand out feeling disoriented. The smoke became black and thick. She couldn't breath.

She fell to the ground, desperate for air. Her hands and knees ached from arthritis and then Victoria knew she sensed an old woman struggling to find a way out of her burning house. The woman called to her dog knowing he was frightened too, desperate not to los her best friend. She called again. No response. She grew tired. The soft, wet grass touched her cheek as Victoria waited for the vision to end. It began to fade when a large tongue licked her face, and a damp nose pressed against her forehead.

She grabbed Benjamin's collar and pulled herself to a sitting position.

Robert knelt beside her and rubbed her back. "You're going to be okay. Breathe slowly."

Victoria squeezed her eyes shut. "She's in the house and she can't get out. It's too late, no one can save her." The image disappeared. The smoke dissipated and became fog again. The spirit of the woman was gone.

He helped her to her feet. "Let me take you home."

"Her dog should have alerted her, but he wasn't there." She gripped his arms and looked into his eyes pleading. "This was real, he killed her. You'll see."

The next day he did see. Robert watched the pathologist transfer the charred body of a seventy-year-old woman onto the stainless steel table. A body of blackened muscles contracted by the heat, smelling like a rotten steak. He prepared himself as the pathologist gathered tools to pry open the body. He no longer could deny that Victoria's vision had been real. Everything she'd seen made sense, except for the arson. This had been another electrical fire; however, the same thing that had bothered Victoria worried him. Nobody heard a dog bark, and no body of a dog had been found. Why did he get the feeling that the dog was the key?

* * *

Grant jangled his keys in his pocket and sighed. He wanted a cigarette. Bad. He hated buildings that didn't allow smoking. Most didn't nowadays. You could eat yourself into a coma, drink until your liver shriveled, but you couldn't burn your lungs every once in a while. Couldn't they at least have a room? He glanced around the table at Melinda and Carroll as they went over the warehouse case. The paper trail from the owner didn't lead far.

"So far no one's claiming the Hope diamond," Carroll said.

Melinda nodded. "And the lab confirmed that the area was soaked with acetone."

"And the company close to that area was Techno Technology. The owner is Hinda Haddad."

Melinda started.

Carroll looked at her puzzled. "What's on your mind?"

"The name sounds familiar." She tapped the pen against her cheek. "I don't know why."

Grant rested his chin in his hand, trying not to picture her pen as a cigarette. "Maybe 'cause it sounds like a terrorist?"

She glared at him angered by the implication. "That's not funny. My sister-in-law is Muslim."

He looked bored. "So is my uncle. So why don't you relax, woman? I was trying to lighten the mood. Everyone's so scared they don't have a sense of humor anymore."

"Making fun—"

He held up his hands in surrender. "Okay, forget it. You're beginning to make me feel guilty." He rested a hand on his chest. "I'm Catholic. Guilt's a hobby of mine. So is collecting rectory jokes. Want to hear some?"

"Your jokes are as bad as your attitude."

He straightened. "I think it's better than your—"

Carroll held up a hand. "Let's try not to get personal, okay?"

Melinda gritted her teeth. "Well he—"

Carroll sent her a warning look.

"All right."

"Now let's get back to the subject. For Techno Technology, business isn't good. They're up to their neck paying off borrowed insurance."

Melinda raised a brow. "That's interesting."

"But not criminal," Grant said. "They haven't made an insurance claim yet."

"We'll have to pay them a visit and see why not."

Carroll stood. "You two have to go. I've got to pick up something." He walked to the door, ran a hand through his hair causing it to stick up more then flashed a wicked grin. "Try not to kill each other."

Grant and Melinda sat and stared at everything in the room but each other then Grant slowly rose to his feet. "We'll take my car."

Melinda sighed and reluctantly followed him.

They drove a while in silence. Around them they heard the whirring siren of a police cruiser whizzing past, the loud horn of a passing truck and the roar of a group of motorcycles weaving between cars. Grant finally said, "I'll do the talking."

Melinda rolled her eyes. "Am I supposed to just sit here and look pretty?"

"Well, you can sit there. The pretty part is up to you."

She looked at him amazed. "Don't you think it's about time you got used to our presence around here?"

He lowered the window and rested an arm on the doorframe. "I'm used to it and I still don't like it."

"We're on the same side." She frowned. "You know you should have both hands on the wheel."

He raised his hands. "Would you like to teach me how to drive? I might have forgotten while crossing the parking lot."

Melinda lunged for the steering wheel. "Elliot! Stop it!"

He grabbed it and chuckled. "Will you relax? I've been driving for a long time. Besides there's no one around us."

"You should always be prepared."

"I am. That's why I wear a seatbelt."

Melinda folded her arms and turned away wondering why good-looking guys were always such jerks. Except for Braxton. There was a man she could understand. A man devoted to his work. Elliot always showed up as though he'd arrived at a party. Unfocused, flippant, ready with a stupid joke and a quick grin that for some reason always made her wonder what other things would put a smile on his face. Not that she allowed herself to entertain that thought long. Elliot didn't have Braxton's finesse, his sense of structure, or his background. She related to that. "Braxton doesn't mind our help," she said.

"Braxton isn't me."

"Yes, he's more mature."

He shrugged. "Probably. I'm still doing the talking."

She let her hands fall to her lap. "Fine. You're such a big baby."

Grant only grinned.

Hinda Haddad lived in a house with her niece, Raisa in a nice middle class neighborhood. For a business that was falling apart they lived in a house that a home and garden magazine would place on the cover. Grant knocked on the door.

A small, birdlike woman with streaks of gray in her dark hair opened the door. She looked at them curious. "Yes?"

Grant flashed his badge and introduced himself and Melinda.

She frowned. "Is something wrong?"

"We'd like to ask you a few questions."

"About what?"

"May we come in?" Melinda asked.

Hinda hesitated then moved aside. She led them to the living room. Grant saw a young woman hurry past. "Who's that?"

"My niece."

"We'd like to speak to her also."

Raisa came into the room with her head down, dark hair hiding her face.

"She's shy," Hinda said. "That's okay," he said.

She settled into the couch. "What is this about?"

"It's about the fire."

"I don't know much about the business."

Melinda and Grant looked at each other perplexed. Grant said, "But we have your signature on corporation papers and loan checks."

Hinda shrugged. "I was merely a puppet. My son, Josef

and his cousin Basam travel a lot and they tell me and my niece what to do and we do it. They are the clever ones. You must speak to them."

"We plan to," Grant said. He asked her some more questions that she politely answered. He soon realized that she was either very devious or ignorant. After Hinda answered another question apologizing for her lack of knowledge, Melinda lost patience. "Ms. Haddad it's hard for me to believe you know so little about the business when your signatures are on important documents."

She nodded keeping her voice calm. "Yes, but as I said we just follow directions."

"When can we speak to Josef and his cousin?" Grant asked.

"I don't know. They are away."

"For business," the niece added.

Grant tapped his pen against his leg. "How far away?"

Hinda shook her head, looking a bit lost. "I don't know. They often travel for business."

"When did they leave?"

Her eyes darted between them then fell. "I don't know."

"Please this is important."

She covered her face and burst into tears. "I don't know. I don't know," she cried. "Please no more questions."

Raisa held her aunt's shoulder and said sadly, "They've disappeared."

"When?" Grant asked.

Hinda rocked and cried. Raisa tried to soothe her.

"Was it the night of the fire?" he persisted. "Or early the next day?"

"I don't know," Hinda moaned, her hands fell into her lap. "I don't know."

"Did you file a missing persons report?"

"No."

"Why not?" Melinda snapped.

Grant pinched her in warning. "Is there a reason you didn't?"

"Because I know he will return. He will contact me when he has the chance."

Grant and Melinda left the house in frustration. In the car, Grant grabbed a cigarette. "Mind if I smoke?"

Melinda rested her head back and briefly shut her eyes. "No."

He rolled down the window, lit the cigarette and inhaled. "Well, that was a bust."

"Completely." She placed a hand on her forehead, fighting an oncoming headache.

"Why haven't they made that nice little insurance claim?"

"You'd think they'd be panting for a check like the other companies." She sat up. "I guess they're playing it cool."

Grant shot her a glance. "You weren't."

"I know." Melinda sighed with regret. "She was so polite and apologetic it drove me crazy. What happened to the woman's movement?"

"It missed her country."

"No, it's probably just me. I get too involved sometime. Especially times like this. I wanted some answers."

"Me too."

"We won't get anything more until they show up."

He stubbed out the cigarette and reached for another.

She frowned. "I've never seen a guy go through a cigarette so fast."

"I'm frustrated, okay?"

"You're also wasting money. You should try to make your cigarettes last. The best way is not to smoke them. What did you say?"

"Nothing you'd want to hear." He lit his cigarette. "Don't give me a lecture. I'm not in the mood." He took a long drag. "They're both gone. This was our last lead."

"Maybe one is dead and the other is in hiding."

"Or the fire wasn't about insurance, but cocaine."

"Or they're innocent and we're making something out of nothing."

"We've run into a brick wall." He fell silent. She looked so disappointed he wanted a way to cheer her up. "How would you like a drink?"

"Who's buying?"

He tapped his ashes. "A gentleman always buys."

"I know, but I'm asking you."

It was her tone rather than her words that made Grant pause with the cigarette to his mouth. Was she teasing him?

A smile tugged on her mouth. "Watch the road."

He moved his gaze from her face. "I am watching the road."

"You weren't before."

"I was distracted."

"Do you distract easily?"

"Not always."

She turned away. "So are you buying the drinks?"

"Yes, I'm buying." He stubbed out his cigarette, trying to sound casual. "I may even include dinner if you're nice."

She grinned. "What do I get if I'm not?"

Yes, she was definitely teasing him and he liked it. He sent her a sly glance. "I'll think of something."

CHAPTER THIRTEEN

All she wanted was a good story. One good story that would put her over the top. A story about heroes or a mystery solved or even a nice sex scandal. Something to get her back on track after she'd nearly ruined her career. Susannah rested her elbow on the restaurant table. The polished veneer felt cool against her skin. In the background the boisterous sound of laughter mixed with hurried footsteps as waiters dashed back and forth.

She groaned at the sight of the notes spread out in front of her. She didn't get juicy stories. All she got were break-ins, school board meetings, fires and a police department that gave her the regular spiel. Chief Braxton still wouldn't speak to her. Now if she were doing the gossip pages he would be an interesting story. Millionaire turned cop. She still remembered his highly publicized divorce to some artist who now lived in Europe.

Yes, Robert Braxton was an interesting character, which was one of the reasons she set out to get to know his assistant at one of her AA meetings.

She poured herself another drink; glad she'd escaped. Although she'd left the group years ago, she'd ended up with a great contact. Unfortunately, he didn't give her much to use. She had to try another tactic. She smiled when Foster approached the table.

He didn't return the expression, staring at her glass. "What are you doing?"

"Relax. It's light."

"You know you're killing yourself."

Susannah waved to a chair. "I already have a Dad. Now sit down."

"What do you want?"

"I want to know if you know anything about the warehouse fire or any of the fires recently?"

His blue eyes hardened. "I told you before. If you want information you need to speak to my boss. I only came to see how you were doing."

"You want to see how I'm doing? Look at me. I'm with the local damn news on a channel nobody watches. I need a story. A big one."

"You're a lot further than a lot of people."

"But not far enough. Just tell me something, anything. Anything juicy. I don't care. Something the public can sink its teeth into."

"I don't have anything."

"Have you thought about my book idea? We could write one together. You're near the action. I'm sure your boss tells you things of interest."

"He's my friend."

She took a long swallow of her drink, the alcohol

dulling any feelings of desperation. "And does your friend know why you started drinking?"

Foster stared at her then said, "Do you want to tell him yourself?"

"Dammit Foster." She threw up her hands. "Don't you know you're sitting on a goldmine?"

"He's my friend and you're not the first reporter who has wanted me to betray that friendship."

"Look, you work for the guy. So he gives you a nice salary, I doubt he considers you a close friend. You're an old, white, alcoholic, divorced, ex-engineer. Your career was shot to hell before he was even born. You've never even touched his level of success, let alone his money. What do you have in common?"

Foster began to stand. "If there's nothing else, I have errands to run."

Susannah ran a hand through her hair resigned. "Fine. Go run your errands."

He sighed. "I'd really like to see you at the next meeting."

She waved a dismissive hand. "I'll think about it. I'll make no guarantees. I'm so important I'll have to check my busy schedule." She laughed at her poor joke. "But I can guarantee you one thing." She lifted her glass. "If there's a story, I'm going to find it and you can't stop me."

Victoria tried to push away the memories of the kiss determined that it meant nothing. Unfortunately, she found herself thinking about it at the oddest times. Like when she was folding his laundry and would hold his shirt up and smell it and remember his lips pressed agains hers. Or when she cleared the dinner dishes and the scent of his cologne still lingered in the room. Or when she passed by his portrait in the great hall, knowing that the artist could have softened his look by making his eyes less hard, giving his jaw more tender brushstrokes.

But despite her imaginings she knew nothing had changed. At least Braxton didn't treat her any different and she didn't dare believe the kiss meant anything more. He couldn't be trusted. Hadn't Dana warned her? Hadn't she learned from her own experience in the past? She couldn't jeopardize her future because of a moment of weakness.

She was the housekeeper, he her employer. Nothing had changed except one thing. Benjamin no longer sat under the willow tree. Instead he followed Robert around the house. She had to remind herself not to do the same and buried herself in work. Then a red corvette roared up the drive, delivering two expected guests and shattered that routine. Victoria learned about their arrival when she found Amanda in the pantry holding a flashlight, reading a book and listening to music.

Victoria pulled off the earphones.

"Hey," Amanda cried.

"What are you doing in here?"

She jumped to her feet and closed the door. "They're here," she said in an urgent whisper.

"Who's here?"

"My cousins. I saw them come up the road and barely made it in here without being caught."

"You're going to have to speak to them sometime. You can't hide until they leave."

"I can try." Victoria was beginning to wonder if that was the Braxton motto.

"If I could, I would hide in the Safe Room, but Uncle told me never to go in there except in an emergency." She flashed an impish grin. "But once I did slid down the trapdoor and found out that it leads you right into the living room." She suddenly made a face. "But they like to sit in the living room so I wouldn't want to go there." She sighed. "Oh, well. You can stay in here with me if you like." She put her earphones back on.

Victoria took them off again. "Don't be silly. I doubt they're that bad."

"They're not bad—they're awful, horrible, and gross." She made a face. "I hate them."

"Shh, you don't mean that."

"I do to-o." She clasped her hands together. "Please don't make me see them."

"You can't hide in the pantry." Victoria pulled her out and closed the door. "Now get ready for dinner."

Amanda went to the fridge and took out bread, peanut butter and jelly and laid them out on the counter.

"What are you doing?" she asked as the girl searched through the drawers.

"I'm making dinner. I am not eating with them and you can't force me." She waved her hands exasperated. "Where's a knife?"

Victoria found a knife and handed it to her. "I wasn' planning to force you."

"Good." She quickly made her sandwich, grabbed bag of chips and a drink. "Could you make sure the coa is clear? *Please*," she begged when Victoria hesitated.

"Only this once." She checked the hallways. "You're clear."

"Thanks." With her stash in hand, Amanda raced to her room.

Victoria heard a few grumbles from the rest of the staff about the new arrivals, but did not see the notorious pair until the next day.

"They want breakfast in their bedroom," Dana announced when Victoria entered the kitchen.

She stopped. "I'm sorry?"

"You heard me. They want you to bring up their breakfast."

"I must have missed the sign saying that this is a hotel."

"That's what they want."

"I'm not walking up those stairs twice just so that they can eat in luxury."

"There's an elevator."

"If they're hungry enough they can come downstairs."

Dana waved a spatula at her. "Watch yourself, Victoria. These two aren't as nice as Mr. Braxton. You don't want to get on their bad side."

"I don't care. I set the table last night, as always, so that they'll come to a lovely breakfast. I will pour the juice, I will get the toast, but I will not be a servant."

"They won't come down."

"Then they will miss their breakfast."

A loud bell rang.

Dana smiled. "That would be Patrice."

Victoria gritted her teeth as the sound crashed against the walls. "She has a bell?"

"Yes."

"Well, she can ring it until her arm falls off."

Dana shook her head, but said nothing.

Janet came into the room. "What are you two doin[g] Are your mouths open so wide that you can't hea[r] Haven't you heard the bell?"

"She won't go," Dana said.

Janet looked at her niece and knew then that it was n[o] use trying to persuade her. Once a Spenser made up h[is] mind there was no changing it.

Janet smoothed the front of her apron and sighe[d.] "Very well then. I'll do it."

Victoria stood in front of the cupboard, preventing h[er] aunt from getting the trays. "You won't go either. We wo[rk] for Mr. Braxton. We keep his house clean, we make su[re] everything runs properly. We don't, however, respond [to] bells like dogs."

Janet sighed defeated. "You only cause trouble f[or] yourself, girl."

She lifted her chin. "Trouble makes you strong."

Katherine came in. "What is going on here?"

"We're working," Victoria said. "Yes, we heard the be[ll.] No, we're not going to answer. Any more questions?"

"You are paid—"

"Yes, I know what I'm paid to do, and it's not [to] answer a bell."

Katherine curled her lip with malicious satisfactio[n.] "You're a bad mix of Jamaican pride and American a[r]rogance. I hope your bags are packed. You won't l[ast] here long." She left.

Dana looked worried. "You know she might be right. Mr. Braxton is very protective about his family."

The bell stopped ringing after a few minutes. Soon after Patrice stormed into the kitchen draped in a pink silk robe and fuzzy high heels. Heated chocolate eyes blazed from a finely sculpted face.

"Have you all gone deaf?" she demanded. "Didn't any of you hear me?"

"Your breakfast is in the dining room," Victoria said quietly.

"I wanted it in my room. I rang my bell."

"Yes, we know. It seemed to make you happy."

She narrowed her eyes. "Who are you?"

"I am Ms. Spenser."

She pointed a manicured nail at her. "You'd better watch yourself or you might find yourself without a job." She spun away her robe trailing behind her.

"Keep your tongue," Janet warned.

"Listen to your aunt," Dana added. "If you mess with Patrice, you'll only end up with claw marks."

Victoria said nothing as she went through the kitchen doors. In the dining room she found a handsome young man poking at his eggs with a bored expression. He had the Braxton features, strong profile, dark piercing eyes, but whether he had the Braxton charm or not was yet to be determined.

"This food is cold," Patrice complained, pushing her plate away. "Tomorrow I expect to have my breakfast served in my bedroom."

"Then your food will be cold tomorrow as well."

She checked her nails. "If you plan on staying in this country long, I suggest you start being nice to me."

"If you plan on staying here long, I suggest you do the same."

"Is that a threat?" She rested a hand on her chest. "Are you threatening me?" She turned to her brother. "You heard that, right? She's threatening me. Wait until Uncle hears about this." She tossed down her napkin in a dramatic display and left, her high heels clicking down the hall.

"You're in for it now," Nicholas drawled. He bit into a slice of bacon. "Patrice in a temper is not a pretty sight for anyone who's not male."

"So I see."

He sat up and put his fingers together in a steeple. "Look, I'll give you a break because you're obviously new here. We like breakfast in our rooms. Preferably at 9:30."

Victoria smiled determined to keep her temper. "Okay, I'll show you where the trays are so that you can carry your food to your rooms."

"No, you don't understand—"

Her smile thinned. "English is not my second language. I understand you perfectly."

"I see." He sat back and studied her. "I bet Uncle didn' know what he was getting when he hired you."

"He got a housekeeper, not a servant. Fortunately, he' clever enough to know the difference."

She picked up Patrice's plate and left.

They came down to breakfast the next day and th mornings after that. That was a small victory for Victori who dreaded being sanctioned by Braxton. Unfortunately, their visit progressively got worse, only fueling the strength of her resolve. She refused to pick up Patrice's dirty clothes from off the floor, no matter how much Janet lectured her.

"I will wash the clothes," Victoria said. "I will iron the clothes. I will even hang up the clothes, but for no amount of money in this world will I pick up some grown girl's underwear."

"You think too high."

"Even Amanda isn't as filthy as her. She has a hamper yet I found her bra hanging from a lampshade. What does she do, fling them about the room?"

"Never mind that. Your job is to clean up."

"Right I clean up, not pick up. Whatever does not end up in the hamper doesn't get washed. Since their parents didn't train them properly we'll have to. When she has only dirty clothes left to wear she'll learn."

Her crusade to tame the shrew became a battle of wills. Patrice would toss an apple cord on the living room carpet; Victoria would smash the core into her pillows. Patrice would stain a cushion; Victoria would shrink one of her blouses.

Braxton called her into his office. Although Victoria had feared a reprimand she was still surprised by the request and went to his office with dread.

"Sit down," he said when she entered.

She did so, ready for combat. She hadn't been alone with him since the kiss and knew that the man who had held her so tenderly that grey morning wasn't sitting before her. The remote expression had returned to his eyes. In that moment, she let her foolish fantasies die. When Benjamin came up to her in greeting, she offered him a quick stroke then folded her arms.

Robert tapped his pen against the desk. He should have expected something like this. He'd known Nicholas and Patrice better than anyone and at times even he wanted to strangle them. But they were family and they were to be treated accordingly from his employees. "I've had complaints. Complaints are tiresome and break up my day, and I'm—"

"A very busy man," Victoria finished.

"Yes." He put down his pen. "I won't beat around the bush. Patrice has said that you've been rude to her."

She raised her brows in feigned surprise. "Oh, did she?"

"She says you won't obey simple requests."

"I obey two things: God and the law, and even that only sometimes."

He rested his arms on the table and kept his voice level. "Well the law of this house is that you make sure my guests are happy. Ms. Anderson has informed me that she has tried on many occasions to make that clear and you ignore her."

"Do you expect me to make your guests happy by picking up after them and bowing to them like a servant? No, Mr. Braxton, I will not."

His jaw twitched. "Are you defying my orders?"

"Are you making them?"

His voice dropped and he lowered his eyes. "If you want to stay on my staff you will do as you're told. I have plenty of guests who come to stay and though I may enjoy your occasional sharp remarks, I know others may not find them so amusing. I cannot afford to have someone who insults my guests."

She leaned forward her eyes blazing. "Why is it insulting to ask for respect? I have the table set. I wash the clothes. I clean the kitchen. I clean the sitting room and tend to the garden. I'm a housekeeper. I may not dress in a suit, but I will not pick up after someone who leaves trash on the ground or who tosses their dirty clothes all over the place."

His eyes met hers. "My niece's habits are not the issue," he said sharply. "Your behavior is."

"There is nothing wrong with my behavior."

"You need to learn to hold your tongue in the presence of those above you."

Fury almost choked her. "Above me?" She repeated unable to believe the words.

"Most systems have a hierarchy. Think of this as a corporation. I'm the CEO and you're a worker. Patrice and Nicholas are managers. Therefore, their situation is above you. She is family which means—"

"She is more important to you than me."

"Don't put words in my mouth," he snapped.

"How could I?" She leaped to her feet. "You have plenty of your own."

His eyes hardened. "Sit down."

"I won't—"

"I said sit!"

She dropped into her chair and crossed her legs. "Are you sure you wouldn't want me to kneel or perhaps I could—?"

"Stop it Ms. Spenser," he said with a thread of warning.

"You may hit your target, but are you prepared for when I fire back?"

She turned away.

Robert took a deep breath. "You can't live by your own rules. Every system needs order. For order to exist there must be compliance, compromise, and—"

She glared at him. "Compassion? Or is that what the generous salary is for? To compensate for the lack of it."

"You're treading on dangerous ground, Ms. Spenser."

"Only because you pushed me there, Mr. Braxton."

"Because you force me. Why do you fight me every step of the way? Everything is a battle with you. Can't you meet me halfway? I am making a simple request. I want you to behave in the manner I pay you to."

She gripped the handles on the chair to keep from jumping up. "I know she is your niece. I know that family is important. I know I'm just a housekeeper that I mean nothing to you." She bit her lip ashamed that she had revealed the pain in her heart. She glanced away, gathered her emotions and began again. "After my parent's died I haven't been important to anyone. So I have to be important to me. Yes, she is prettier. Yes, she is richer. She may even be smarter, but the day I consider a dirty, spoiled, *hitey titey*, overgrown girl above me, is the day the river turns to sugar."

"She's above you in station, not in worth."

"But the treatment is the same."

Robert spoke softly, though his own temper was read to snap. "I respect your opinion, but where would I be if have no control over my staff? If they offer no respect t the orders I give them? This is my home. I've made m position clear. I give orders and I expect them to be followed. I create the laws of the land here. My land. Chaos ensues where rules are ignored. If someone can't abide by my rules I invite them to go elsewhere."

Victoria held back tears. She was being fired. All that she had become used to, her home, her job, and the staff was being taken away from her. She wasn't surprised. Somehow it all seemed too good to be true. She could sense his frustration and knew the only option was to leave.

She could relent and bow to the whims of Patrice, but her pride would not allow her to do so. Wasn't it the same at Uncle William's house where her cousins taunted and teased her mercilessly and she had to endure? As a child she had no choice. She was a woman now.

She clasped her hands in her lap to keep them from trembling. She fought the tears tightening her throat. "Thank you, Mr. Braxton." She kept her eyes lowered. "I understand now."

Robert visibly relaxed, relieved that all signs of temper had gone. He was glad that he had gotten through to her. 'Don't worry. They shouldn't be here too long."

Victoria nodded then left. She walked down the hall feeling numb, feeling the weight of defeat. She saw Nicholas and Patrice sitting in the living room. Patrice looked up at her and smirked as she let some cigarette ashes drop on the floor. Her numbness left her as fury took hold. No, she couldn't stay in this house where she was below such a dreadful woman. She stormed through the kitchen to the exit.

"Where are you going in such a rush?" Janet asked.

"I'm leaving."

"Why?"

She shoved open the door. "Because he fired me."

"Good," Katherine said.

Victoria halted then marched up to her. "You may lift your nose, but your head only reach high enough to touch their bottom and do this." She kissed the air.

Katherine gasped. "Don't you—"

"You think because you act like them that you are one of them." She wagged a finger. "Don't fool yourself. You work here. You could lose your job as quickly as I could. That makes us equal."

A cool smile touched her lips. "No, we are not equal. As you can see I still have a job."

Victoria spun on her heel and left.

"Wait!" Janet cried.

But she didn't slow down. She marched to the house with building anger, brushing back hot tears.

"What happened?" Janet asked when she entered Victoria's room.

"He said they're above me." She pulled a suitcase from under the bed. "How could that woman be above me?"

Janet sat on the bed her voice sad. "For all the obvious reasons."

She flung open a closet. "Well then, let me find my kind. I'll make a living with the rest of the bottom feeders."

"You're just in a temper. Give yourself time to cool down. I'm sure if you apologize for whatever you said he'll give you your job back."

"A Spenser doesn't grovel."

"Nor do we spin gold, child. How will you live?"

"I'll find work." She tossed some shirts in the suitcase. "I'll see if the nursery in town needs hired help. I'll work as a waitress, I'll clean gutters, but I won't work here."

"This is a great place to work."

"How can I work at a place where I'm expected to kiss the very feet that kick me? I've done it all my life. I won't do it anymore."

Janet grabbed the iron bedpost. "You can't afford your pride, Victoria."

She opened her drawer and began taking things out.

"You're young and you'll soon learn that we are all given positions in this world. You can't think yourself too high. I kept my thoughts to myself and attained this house, a car, a good income, and the ability to send money back home."

"I want to do that too, but not like this. I don't belong Aunty. I never do. No matter how hard I try. I always cause trouble." She stuffed her suitcase. "Will you drive me to town?"

"Victoria, please."

She took her aunt's hands and sat on the bed, feeling the heaviness of her aunt's sadness. It compounded her own. "I admire you more than anybody I've ever known. You've been in my life for a short while, yet you fill the majority of my heart. You took me in when no one else would. You were the first to treat me like family, to give me a home and work. You didn't make me feel bad. I thank you and I will live in this world with the hope of making you proud.

"But all my life I've been told I'm less than because of

something I can't control. Is it wrong to ask to be treated with a little dignity? Because we are small does that give anyone the right to crush us? No money is worth my self-respect." She kissed her aunt's hand. "I will survive. I always have."

Janet hugged her and whispered. "Please don't leave. The house will be empty without you."

Victoria drew away glancing at her room. She'd hate to leave the safety of this. "Perhaps I'll just work in town. I could use the car and come back and forth and if I can't find anything in town... I'll find something."

"Finding work isn't that simple." Janet stood and went to the door. "We will talk more tomorrow. Perhaps you'll think more clearly in the morning."

Victoria sat on the bed and whispered, "I'm thinking clearly now."

Janet left that evening. Probably for church, she didn't say where she was going. Victoria lay on the couch and stared at the ceiling, repeating all that her aunt had said, but Braxton's words forced them into the background. He was like her Aunt Margaret, who saw her as a worker rather than as a person. All that time she had spent with him, sharing dessert, speaking at Bailey's gravesite, had been an illusion.

Victoria closed her eyes ashamed she was foolish to believe it could be anything else. She had barely finished secondary school; he had advanced degrees. He'd been born into money and privilege; she couldn't even claim her father's name.

"She doesn't even look like a Spenser," she remembered her grandmother telling her mother. "Too much of that Taylor blood. Did I not tell you not to run off with that man?"

"Yes, Mummy."

"And now you're back here and want to give his child our name?"

She nodded. Her mother could give her the name, but needed it to be recognized by other family members.

Victoria recalled her grandmother's long fingers as they grasped her chin. The older woman peered into her face. "It's not your fault your mother slept with the devil. You'll never be anything, but at least you'll have a good name."

Victoria opened her eyes. Yes, she did have a good name. And although she tried to live up to that name, she continued to fail. Spenser pride. Yes, she knew the Spensers had their pride, but she knew hers came from a dark place in her heart. A Taylor place.

She knew no matter the outcome she could not go back into that mansion with its cold paintings on the walls that mirrored the hearts of the people inside. She could not pretend that it didn't hurt when Nicholas or Patrice spoke rudely or when Katharine with her elegant manners and perfect diction would correct a phrase or word she said. Yes, she needed to leave that house and everyone in it—especially him.

Braxton, Braxton, Braxton. Why couldn't she get him out of her mind? Why did what he thought of her matter? He did not see her as important and he never would. She didn't blame him...sometimes she didn't feel important. He probably still thought she was crazy.

He hadn't mentioned anything about her vision. She discovered she'd been right by watching the news. It didn't matter. Nothing mattered.

Victoria wrapped her arms around herself. She fought the familiar feelings of loneliness and rested her head on the couch. She drifted off to sleep.

She jumped when someone pounded on the front door. She looked through the peephole then opened the door surprised to see Robert standing there. "What do you want?" she asked.

He blinked. "What do you mean what do I want? You called me."

"No, I didn't."

"Yes, you did. I heard you. You called me three times."

She rested a hip against the doorframe. "No, I didn't."

His voice grew insistent. "Yes, you did."

"Did anyone else hear me calling you?"

"I don't know. I haven't spoken to anyone." He rubbed his forehead. "You called me. If you've forgotten the reason why, that's fine. Why are you looking at me like that?"

"I didn't call you." She straightened. "But I did think about you."

He nodded. "You thought about me then you called me. I understand."

She shook her head. "No, I just thought about you."

His face changed at the implication. He took a step back and held up his hands. "Oh no. You can't pull that stuff with me. I have absolutely no psychic abilities. You're the empath not me."

"Then why are you here?"

"Because…" He shook his head frustrated. "Look, I know you're upset. Why do you want to leave?"

Victoria began to smile. "If you haven't spoken to anyone how did you know that I was leaving?"

Robert thought for a moment then waved his hand as though brushing the thought aside. "It's a simple deduction that's all. However, that's not the point." He rested a hand on either side of the doorframe. "Why are you upset? I thought we'd come to an under-standing."

"We had."

"Then why are you leaving?"

She turned. "Because you gave me no choice."

He came inside and closed the door. "I gave you the choice to obey a simple order. But you have such little respect for me that you can't even do that."

She stared at him surprised. She'd never heard that tone before. She'd heard him angry, demanding, but never with such sad bitterness. "I do respect you, but I can't stay." She shrugged not knowing what else to say.

"Don't leave because of this. They won't stay forever."

Victoria suddenly felt tired. "It's not just this. It's everything." She walked to the stairs. "Everything I do is wrong and everything I say is wrong. Nobody believes me. Now good night." She walked up the stairs.

"I believe you." The words, softly spoken, shot through the room as though he'd shouted them.

She spun around. "What?" She took a step toward him then stopped. "What did you say?"

"I said I believe you."

Victoria gripped the front of her blouse and sat down

hard on the stairs. Disbelief made her legs weak while an unbelievable joy filled her. "You do?"

"Yes." Robert glanced away and grasped the newel post as though searching for words. "There was a fire and an old woman died. And all the evidence says accidental, but something bothers me. Everyone says she had a dog, but I don't know why the dog didn't bark and a body of a dog hasn't been found. So I'm thinking that it was a cleverly set up arson, though I can't figure out why, since she had no money or anyone who'd want her dead." He waved his hand exasperated. "And I have all these questions and if you leave…" He faced her again. "I'll have nothing."

"You believe me," she said, treasuring the words. She covered her face, wanting to cry, but too stunned to do so. "You really believe me."

"Yes." The corner of his mouth kicked up. "Would you like me to write it down?"

She let her hands fall as a sense of caution entered her joy. She had to be careful. She stood then took a step toward him. "Another man once said he believed me and I thought all my dreams had come true. He made feel special. Finally someone in this world believed me. Believed *in* me. Someone who thought I was a good person. But it was just a trick. He wanted to see what I was like. He found out." She hugged herself remembering his cold touch and cruel words. "I think he was disappointed." Her lips twisted in a cynical smile. "I'm glad."

"And you think I'm like him?"

"No, you never pretended to believe me and that' what makes you different and why I can't believe wha you've just said." She looked at him, weary. "Or maybe I'm afraid to."

"You don't have to be afraid of me."

"I think you're more dangerous to me that he was."

"Why?"

She couldn't tell him why. She couldn't admit the reason to herself. She'd been vulnerable to the emotions of others for so long, but never this vulnerable to her own.

He spoke in a whisper. "I want you to stay."

"But Patrice—"

"I'll handle Patrice. I can barely stand her myself." He leaned against the wall and stared up at her with a grin. "Remember when I said people are like medicine? Think of her as antacid."

"Actually arsenic comes to mind."

She expected him to smile. He didn't. His gaze intensified instead. "Please stay."

"I can't."

"Yes, you can."

Could she trust him? Dare she trust him? A man who confused her, but who she knew in her heart was a good man. She should leave, but wasn't ready to say goodbye... not yet. She took a deep breath. "Okay. I'll stay."

"Good."

Neither moved.

Victoria let her arms fall to her sides and turned.

"Don't," he said.

She glanced over her shoulder. "What?"

Robert walked up the steps until he stood behind her.

"I notice the house is quiet," he said his breathe warm against her cheek.

Victoria gripped the railing. "My aunt isn't here."

"I know." He spun her around and claimed her mouth. The feel of his lips again assailed her with unfamiliar feelings that gripped her as strongly as his hands did. Feelings of such exquisite desire filled her, she was almost ashamed to acknowledge them, but too enthralled to deny them.

His arms wrapped around her waist like a curling vine, yet she felt no fear. He was strong, he was fierce, but his mouth was too tender for her to fear him. She pressed her hand against his chest, whether to restrain herself or him she wasn't sure, but it only succeeded in exciting her as she felt his beating heart beneath her palm, racing as fast as her own. She drew back breathless. "Remember who you are."

His voice broke with huskiness. "You can remind me later."

He kissed her again, slipping his tongue into her mouth eager to taste every part of her. He groaned deep in his throat when she attempted to do the same. He knew he should stop, but couldn't. He had yielded to temptation, determined to understand his attraction to her, determined to find the answer that would stop his curiosity. His curiosity only grew. He'd touched her, tasted her, and held her only to realize that it wasn't enough. He broke away and took her hand. He raced up the stairs.

"What are you doing?" Victoria asked.

He didn't reply. Instead he darted into a bedroom.

He halted in the doorway as he surveyed the strict decor. "Oh no."

"This is my aunt's room."

He sighed with relief. "Good. I was worried for a minute." He backed out of the room. "It's sort of hard to make love with a picture of Jesus staring down at you."

"Come here." She pulled him inside her room. He closed the door with his foot, grabbed her wrist and pulled her close. He kissed her again—quick, but just as heated. She moaned deep in her throat as he pressed her tighter against him.

"Careful Mr. Braxton." She loosened his shirt from his trousers.

"My name is Robert," he growled. " You'll be saying it a few more times before the night is over."

She slid her hand up his chest, teasing a taunt nipple with her fingers. "Perhaps."

"And what might your name be Ms. Spenser?"

Victoria kissed the side of his throat and whispered. "Doesn't matter. Before the night is over you'll be too exhausted to say it."

"Is that a promise?"

She began to unbutton his shirt. "It's a guarantee."

They quickly shed their clothes and fell on the bed. Victoria saddled his hips while Robert stared at up at her. "At last I get to meet them," he said.

"Meet who?"

He lifted her breasts and kissed each nipple. "My new best friends." He sighed with pleasure and cupped them in his palms. "Now what should I call you?"

"You're being silly."

He playfully frowned at her. "Excuse me, Miss, but this is a private conversation."

"I don't think they'll mind the interruption." She buried her face in his neck and moved against him. He moaned. She gently nipped his earlobe. "Are you ready?"

"Don't I feel ready?"

She clasped the erection pressing against her thigh. "You feel great."

His voice deepened more. "Umm, we may have one problem."

She sat up. "What?"

"My little friend has forgotten his hat."

Victoria laughed. "And you can't enter church without a hat."

Robert frowned. "What?"

"Never mind," she said still laughing to herself. She jumped up. "I think I have something." She opened her closet and dug inside a bag. She returned to the bed and tore open the foil packet. "I borrowed my uncle's suitcase and found a whole bunch of these." She saddled him again. "His friend is always well dressed."

He stared at her appalled. "You want me to wear a condom you *found*?"

She lowered her gaze and slowly ran her hand up and down his erection as he had the orchid stem. "Would you rather go home?"

He snatched the condom from her, rolled it on then changed their positions. "No, I don't plan to leave anytime soon."

"Really?"

"In fact I think I would like to start a garden. Let me

survey the land." He skimmed his hand over her stomach. "I've never dealt with this much land before."

"Too much for you?" she challenged.

"No." His eyes caressed her as his hand descended. "So beautiful. Such rich land and soft grass." He ran his hand through her triangle of hair then opened the lips of her center as though peering into the petals of a flower. He stroked inside. "Yes, the land is rich and moist." He slipped a finger inside. Victoria writhed with gathering desire, remembering another time his finger had sunk into soil, feeling the sweet agony of her arousal.

Robert saw the passion in her eyes and his grew stronger. "I don't think I can wait anymore."

"You don't have to," she gasped. "Please."

"Time to plant." He entered her with a little less control than he'd planned and felt her wince. "Sorry."

"I think your tool is too big."

"Am I hurting you?"

She adjusted to him. "No, I just have to get used to you." She ran a hand down his thigh. "I thought all men were created equal. I think you just blew that theory."

"Is that good or bad?"

She placed a finger over his mouth. "Stop talking and let me find out."

She did. He stirred passion, her body exploding at his touch. "I didn't know you could do that with a garden tool."

"I know how to use mine."

She smiled and pinched his thigh playfully. "How many gardens have you made?"

He brushed his nose against her neck, inhaling her

scent. "I don't remember anymore." At that moment he couldn't think, but felt everything. He felt as though his skin was exposed—sensitive to every touch, every movement of the woman beneath him as though her feelings were also his own. He could feel the cotton sheets; smell the scent of wisteria outside her window. There was such fire in her, and it blazed past any darkness inside him.

"When my grandfather taught me about the birds and the bees. I think he left out flashpoint."

"What is that?"

"The temperature at which something will ignite. I think I'm on fire."

"Want me to put out the fire?"

"No, baby, just let me burn."

They both thought they would burn as their lovemaking intensified. Soon they had no energy to speak as their bodies said and did all that they couldn't. They collapsed panting, every part aching with ecstasy. Victoria rested her cheek against the sheen of sweat on his back. His heat threatened to meld her to him; she didn't care. "You can't stay here," she said, stroking his thigh.

"I know, but I like what you're doing."

"Me too." She cupped his bottom. "You're very well made."

"Thank you."

"You know there are other ways to start a garden."

He rolled onto his back and stared at her with interest. "Is that right?" He reached up and tenderly brushed his fingers against her jaw. "I'd be interested to find out."

"You're not too tired?"

"I'm in great shape, remember?"

Victoria opened her mouth to respond then heard the sound of a car drive up to the house.

They both sat up. Victoria stared at Robert panicked. "My aunt's home."

He swore.

They scrambled out of bed.

Robert frantically searched the room. "Where are my clothes?"

"I don't know. I have to find mine."

He grabbed his shirt from on top of the closet door. "How the hell did this end up here?"

"Who cares?" She tossed his trousers at him. "Get dressed."

He quickly buttoned his shirt. "I am."

She wiggled into her jeans then stared at him. "Why are you taking so long?"

He shot her a glance as he slowly zipped up his trousers. "Darling, there are certain things a man learns not to rush."

She turned away. "What are we going to say?"

He tucked his shirt into his trousers then opened the door. "Don't worry. I'll handle this."

Robert reached the bottom of the stairs just as Janet opened the door. She stared at him stunned. "Mr. Braxton. What are you doing here?"

"Talking to Victoria. I discovered she was upset and thinking of leaving. I gave her a reason to stay."

Janet looked at her niece. "I hope it was a good one."

Victoria bit her lip unable to look at him. "Don't worry aunty, it was the best."

CHAPTER FOURTEEN

Katherine stood at the second-story window in the corridor and saw Robert coming from the carriage house. She glanced at her watch and frowned. He'd stayed there a long time. Had he given Victoria two weeks notice? Very likely. He was a fair sensible man. He knew she'd need time to find another place of employment. Katharine prided herself on being discreet, but was too curious not to wonder what had happened between them. She met Robert as he came through the door.

"Is everything all right, Mr. Braxton?"

"Yes. Why?"

"I know Ms. Spenser left here in a hurry."

"She's okay now."

Katherine blinked in surprise. "Does that mean she's staying?"

"Yes." He walked past her.

Katherine listened to his fading footsteps trying to fight a seething anger. *She was staying!* Victoria was cunning, but she wouldn't succeed. She had overwhelmed Braxton and the man was too kindhearted to know that. She'd heard Victoria and Braxton talking before. Victoria obviously had impressed him with her unusual ability. But what had caught her interest was who her father was—is. Such knowledge could prove useful.

Katherine turned toward her room then saw a card on the floor below where Foster hung his jacket. She picked it up to return it then read the name. *Susannah Rhodes.* The reporter. Hmm. She felt her anger subside. This could prove interesting. She pushed the card into her pocket. Victoria needed to go. She was such an uncouth young woman.

Katherine wrinkled her nose in distaste. She'd once seen her covered in mud laughing with Foster and talking to the gardening crew as though she were one of them. Most of them were foreigners with few English skills. Heaven knows what she could find to say to them.

Dana had also fallen under her spell. She'd spotted Victoria teaching her a new recipe and the girl always entered the kitchen with awe, as though she'd never seen it before. But what really concerned her was Amanda. Amanda thought Victoria was wonderful and blew into her flute determined to one day play exactly like her. Katherine doubted her mother would approve Amanda having such a role model.

She certainly didn't. Victoria had ambitions. Her kind usually did and Katherine knew Victoria was not good for r. Braxton. Since he didn't know that, she would have show him.

Katherine went into her room and closed the door. She

picked up the phone. When Susannah answered, Katherine said, "I think I've got an interesting story for you."

"Come on," Janet urged the next morning. "Why are you taking so long?"

Victoria sat at the breakfast table paralyzed. She'd never felt so alive, so refreshed. She'd slept so soundly. Yet how could she see him again after last night? How could she pretend that everything was the same? That he had not held her in his arms, that she had not invited him inside her? She took a deep breath. She would have to. She had to face him as her employer, Mr. Braxton, and nothing else. She had to remember who she was—who he was.

"Victoria!"

She leapt to her feet. "Yes, Aunty, I'm coming."

A wave of relief mingled with disappointment when she learned Braxton had left early. Delight replaced her disappointment when she the look of shock on Patrice's face at breakfast.

Patrice dropped her fork, causing scrambled eggs to fall in her lap and gaped at her. "What are you doing here?" she demanded.

"You would think the uniform made it obvious," Victoria said.

She glared at her determined to make Victoria's days as miserable as possible. She piled up her hamper with clothes, both dirty and clean; demanded that each side order be put on a separate plate; and had her polish her shoes—twice. Victoria worked as if Patrice were the most generous and pleasing guest she'd ever encountered.

Complimenting her on her clothes, her sense of style, and praising her kindness. This only irritated Patrice even more, so she sought to anger Victoria by attacking her vanity.

"You know you really should do something with your hair," she said, watching Victoria clear the dinner plates. She lit a cigarette and took a drag. She exhaled and watched the smoke drift up to the ceiling. "You have so much of it and it really doesn't do much for you. Your face isn't pretty enough to carry it off. Since you're so big, you end up looking like a mushroom." Patrice watched her out of the corner of her eye. Victoria appeared unaffected so she continued. "I would suggest my hairstylist, but you wouldn't be able to afford it." She tapped her cigarette against the ashtray. "I'm going to get rid of my wardrobe. Everything in it bores me. I've already had it for a year. I'm thinking of donating it. My mother can't believe how generous I am, but I love giving to charity." She pointed the cigarette at Victoria. "I would give some of my dresses to you, but unfortunately you don't have the figure for it. I have this gorgeous silk dress, but it you wouldn't be able to fit it."

"Yes, pity. I would have been able to fit it when I was twelve."

Patrice narrowed her eyes. "There's no need to be jealous."

"I'm not."

She walked up to her and poked her in the shoulder. "You'd better be careful. Family means everything to Uncle Robert. I don't know what you did to persuade him to let you stay, but let me tell you, he can get that on a street corner."

Victoria lifted a knife and let it glint wickedly in the light. "You can also find dead bodies there, so don't tempt me."

She backed away. "You're crazy."

Victoria ran her thumb over the edge of the blade. "Yes, I've been accused of that before."

Patrice raced out of the room.

Victoria found solace outside. She loved getting out of the house to work in the garden with Foster. She also learned the names of other members of the garden crew that showed up once a week to maintain the lawn. She enjoyed listening to Foster sing his bawdy lyrics off key, and took the opportunity to bask in the still day with the sun's warmth coating her skin.

What truly excited her was the challenge of saving the garden. She imagined that they were two doctors working to save the life of a patient with a rare disease. They poured over books, asked different nurseries for advice, and went online to find the cause and a possible cure. Unfortunately, despite all their efforts, their patient continued to die. Each treatment became more expensive and time was running out with the contest only a month away.

Victoria thought the treatments were useless, giving the promise of miracles in long, foreign words, but only succeeding in disappointing them. She kept her thoughts to herself, not wanting to cause any more trouble with Braxton because many of the suggested treatments had come from him. She did try to convince Foster of her idea, but he wouldn't do anything without Braxton's say so.

Victoria fought feelings of frustration. She wanted to be a dutiful employee, but the task was becoming difficult; however, she continued to say nothing and did as told. As Foster grew more depressed, however, she worried that this set back might send him into a bar and into the waiting arms of a beer that would calm all the sorrow of losing his beautiful garden.

She had to do something to end the devastation of the garden and to revive Foster's hope. After a night of endless pacing and weighing all the pros and cons, she decided it was time to share her idea. It had been two days since she'd seen Braxton. She had to face that what had happened between them meant nothing. She had taken that risk and would have to deal with the consequences.

There was no reply when she knocked on his study door. She chewed her lower lip, knowing she still had the chance to turn back. But she opened it and peeked inside. Braxton was asleep at his desk, resting his head on his arms. Papers lay scattered around him, a mug of coffee sat near his elbow and a large volume sat open, hanging precariously off the desk.

Her heart shifted and she made a move to go to him then stopped herself. Benjamin lifted his head and wagged his tail. She raised her hand to knock then changed her mind and started to close the door.

"It's still dying, isn't it?" he asked in a muffled voice.

She wanted to lie and tell him that the garden was slowly responding to the treatments. She would have done anything to have it be true. But he had only to look outside and see that the garden was a disaster. She walked in and closed the door. "Yes, it is."

Robert didn't raise his head. "The man at the State Department of Agriculture Horticulture division said, if the treatment they recommended did not work, there was only one thing to do."

Victoria took a seat, clasping her hands together. She squelched the hurt she felt that he wouldn't look at her. She would be as distance as he was. At least something could be done with the garden. The garden. She had to focus on the garden. "What is it?"

He paused. "We have to dig up all the plants."

"Dig up *all* the plants?" her voice cracked in dis- belief.

"That's right. And create a new irrigation system, possibly import new soil."

"That is utter nonsense!"

He raised his head and stared at her, interest entering his sleepy gaze. "You have a better idea?" he asked doubtful.

She straightened. "Yes. I can solve this problem without doing that."

He rested his cheek against his hand, resigned. "How?"

She told him the solution. He stared at her for a moment, considered her statement then burst into laughter.

"It will work," she said, stung by his laughter." You've already spent too much money and we've wasted enough time."

He sobered, but his eyes danced. "And you think a

bunch of herbs and water will do the job scientifically tested pesticides couldn't do?"

"Yes."

"And if that doesn't work, what are we going to use? Pixie dust?" He laughed again.

She frowned. "I'm serious."

He rubbed a smile from his mouth. "So am I. I have some strange exotic insect that is feasting on my plants and you think a couple of herbs boiled in water will solve all my problems. Should I ask what type of cauldron you're planning to use?"

"What are you talking about?"

"I'm wondering how you plan to prepare your magic potion."

"It's not a magic potion. I don't understand what you find so unbelievable about my suggestion. Nature has its own defenses, but we usually forget about them. Most medicines are made out of herbs. Why are you so skeptical?"

"Because I don't understand it. I like things to have solutions that follow a logical direction. If you have aphids you spray with insectidal soap. If you have caterpillars you cut down and burn the webs. If you have, a fireblight infestation, you prune out, destroy infected stems, and spray with bactericide. Simple cause, simple solution."

"This solution is simple. I just need—"

Robert waved his hand. "Please don't explain it, it won't make sense to me anyway."

"So will you let me try?"

He shrugged impatiently. "Fine. Go ahead. If we

even place in this contest I'll walk around with a rose in my teeth."

"You won't regret it." She stood.

He rested his head back down. "That has yet to be seen."

Victoria reached out to touch his hair then jerked her head back. He'd made no gesture that anything had changed between them. She had to remember that. She wasn't important to him. Her heart twisted with pain then she straightened. She had no room for self-pity. It was okay. She'd taken a risk and didn't regret it. She would think about the garden. Only about the garden. That sad, dying garden. She turned to the door.

He spoke again before she opened it. "How are you?"

"I'm fine," she said without inflection.

"It's been a week, hasn't it?"

"A week since what?"

He winced. "Ouch. You really know how to wound a man's ego."

"Oh that. Only a couple days ago."

"Really?" He lifted his head and yawned. "Seems longer. My bed is just not the same anymore. I actually entertained the thought of kidnapping you."

She smiled.

"I'm not trying to be funny. I haven't been able to sleep."

Her smile fell. She'd been sleeping perfectly. The best she had in a long time. "What do you mean?"

"I mean I can't sleep."

Her eyes widened. "Oh no."

"Oh no what?"

Had she some how projected her feelings to him? That was impossible. She fell into a chair and searched for words. "Just...uh...that's not good."

"Yes, I know. The warehouse case has reached a dead end and I have two accidental fires that may not be accidental. I have this sense that something's wrong. That old woman's death bothers me. Why are you looking at me like that?"

She shrugged attempting to look innocent. "Like what?"

"As thought I have a fatal disease. I have had sleepless nights before."

"Of course you have." He looked exhausted. She hoped it wasn't her fault. "Besides not sleeping is everything else fine? Are you sure you're all right?"

He was silent so long she wasn't sure he would answer her. "I just came back from taking Nicholas and Patrice out."

"I see."

"You'll be happy to know that after a rather long discussion, Patrice has decided to leave."

She tightened her fists to keep from jumping for joy. "Oh."

He glanced at his watch. "I have about a day before the phone starts ringing and my brother asks me what I did to upset his little girl. That would be my eldest brother, Timothy, the lawyer who can badger anyone until they wished they were in a coma. Patrice is DLG."

"DLG?"

"Daddy's Little Girl. He will find it upsetting that she's decided to leave. "

"I'm sorry."

He sent her a wicked glance, knowing she wasn't sorry at all. "Sure you are." He pushed his chair from the desk and held out his hand. The look he sent her told her she'd been wrong. Things had changed between them. "Come here, Victoria."

She jumped up and stood behind the chair. "I can't, Mr. Braxton."

"Robert," he said. "Just for a minute."

She gripped the chair. "I can't." Not until she could figure out what was wrong with him.

He frowned and came from behind his desk. "Why not?"

She backed away. "I have to go."

He reached for her. "All I wanted—"

She slipped out of his grasp and opened the door. "I have to go."

Victoria raced down the hall. When she saw her aunt, she grabbed her shoulders and said in a rush, "I've done something awful."

"What?"

She opened her mouth, but didn't know what to say. She couldn't tell her that she'd slept with her boss and somehow transferred her feelings to him. She chewed her lower lip. What if it wasn't that? What if he was somehow able to read her emotions? She released her aunt and held out her palms. "Let me tell you a story."

Janet waved her away. "I don't have time for stories."

"It's a quick one."

"Not even a quick one." She pushed past her. Victoria stood in the hall defeated. The only thing she could do was stay away from him for a while. That might help. She would focus on the garden until she got her emotions under control. Yes, that would be a soothing, calm activity. Now that Patrice was gone she could focus.

"You look like hell," Grant said as he and Robert stood in the backyard of the burned woman's residence.

"Thank you." Robert scratched his chin. "This case is driving me crazy."

"It was an electrical fire. What's the problem?"

"Victoria said it was arson."

Grant stared at him surprised. "You believe her now?"

"Yes."

"Great. How did she say it started?"

"Electrical."

Grant began to speak, stopped, shook his head then d, "So what's the problem? Unless she can tell us some- ng that hints at arson, we can't say it was arson. Did she how he did it?"

No. But she felt the woman's pain."

It's a tragedy, but it's an old house. At least it was. The nan didn't regularly check her fire alarm like most ple so—."

Her dog should have alarmed her."

What?"

he dog didn't bark."

ant shrugged. "It probably ran away."

hat if it was kidnapped so she wouldn't be warned?"

he had no money, no family. There was no reason l her. I trust Victoria as much as you do, but if we can't prove it we have to let it sit. There's nothing we can do."

"We need to find that dog."

Grant heard the determination in Robert's voice and began to grin. "Do you think he started it?"

Robert shot him a look of disgust then walked to his car.

That evening Victoria went into the library. She loved its antique bookshelves and display cabinets carrying souvenirs from different countries. At times she imagined herself sitting on the couch or in one of the vintage French chairs that were placed about. She could picture Braxton scribbling notes at the large writing desk in the corner and Amanda spinning the standing globe guessing where her parents would holiday next.

Victoria pushed the thoughts aside and searched the shelves to find books on herbs that were similar to those she found back home.

She pulled down a few books and flipped through them, humming to herself as ideas ran through her mind. It took her a moment to realize she wasn't the only one occupying the room. She turned when she heard glass being carefully set down.

"Well, well, well," Nicholas drawled, stretched languidly on the couch. "What are you so excited about?"

She snapped the book shut and replaced it on the shelf. "Nothing."

"Celebrating your victory on getting rid of Patric He raised his glass in a toast and took a sip. "I do blame you."

She walked past him, determined to make a quick exit.

He grabbed her wrist, seizing it in a solid grip. "Where are you off to? You just came in here. You don't need to keep your victory a secret. Why don't we celebrate together?"

She tried to twist her wrist free, feeling the burn of his palm against her skin. "I have work to do."

"You work too much." His eyes trailed the length of her. "Although I haven't seen you around much. I like you in jeans much better than that uniform. Uncle Robert has no sense of fashion. Now if you belonged to me, I'd have you in a dress that showed off that nice figure of yours."

She struggled to pull her wrist away, but his grip tightened. "I don't belong to anyone."

"You would if the price were right. Isn't Uncle Robert paying you enough?"

Victoria grabbed the glass on the side table and lashed him in the face. Surprised, Nicholas loosened his grip. She yanked her wrist free and ran to door. He blocked her path—as large and fierce as Braxton had been, but pulsing with a masculinity that was pure menace. "Don't be shy," he said gently, his icy eyes belying his tone. "Natalie wasn't shy. I'll make it worth your while."

Rage and fear coursed through her. "Open the door."

He smiled coldly. "Sorry, darling, you don't make the orders around here."

She backed away as he came towards her, looming over like a wolverine over its prey. She could smell the scent of too much Chablis. Her eyes surveyed the room for something she could turn into a weapon, but even a thick encyclopedia would not be strong enough to deter him. "I'm warning you."

"Good, I like warnings. They make everything that much more exciting."

Her eyes fell on a statue, sitting on the writing desk. She ran towards it. Nicholas rushed forward and grabbed her. She fought with such violence he lost his balance. They both fell on the large Oriental rug, which softened their fall. She wiggled back. The rug fibers burned her skin. She grabbed the leg of the cabinet.

"You may take me down," she said. "But this is coming with me."

"You wouldn't dare."

"Try me." One touch from him and she'd pull the heavy, wooden cabinet until it came crashing down, shattering everything inside.

Nicholas hesitated, glancing at the cabinet then at the determination in her eyes. He loosened his grip, but didn't release her. "You're crazy."

Victoria narrowed her eyes and strengthened her hold. She began to pull the cabinet towards them. It squeaked as it scrapped across the floor. "Would you like to find out how crazy?"

He immediately released his hold and stood in disgust. "You're no fun."

She scrambled to her feet. As far as she was concerned, she hoped he thought she was the greatest bore of the century. She ran to the door. He grabbed her arm and pressed his face close to hers. "I wouldn't tell anyone about our little chat." He glanced down at her. "Nobody would believe you anyway."

Victoria yanked her arm free and darted out of the room. She ran down the hall, remembering her joy and how Nicholas had replaced it with fear. She had to get out of the house. She turned the corner and crashed into Robert, coming out of the dinning room.

He grabbed her by the shoulders to steady her, but the action only brought back memories of other hands trying to restrain her—ones that were too big and too powerful to fight as they bit into her skin. She panicked and struggled against him.

He shook her. "Victoria, stop it!"

The hard command sliced through her terror. She looked up at his worried, dark eyes and knew she was safe.

"Is there a fire?" he asked. "Has something happened?"

She shook her head and let her eyes fall, unable to speak or look at him. The significance of what had happened made her mute. Robert gathered her close, Victoria began to pull away, but he held her tighter. "I'm here, Victoria. You're safe."

Whether it was the sound of her name on his lips or his arms around her, she believed him. She nestled against his strength, seeking to gain power from him. She moved her cheek against the soft cotton of his shirt and slowly felt her fear slip away.

Robert continued to hold her. He glanced around the hall, in an effort to figure out what had scared her, but the house was quiet. There was no smell of smoke, no shouts of dismay. Nothing to indicate that something was wrong. Nevertheless, he knew something was the matter. He'd held her before and never felt such fear. Fear so terrible it seemed to crawl over him. She trembled in his arms like a bird caught in a net. He shut his eyes for a moment to check his anger. He had to fight the impulse to find and destroy whatever had frightened her. "Can you tell me what's wrong?"

Tears of anger swelled, blurring her vision. She couldn't tell him what was wrong. She couldn't share what had happened. How could she explain what his nephew had attempted? He might ask her why she hadn't screamed, why she hadn't called anyone. He might not believe her. If he asked Nicholas about it, he would lie. Would Braxton take her word over one of his family? He had already gotten rid of Patrice because of her. How could he get rid of Nicholas too?

She felt him sigh, sensing his frustration. "Victoria, what happened?" he asked tenderly. "Did a big bird swoop down and try to eat you?"

A vulture perhaps. With your last name. "It's nothing Mr. Braxton."

"So it's still Mr. Braxton, huh? Come." He led her to his study. "Sit down."

She fell into a chair. A sense of vulnerability slithered over her now that she was free from the safety of his arms. She gripped the handles of the chair to keep herself from shaking.

He sat on the edge of his desk and assessed her with hard, critical eyes. His voice remained so "What happened?"

"I saw a spider," she managed in a cool voice.

He rubbed a brow. "A spider?"

"Yes. A big, black, hairy one the size of my palm

was cleaning the cobwebs and it fell on me. I just got scared and ran."

He frowned. "You're afraid of spiders?"

"Yes."

"All kinds? Or just the ones you make up?"

She stiffened. "Are you laughing at me?"

"No, I don't believe you."

Her grip on the handles tightened. "I can't help that."

"Sure you can. You can tell me the truth."

"That is the truth."

"A big, hairy spider brought you to tears?" He quirked a brow at her surprised. "Oh, you thought I didn't see them?"

"I was just scared."

He rested his hands on the desk and tapped his fingers against it. To Victoria it sounded like a warrior's drumbeat. He was on the hunt for the truth. "I know that you were scared. I want to know why."

"I told you why. So if you are finished with your questions, I'll leave. I don't have time to convince you of my honesty. I have work to do. "

"Don't worry," he said, lightly. " I won't tell your boss." He continued to study her with dark, unreadable eyes. "Have you made any progress with the garden?"

The abrupt change in topic confused her. "Garden?"

"Yes, the one you've been working on outside."

"I haven't been able to do anything yet. I was in the library looking at different herbs and was going to write one down when…"

"That big hairy spider attacked you?" he finished dully. "Wow. How did you do that?"

"Do what?"

"Look at the books and clean the cobwebs at the same time?"

She folded her arms and glared at him. "May I leave now?"

He leaned forward and lowered his voice. "I'm not the enemy. I just want to know what happened."

"I was frightened by a spider," she said evenly. She let her arms fall.

"Fine. Since spiders scare you so much, I suggest you stop cleaning cobwebs. They have a strange habit of making them."

She went to the door.

"Victoria," her name burst from his lips as a plea. For a moment he stared at her vulnerable and her heart shifted. "Have I done something wrong?"

She folded her arms again. She couldn't trust him yet. She couldn't trust anyone not even herself. "No."

"Then why have you been avoiding me?"

"I've been busy."

He nodded; a shutter came over his face and she knew she had failed him. "I can't explain—"

"Doesn't matter," he said polite, but distan "That's fine."

"No I—"

He changed the topic. "So is that a new style?"

"What?"

He gestured to her ear. "Wearing one earring. I usua see you with two."

She reached up to her left ear and felt nothing. S jumped to her feet, panic washing over her in waves. "

my God. I've lost it!" She was out the door before Robert could stop her. He found her crawling on the ground in the library, her hands frantically sweeping the floor.

"I have to find it," she cried. "It was my mother's."

"Relax," he said calmly. "We will find it eventually."

"No. I have to find it now."

He lifted her off the ground and turned her to him. His eyes clung to hers. "I will find it," he said slowly. "It's not gone. It's just been misplaced. You will get it back. You have my word." He took her hand and felt her wince. He glanced down and noticed redness on her wrist. "What's this?"

She furrowed her brows. "I think it's called a bruise."

He shook his head unable to stop a smile. "Always ready with a quick reply. You must be feeling better. Did the spider bite you?"

"No."

"Then how did you get it?"

"I don't know. I got it caught."

"Got it caught in somebody's hand perhaps?" His finger grazed over the crescent shaped marks. "These look like fingernails."

She shrugged.

He stroked the bruise with his thumb. His voice was low edged with steel. "Some of the men working here have a strange respect for women. You're very friendly and that can be…" He searched for the right word. "Misinterpreted. I won't promise I won't fire him on the spot, but if one of the workers—"

"They've always treated me with respect," she said quickly. She didn't want him casting suspicion on them.

"I bruise very easily. Sometimes Aunt Janet grabs me to tell me to slow down or Foster takes my arm to stop me from doing something. The bruise always goes away so I don't take notice."

Robert fell quiet, continuing to caress her wrist. He finally lifted his eyes and his steady gaze traveled over her face with such gentleness her heart melted. "If that spider scares you again, you come to me. Understand?"

"Yes." Victoria swallowed, feeling the weight of his hurt and confusion as he released her to go.

Of all the people in the world she didn't want to hurt him. She couldn't let him leave thinking he'd done something wrong. She bit her lip then grabbed his collar and kissed him. "You haven't done anything wrong," she whispered against his lips. "I think you're wonderful." She took a step back; he stopped her and crushed her to him. "That's nice to know."

His mouth covered hers, massaging her lips with demanding mastery. Victoria felt a new panic rising inside her. It filled her with a delicious anxiety, causing her entire body to tingle as she recognized his power and her weakness to him. She was at his will unable to resist him. Instead of the heat of the previous kiss, this one was slow and soothing, healing the wounds that Nicholas had inflicted moments before.

Her knees weakened as the kiss deepened and his hands curled around her waist. She wrapped her arms around his neck to keep herself from falling into the abyss of joy, calling to her. She pressed herself against the solid length of him as his moist lips slid to her neck.

"We mustn't do this here," she said.

"I know," he replied in husky tones. He swept her into his arms and rested her on the couch. His eyes smoldered with an inner fire. "But I can't stop." His lips were on hers again. She traced an S pattern down his chest, undoing the buttons of his shirt. She kissed the base of his throat and curved into him as his powerful hands made a sensuous trail up her body.

"Victoria," he moaned.

She touched the sensitive part of his ear with her lips and whispered, "I love how you say my name."

"I'll say it some more." He buried his face in her neck and sighed, enjoying her softness. He could hold her forever. He reluctantly drew away before he went too far. He gathered his control and walked to the door.

"Robert."

He spun around and stared at her. Her voice was a whisper, but it rang in his ears. He never realized how much he needed to hear her say his name. It called to something deep inside him. It woke a man who'd been sleeping inside him living in a cold, dark cell for years. He took a step towards her, the depths of his need for her propelling him forward, seeking her promise of warmth. He closed the distance between them and kissed her again. "This isn't good," he said letting desire rule him.

"It feels good."

He fell on the couch and pulled her on his lap, feeling her soft bottom, pressing against the hard bulge in his trousers. He ran his hand through her hair, deepening his kiss.

Someone knocked on the door then opened it. Robert

jumped to his feet; Victoria fell on the ground. Foster entered the room.

"Yes?" Robert snapped.

Foster ignored the tone. "I have to talk to you."

"I'll meet you in the study."

"Okay." He nodded then closed the door.

Robert held his hand out to Victoria and began to help her up.

Foster opened the door again. "And Braxton?"

He dropped Victoria. His eyes flashed with annoyance. "Yes?"

"It's urgent."

"I'll be right there," he said between clenched teeth.

"Okay." Foster didn't move.

"Is that all?"

"Yes."

Robert's voice chilled with a layer of ice. "Then I suggest you leave."

Foster nodded then closed the door.

He helped Victoria up. "Are you okay?"

She rubbed her sore bottom. "From the first or the second time you dropped me?"

"I'm sorry." He bent over her. "Want me to kiss it and make it better?"

She pushed him away, trying not to laugh. "Stop it and go."

He smiled and left the room, whistling.

A few moments later, Robert walked into his study in a good mood. "So Foster what's so urgent?"

"Susannah Rhodes is doing a story on you."

His good mood died. "Why?"

"She knows about you and Ms. Spenser."

His eyes widened. "How could she know about that? What was she doing? Peering through the bedroom window?"

Foster delicately cleared his throat. "No, I mean that she knows you're using Ms. Spenser's psychic abilities to aid you in a case."

Heat rushed to his face. Robert sat on the edge of the desk and shrugged trying to be nonchalant. "Okay. I'll deal with that."

"She also knows who Ms. Spenser's father is."

He jumped to his feet. "How much does she want?"

Foster brushed lint from his trousers. "She doesn't want money. She wants fame and you're her ticket there. Her story airs tonight."

That evening Robert watched the report in disbelief. Susannah Rhodes either had a good contact or was very good at guessing. She knew everything. She spoke about Victoria's background and how she thought the recent fires were connected to one firestarter though investigators classified them as accidental.

When the phone rang, he absently picked it up. "Braxton."

Grant came on the line. "Are you watching—"

"Yes."

"How did she find out—"

He ran a tired hand down his face. "I don't know."

Grant exhaled. "This is bad."

It got worse. The next day the commissioner called

Robert into his office. Commissioner Wesley Pinkel was a big man with a big voice. He used it on Robert.

"Tell me this isn't true, Braxton. Tell me one of my top investigators is not using the help of a damn psychic to help him with a case." Robert opened his mouth, but Pinkel continued. "And not just any psychic, but one with a damn murderer in the family."

Robert stared at him, reserved. "She merely gave me some clues."

"If we wanted officers that believed in New Age hoodoo voodoo shit we would have recruited them by looking at their palms. Or maybe we'd scrye for them on our lunchbreak."

"I didn't use her in the crucial part of the investigation I am loyal to the scientific practices—"

"Braxton, I listen to enough shit from the people who work for me. I don't want to listen to yours too. That fact is you've involved a psychic in cases that are none of her business and were careless enough not to keep it under wraps."

Robert stared at Pinkel unfased by his anger. "We work for the public. If they have knowledge of any type it is our duty to follow their lead."

"Bullshit. Do you know what this story has done? We had a few buildings burn down and were able to assure the public they were isolated instances. Now the public thinks some lunatic may be setting things on fire and they're in a panic."

"It's not hard to scare the public."

Pinkel narrowed his eyes. "It's also gotten a lot of important people breathing down my neck. I don't like that. So you're going to have to do something." He leaned back. "I've known your family a long time. You're used to the press and you know the danger of bad press. You're a smart guy, Braxton. I don't need to tell you how this system works. You either tell the public they have nothing to fear or you find a damn suspect and charge him with something."

"I don't—."

"This isn't a suggestion. I don't care whether your psychic is right or wrong or whether your investigation is going badly or smoothly. You'd better find a way to make this trouble go away or I will."

When Robert reached home, there were cameras and reporters close, but not close enough to his property that he could charge them with trespassing. He ignored their barrage of questions and drove up the drive. Katherine came up to him. "I'm sorry Mr. Braxton I can't get them to leave. They want to speak to Ms. Spenser."

"I know."

"Perhaps her presence here isn't the best for you. This must be very stressful."

He gently squeezed her shoulder. "I'll deal with it. Don't worry." He marched past her, feeling as though he'd aged ten years.

Katherine watched him satisfied. Mr. Braxton would soon see that Victoria was a liability and then she'd have to pack her bags. Fortunately, Susannah promised not to reveal her source. Everything would work out soon, she had to be patient. Katherine walked up to Amanda's room, humming.

* * *

Susannah threw her glass against the wall and let out a scream. Channel Four! Channel Four! She breaks a story and Braxton decides to do an exclusive interview with Mandy Roberts of Channel Four! He even brought on his big, fat maid. For some reason the camera loved her. She could picture the camera operator drooling trying not to zoom in on her front. Women paid for a set like that. It wasn't just her body that was good on film, however, she also had fantastic photogenic features. She knew exactly how she would have edited this story. God, all the questions she would love to ask them.

But this wasn't her interview. She'd had to be content with the press conference held three days ago. She clenched her teeth as she stared at the screen. That little hussy was taking all the glory that should have been hers. Mandy looked like a stupid tart, trying to appear interesting, though everyone knew she was riding on the hard work of someone else.

Then there was Braxton, looking attentive and helpful, giving the best sound bites a producer could want, but, then again, Braxton knew how to use the press.

Susannah pressed the off button and sunk into her couch. Fine he'd never get good coverage from her again. She'd find another way to get what she deserved and to make sure he got what he deserved, too.

Victoria sat in the now quiet sitting room, gripping the seat cushion. It was over. The makeup artist, camera crew and reporter were gone. They wouldn't come back. She'd told her story and now they had no more use for her. It was over. Over. But she knew that wasn't true. Now the entire country knew who she was. Who her father was. She no longer had a place to hide. No matter where she went there would be whispers, snickers, and cruel remarks. There was no place to turn no place where she would be safe.

Robert came into the room, rubbing the back of his neck, looking weary. "I'm glad that's over. You did a great job."

She couldn't look at him. He wasn't safe either. His job was be in trouble because of her.

"They'll run the story a couple of times then the interest will die down. Thank God for a fickle public."

She began to tremble.

He stared at her alarmed. "Hey, hey. It's okay now." He gathered her in his arms. "You're okay. It's over."

She buried her face in his chest, trying to gather strength. "They all now know." She stared up at him. "What if the family of one of the victims wants revenge? What if my father's out there somewhere and tries to contact me? What will I do?"

He gently rocked her. "You'll be okay. I'm here."

She sniffed. "What can you do? Everywhere I go people will know. They'll know that—"

"They'll know that you're not Vernon Taylor and that you're trying to help the police find a possible firestar—" He cupped her face; his eyes clung to hers. "I won't anything happen to you."

"You can't—"

"I can. Trust me, I can."

Her panic began to dissolve. He meant it. He would

be there for her. She'd never had someone say that to her. She stared at him as though seeing him for the first time. She stripped through the layers of his façade—his good looks, his past, his wealth—and found the most beautiful, generous spirit she'd ever known. She threw her arms around him, wishing she could say what her heart now knew. She loved him.

Robert stroked her back. "You're going to be okay."

"I know." Victoria shut her eyes, briefly imagining he was hers. "Thank you."

He drew back. "I have to go."

She released him. "Yes."

He smiled then stood. "If there's anything you need. Call me."

She nodded. He looked at her as though he wanted to say more then left.

Victoria fell back on the couch all her energy leaving her. She closed her eyes, gathering the truth close to her chest as if it were a treasure. She loved him. She loved Robert (for he could never be Braxton to her again) and there was nothing she could do about it. Nothing she wanted to do. Her love was something she would carry like a precious jewel. It would be something else of value she would carry around with her like her mother's earring.

Now someone else would be in her fantasies, she wouldn't be alone. In her dreams she would belong someone, she would matter to him. She would not t him how she felt. She would show him by pouring all h love into his garden and making it grow.

She spent the next two days mixing the solution. S wanted to combine the right herbs, add the correct le of water, and boil it for the right length of time. Janet scolded her for smelling up the kitchen with her concoction. So she continued her experiment outside, creating a laboratory in the backyard. She worked into the night.

When she was certain the mixture was right, she and Foster washed the plants down. They then added a paste and mixed it into the soil so the sun would bake it into the ground. All the nourishment would gather into the roots, kill off the insect, and offer the plants the needed defense against another attack. All they could do now was wait.

Victoria lay on her bed, smiling to herself as she imagined Robert's face when he saw that his garden was flourishing. She knew her plan would work and that they would win.

Then it rained.

CHAPTER FIFTEEN

Robert heard a click as he walked with Grant into the police station. He turned and saw Caprican grinning. He took a menacing step toward him. "What are you doing?"

Caprican waved his camera. "Taking a picture of a hypocrite. Is this how you received your information for the Tract case? Perhaps it was a crystal ball that time." He laughed. "Now I understand why you helped him get off. You seem to like helping killers or at least their relatives."

Robert lunged at him; Grant held him back.

Caprican shook his head. "You're a fraud, Braxton. And now everyone knows it. But we all know it doesn't matter if you lose your job anyway. You just need to make a large donation somewhere and everything is all right again. You can fool the public, but you can't fool me."

Grant grabbed Robert's shoulder. "Come on. He's not worth it."

Robert turned away with effort.

Caprican shouted after him. "Careful not to make your maid angry, Braxton. She just might 'see' your house burn."

Moments later Robert sat in Grant's office, staring blindly at the notes in front of him.

Grant sat back in his chair. "So what do you think?"

Robert blinked. "About what?"

Grant shook his head. "You shouldn't let him get to you."

His voice fell. "He's right though. I am a fraud."

"No, you're not."

"I told the public there was nothing to worry about."

Grant stretched out his legs. "And you're right. They don't have to."

"I'm not so sure. He killed an old woman."

"We don't know that."

"I do."

Grant wanted to argue, but trusted Robert's instinct. "Look, whoever this guy is, we'll find him. A rookie cruising the warehouse district saw a subject near the area during the fire."

Robert's eyes lit up with interest. "Did he get a name?"

"No."

"Did he get a description?"

"No. He didn't pay close attention. The rookie said the subject didn't look drunk or anything and didn't appear to have any injuries. Probably was just a vagrant."

Robert tried not to groan. "Wonderful. That will be easy to find. First let's start looking for speckled pebble on the beach."

"That's what I thought until I got a phone call this morning. A guy wants to see me and talk about the case. He'll meet me on the corner of Parks. He didn't tell me who he was, but he said he'd be able to pick me out."

Robert shrugged though his hopes lifted. "It's better than nothing."

Grant grinned. "I thought that might make you happy."

Wilkins rolled his wheelchair towards Parks. The cop would probably be on time and he wanted to be there to meet him. Besides the neighborhood was bad, and no one in their right mind would hang out long. He knew the streets. He'd spent half his adult life on them. That's why he knew that the guy he saw a couple months ago would interest the police.

Wilkins sighed. He'd thought the cops would be offering a reward by now, however. He certainly had good info about the fire, and he would share it for the right price. Maybe they'd put him on TV or something for breaking the case. He wouldn't mind fifteen minutes of fame. Then he could tell everyone in this neighborhood to kiss his ass.

He didn't care that no one else liked him. He knew life wasn't about that. Life was about getting all that you could get, and today he might get a little help for his information about a possible suspect. He'd seen a guy watching the building before it blew. He left when the fire truck came. He could even describe him. Big black guy too well dressed to be from around here with huge construction boots. But he knew something even more important. He knew the guy's license plate.

Wilkins approached a street corner and rushed forward as the walking sign changed. He wheeled into the street. A truck screeched to a halt and blared its horn. Wilkins flashed the bird and shouted some obscenities then moved forward. He didn't see Emilia Reeds in her new car coming around the corner. She didn't see him until too late.

Robert pounded his pillow. He couldn't sleep. It wasn't unusual. He'd had plenty of sleepless nights since Victoria had come into his life, but somehow this night was different. He listened to the rain pounding on the roof and tapping the windows. The continuous sound should have calmed him, but he found the sound distracting. Tonight he was restless. He flipped on the lights and stared at Benjamin who was curled up at the end of his bed. The dog watched him through narrow eyes.

"Don't worry about me. I'm just going crazy," he said as he pulled on a pair of jeans. He grabbed a shirt. "A nice quiet night, and all I hear is her voice saying my name over and over again."

Benjamin yawned and stretched.

"There's no need for you to lose sleep, too," he said, patting the dog's golden head. Benjamin jumped down and walked to the door. "Okay, if you insist." Robert opened the door and went to his study. He worked on his notes for the three fires. Only one now could be considered arson. What was the reason?

He was adding another section to his notes when Benjamin suddenly raised his head as if something had startled him. Robert, buried in his thoughts, just glanced at him. A few moments later, Benjamin went to the door and began to whine.

"It's just the wind," Robert mumbled.

Benjamin pawed the door. Robert put down his pen. "Okay, let's see what's going on." He opened the door and heard the sound that had startled Benjamin—a crackling sound like something moving at the side of the house. He grabbed his boots and mackintosh.

"Stay," he ordered the dog before he opened the door. "I'm not in the mood for a wet dog."

Benjamin looked disappointed, but sat in front of the door as Robert went to investigate. His flashlight pierced the darkness and fell on nothing as he walked around the house. Then it hit a slick, rain soaked figure. He saw Victoria frantically trying to cover the plants with plastic bags, desperation evident in her movements.

He didn't ask questions just fell down beside her and imitated her actions. Unfortunately, there was too much ground to cover and too much rain to fight, pounding their confidence into the ground like hammers. After half an hour, he stopped and raised his head to the sky letting the rain hit his face and admitted defeat.

He reluctantly stood. "Come on."

She grabbed another bag and began to cover a row of plants. "No, we can't stop."

He reached for her, but she pulled away. He wiped the rain from his face. "We've saved all that we could and we can't do anymore."

"No. I won't stop."

He was tired, he was wet, and he wanted to

inside, but he couldn't leave her out here alone. He lifted her up.

She fought against him. "Let me alone, I'm not finished yet."

"It's over."

"No." She tried to pull away desperate to save what she could, but Robert only held her tighter until his words penetrated. She soon sagged against him, facing the truth. Nothing more could be done.

He steered her away from the sight of the billowing plastic bags that moved like slick black wings in the wind, and the muddy garden bed that resembled a raging brown river, washing all her treatment away. "Come on."

They entered the kitchen. Benjamin met them there demanding attention by brushing up against them. Once he received the proper strokes, he sat in the corner and went to sleep. Robert led her to a chair then heated up some apple cider. He glanced at Victoria. She sat quietly with her head bent, her hood covering her face.

He pushed back her hood and handed her the cider. "Drink this. It will warm you."

She held the mug in her hands, but didn't drink it. She just allowed the heat to warm her hands, but it couldn't warm the cold place in her heart. "I failed," she said softly.

"You didn't fail." He took the mug from her and helped her out of her mackintosh. She didn't notice as she sat like a rag doll with her thoughts far away.

"I should have anticipated the rain," she said in a distant voice. "I should have listened to the weather. I should have put mulch down. That would have protected it. I just thought the sun might do good. But I was wrong. I should have thought of the rain. Now the garden is ruined." She bit her lip. "I've failed you, Foster, and everyone. I've only caused trouble."

"You haven't failed anyone. Certainly not me. I should have listened to you sooner."

"But I should have been more persuasive."

"I should have been easier to persuade."

"But I should have—"

He held up a hand. "Let's not turn this into a competition of who's the most to blame. If we need to place blame, let's blame Mother Nature. I have a few choice words for her." He took a sip of his drink, resigned. "The garden show will come again."

Victoria didn't respond. Robert watched a stream of water drip from her hair, slide down her nose and splash on the table. He searched his mind for something to lighten her spirits. Here she was, the reason he's had sleepless nights, looking as helpless and sad as a butterfly with a broken wing. All he wanted to do was hold her but he had to resist. His fingers tightened around his mug and he looked around for something else to think of.

His gaze fell to the kitchen floor. He feigned a groan. "My housekeeper is going to kill us."

She stared at him puzzled.

"Look at those footprints."

Victoria turned and saw the trail of mud, marring the tile floor. She couldn't stop a smile. "She'll forgive us after a stern lecture." Her brief humor died and she lowered her eyes.

"Don't put this all on yourself. You didn't have to

at you did. You didn't have to try and save them all
your own."

"I wanted to give them the chance to survive. They were
ing so hard and now…" Her words trail off.

'Now it's over," he said flatly.

Yes, now it was over. The token of her affection had
en washed away by a simple spring rain. All the days
d nights tending to the garden and imagining
bert's face when he saw it, had been swept away. If
ly she hadn't done it her way. Tears clouded her
ion and she bit her lip to keep her chin from trem-
ng. She had failed her Aunt Margaret too. She'd
own Trevor had a drinking problem and had been
rned to always leave the shop after him, but one
ght she wanted to go out and be free so she had just
en him a firm warning not to drink and left the
re. Only to come back and see it in flames.

f she had tended to the garden as he'd suggested,
rhaps it would have been better off. Why did she believe
r way was the only right way? Sure the other suggestion
uld have been costly, but it might have worked to. Was
e destined to disappoint those she loved?

Robert reached out and cupped her chin. Tears
pped onto his palm. "Don't," he said gently.

She covered her face. "I wish I hadn't said anything. I
h we had just taken all the plants out and—"

"It might not have worked either." He removed her
nds and wiped her tears away with his thumb. "Don't
le your face from me. There's no need to be ashamed.
now how you feel."

She looked at him in disbelief.

"I know how disappointment feels. I was one until I was eighteen."

She shook her head. "No, not you."

He nodded. "Yes, me."

"I can't imagine you disappointing anyone."

He sat back in his chair. "I was the youngest of five. By the time I came around my siblings had excelled in everything of importance: Timothy was the orator, Jerome the athlete, and JB the scientist."

"That's only three. You forgot Amanda's mother."

He lifted his mug and gazed slyly at her over the rim. "No, I didn't."

"You didn't worry about her?"

"She was a girl. Besides, if she hadn't pretty—"

"Let's not have that conversation again."

"It's true. She would probably still be living at home if we hadn't gotten her married off. I love my sister, but she's a flake."

"Is that why you have Amanda?"

He avoided her eyes. "One of the reasons."

"What's the other reason?"

He set down his mug. "Her last name wasn't Hargrove at first. Serena got pregnant and had a baby girl. Then she found a man that would take care of her, but didn't want to raise another man's child."

Victoria wrinkled her nose. "That sounds selfish."

"I'm afraid Braxtons aren't too clever when it comes to marriage partners. Anyway, Serena was in love and desperate, so she came to her loving brother with the dilemma."

"She came to you first?"

"No. I was her last choice. I was the disappointment remember? No, first she went to Timothy who suggested she give the child up for adoption; Jerome thought she should dump Hargrove and find someone willing to help her raise Amanda; JB wanted her to find the father and sue for child support. She didn't like any of the suggestions so she finally came to her baby brother."

"And what did you say?"

He clasped his hands behind his head. "I said she could marry Hargrove, have him legally adopt Amanda so she would have a last name, and that I would raise her."

"Why did Hargrove have to give her a name? Why not adopt her yourself and let her be a Braxton?"

"For the sake of appearances. Serena didn't want Amanda asking questions about her father. She wanted her to think Hargrove was her father so there wouldn't be any awkward moments when she was older."

Victoria frowned. "But that will be awful if Amanda finds out."

"She already knows."

"She does?"

He let his hands fall. "I told her. Not all the details, but I put everything in very simple terms. She knew I was her uncle. When she began asking about her parents, I told her that her mother and stepfather liked to travel and that she'll stay with me until she's grown. She said 'Oh', asked a few questions then nodded her head and went back to Candyland."

"Candyland?"

"She was five at the time. She has yet to ask about her real father. She doesn't seem interested."

Victoria rested her chin in her hand. "You're not a disappointment at all. Your family must be very proud. Besides you're a success now."

"Depends on what you define as success," he said grimly.

"You're rich and have an excellent career."

"Everyone in my family is rich and using a shovel as your main tool of business isn't exactly impressive. I'm also divorced with no kids."

"You take care of Amanda and allow other relations to visit."

He rubbed his chin thoughtfully. "Which probably explains why I have no children of my own."

"But you do want to have your own someday, right?"

"No."

She blinked at the certainty of his tone. "Why not?"

He finished off his drink and placed the mug down. "Because I'd like to be married to the mother of my children and I have no plans to get married again."

"Was your marriage really so terrible?"

He began to smile in amusement. "Clever. You got me to talk about Amanda, but you're not going to coax me into talking about my ex-wife."

"I was just asking."

He tweaked her chin, indulgent. "Of course you were." He stood. "You look tired. Go to bed. I'll take care of in here."

Her brows furrowed. "What are you going to do?"

"Clean the floor, of course."

She stared at him, trying to figure out if it was a joke

ut saw that he was serious. "I can do that early tomorrow,"
he offered.

"Go to bed. I can handle it."

She shrugged. She was tired anyway. If he wanted to
do one of her duties, who was she to argue? "Okay." She
grabbed her mackintosh and watched him curious to see
what he would do next. He didn't do anything. He stood
in the middle of the kitchen looking hesitant. "What's
wrong?" she asked.

He grinned sheepishly. "Where's the mop?"

She put her coat down, opened the cupboard and
handed him the mop and bucket.

"Take off your shoes," she suggested, as he headed
to the sink.

"Why?"

"Because you're tracking more mud."

"Oh." He kicked off his shoes then filled the bucket
with water. He dipped the mop in.

"That's just water," she said appalled as he began to
mop.

He scowled. "I know that."

She folded her arms and quirked a brow. "You do
realize we use soap too, right?"

He blinked. "Sure."

"I'll get it." She got the cleaning solution out from
under the sink, mixed it with the water then handed him
the bucket. "Okay, now you're all set. Start from the
corner out."

"I know that." He swung the mop in a wide sweeping
motion, splashing the floorboard and cupboards

across the room. He repeated the motion, splashing the other side.

She ran to him and grabbed his arm before he did anymore damage. "Stop, stop! What are you doing?"

"Mopping," he replied, offended.

"Try to keep the mop on the ground." She took it from him and demonstrated. "Like this."

He took the mop from her. "Fine."

"Don't push so hard, you'll damage the tile."

He pounded the mop against the floor. "Look. Do need a certificate to do this? Or will common sense do?"

"Common sense and a bit of grace." She tried to take the mop from him. "Here. Let me do it."

He maintained his grip. "No," he said firmly. " can do it."

She kissed her teeth. "You're so stubborn."

He ignored her.

Victoria watched him trying not to wince. He splashed too much water on the ground, missed sections and generally created a bigger mess than before by making the floor wet and muddy instead of clean. But he did the task with such a genuine intent that she began to smile. "You're trying to make me feel better, aren't you?"

"No, I'm just making an idiot of myself," he grumbled.

She laughed. "You're doing both remarkably well."

He looked up; his eyes pierced into hers. "Getting you to laugh is worth it."

She sighed as the heat of his gaze warmed her, dissolving the pain of disappointment. "I just wanted to make up for everything."

He set the mop aside and stood in front of her. "Why?

She took a step back until she hit the island. "I n't know."

He trapped her against the island. "You don't have to ke up for anything."

"Then why does it all feel like my fault?"

"Because you care." He lifted her onto the island. His pression grew serious. "Thanks for what you did."

She shook her head. "But I didn't do anything."

"Yes, you believed in what I was trying to do. I don't ays get that and it means a lot to me." He pressed fingers against her lip before she could protest. y *you're welcome*."

She reluctantly smiled, accepting his praise. u're welcome."

"You're not going to believe this," Grant said to Robert w days later.

"What?"

"Some homeless guy in a wheelchair got run over by a "

"You're kidding."

"Nope. You'd think he'd have the sense not the park chair in the middle of the road."

Robert crumbled up paper and threw it at him. "You're ck man."

Grant ducked then held up his hands in surrender. k humor is part of the job, didn't you get the memo?"

"You need help."

"Melinda doesn't think so."

He waved his hands as though fending off bad news. n't tell me. I still want to respect her."

Grant laughed. "You can still respect her. She's determined to find out about CHC, though it doesn't seem to exist anywhere. But I also have good news."

"You said you had good news before and the guy didn't show up."

"This is real good news about the warehouse fire."

"What?"

"That nurse I spoke to from Memorial Hospital a couple months ago called. She'd missed the second page. There was a fire injury report that night. Guess who it was."

"Josef Haddad."

"Exactly. Now here's the bad news."

Robert frowned. "You should have told me that first."

"She said his injuries were extensive and that he refused treatment. She believes he probably died of his wounds."

Victoria looked at her aunt across the curried chicken with rice set on the dinner table surprised by how quiet she was. She'd been quiet for the past few days. Her skin looked pale and her eyes tired.

"Are you unwell, Aunty?" Victoria asked, feeling a panic she kept from her voice.

"I'm all right," Janet said. "A touch of cold, perhaps."

She accepted the explanation and nodded. "Oh."

After dinner, Victoria washed the dishes and tried to think of remedies to ease her aunt's discomfort. She was eager to find something besides her problems to focus on. She went to Dana's herb garden and picked some herbs and made a paste, which she put on Janet's chest

When that gave her no relief, she made peppermint tea. She also prepared a lavender bath and made some broth. She tried to persuade her aunt to take time off, but Janet argued that she had never missed a day of work and wouldn't start now.

"I have a cold not a fatal illness," Janet complained as Victoria draped a shawl around her and handed her a cup of tea. "I'm fine." She paused. "I worry about you though."

Victoria tucked the shawl around her. "There's nothing to worry about."

"Is that why you can't look me in the eye?"

"You need to focus on getting well."

Janet put her cup down. "You have a tender affection for Mr. Braxton. I had hoped…" She sighed. "But that's the way it is. You love him, don't you?"

Victoria sat next to her. "Don't worry. I won't embarrass you."

"Don't tell me not fi worry when I already do," she snapped. "I can't look out for you forever. Your temper is too hot and your heart too soft."

She tapped her forehead. "Ah, but I have the sense of Spenser."

"Sense is not something you have. It's something you use."

She looked down and pulled lint off her jeans. "Yes, I know."

"Our first loves are usually our most foolish ones. I fancied myself in love once with a mechanic from Trinidad. All he had to offer me was a smile and a broken heart. It was painful to leave him, but later I was glad I did.

He now has seven children and no wife. Could you imagine that kind of life for me?"

Victoria shook her head. "Is that why you never married?"

"I did marry."

"What?" she sputtered.

"Yes. It was a secret ceremony. We didn't want anyone to know because there would have been talk. He was much older than me you see. But he said he loved me with all his heart and promised to marry me and take care of me. Though I didn't love him, I married him, and later grew to love him so very much."

"What happened? Where is he?"

"We had five wonderful years together then he died. Fortunately, he kept his word and I was well taken care of. So you see the first time is full of heartache and the second full of joy. The young are usually too impatient to wait."

"What was his name?" she asked too eager for her aunt to finish the story to care about the message. "What was he like? Do you have a picture? When did you get married?"

Janet shook her head faintly amused. "Why do you ask the wrong questions?"

"But Aunty this is important. Who was he?"

"Perhaps I'll tell you one day, but not tonight." She absently rubbed her shoulder. "I think I'll go to bed."

The next day Janet hadn't improved and Victoria sensed something was wrong. When she saw Robert sitting at his writing desk in the library, she approached him.

"Mr. Braxton?"

He kept his head lowered and continued writing. "We're alone, Ms. Spenser."

"I know."

"That means you can call me Robert." He looked up from his work and began to smile then stopped. "What's wrong?"

"My aunt has been feeling ill recently. May she take a few days?"

"Of course she can. You don't need to ask me. She knows that."

"She won't unless you tell her to. I tried to convince her, but she won't listen."

He rubbed his chin. "A stubborn Spenser? Now there's a rarity."

"Will you say something to her?"

He pushed his papers away and stood. "I'll do it right now. Where is she?"

"In the dinning room hunched over her notes. She's setting up next week's schedule."

"All right." He gave her a mock salute and went to the door.

"Be your most domineering," she suggested. "Otherwise she'll argue."

He rubbed his chin again. "An arguing Spenser? Now there's—"

Victoria pushed him out the door. "Stop your foolishness. Just go."

Robert grabbed onto the doorframe. "Don't I get a kiss first?"

"Why?"

"You're sending me off to battle. I may not return."

She kissed him on the nose. When he began to protest, she covered his mouth. "You'll get the rest if you succeed."

He winked. "This will take less than a minute. Wait here."

Robert found Janet exactly as Victoria had described, hunched over her clipboard and scribbling notes down. She looked a little tired, but otherwise fine.

He pulled out a chair and sat. "Ms. Janet, I've been told you haven't been feeling well."

Janet pushed her notes aside and sat straight with her hands clasped in front of her. "I'm fine, Mr. Braxton."

"Fine isn't good enough. I want you to take off a week and look after yourself."

Her mouth fell open. "But Mr. Braxton—"

He lifted a brow. "You notice I didn't form that into a question."

She nodded, accepting his order. "Yes. Thank you."

"I could schedule you to have some time away. Time in a nice spa perhaps or a something in the mountains?"

"No, no. I'll be fine at home. Thank you."

"If you don't feel better after your rest, I want you to see a doctor. You're never sick and I want to find out if anything's wrong."

"I'm sure I'll be fine after a week." She hesitated. "A week is a long time."

He patted her hand. "You'll still get paid and I'll hire someone from The Agency so don't worry about anything."

"Thank you." She went back to her scribbling.

He pulled the clipboard away from her and stood. "Your week starts now."

"Yes, Mr. Braxton."

Robert returned to the library, Victoria jumped to her feet when she saw him.

"She's to take off a week," he replied to her silent question.

"Did she argue?"

He smiled. "She tried." He handed her the clipboard. She held it to her chest. "Oh, good. Thank you."

"If you're in the mood, try to convince her to go to a spa. I know a few resorts my mother likes to visit when she needs a rest. I'll pay for everything."

"That's very generous, but she won't go."

"The offer is always open. I'll be calling The Agency to send someone to take over her duties. I don't want everything falling on you."

"Thank you." She moved to the door.

He blocked her path. "You're forgetting something."

"What?"

"My kiss."

She blinked her eyes innocently. "But I'm on duty, Mr. Braxton."

"No, you're not." He reached for her.

She slipped out of his grasp and escaped through the door.

"I will hold you to your promise, Ms. Spenser," he called after her.

She laughed.

That night Victoria felt a feeling of restlessness again as she set the table for dinner in the carriage house. She had to talk to her aunt about Robert and what she should do if there happened to be another fire. Her aunt always had useful advice. Victoria jumped when she heard a loud crash in the kitchen. She ran inside and found Janet on the ground grimacing. Soup stained the white tile red.

Victoria grabbed the phone and called an ambulance. When the dispatcher told her to stay on the line, she dropped the receiver and lifted her aunt from the floor. She cradled her in her arms.

"You must hold on," she said hiding any panic from her voice, wishing she knew a way to ease her pain. "You'll be okay."

Janet looked up at her suddenly looking very old. "No, I won't."

Tears blurred her vision as her heart slowly shattered. "Yes, you will. You have to be. You can't leave me. You're all I have."

"Victoria—"

She placed fingers over her lips. "Don't speak, Aunty. You need to keep your energy. You need—"

Janet grabbed her arm. "Listen. I don't need tears. I've lived a good life. I was happy."

"But I need you."

"And there are others who need you. Stay strong for me. Always remember you're a Spenser. Use your gift for good and remember…" Her eyes rolled to the back of her head and her breath faded away.

CHAPTER SIXTEEN

Victoria had hoped for a day with no sunshine, but the sun shone bright through the melancholy breeze. The scent of honeysuckle drifted towards her as it clung to a nearby headstone. She did not see the faces of the other mourners, or hear their curious whispers and hushed voices. She'd created a cocoon so that the only emotions she could feel were her own.

Death was no stranger to her, yet its presence always came as a surprise. She knew no one belonged to her, yet felt an anger that her dear aunt would be taken from her so soon.

Victoria didn't remember when the ceremony ended, or when everyone left. She didn't care. She stood alone by the burial site, wishing the bright sun could warm the coldness inside her. The one person who had cared about her was gone. How cruel irony was. She could feel so many things, but had not sensed her aunt's sickness. If only she'd had more warning, but she'd noticed too late. She was always too late.

She kneeled and touched the dirt. All this time of digging and planting she never would have guessed she would end up putting her aunt in the ground. For a moment she wanted to crawl in with her and have it all end. She had no one now. No one she belonged to. She was truly alone. There would be no one to scold her, no one to talk to, no one to come home to, and no one to claim her as family. She felt useless.

Oh, that she could turn to dust as well.

"Now that would be foolish."

Victoria turned at the sound of the low voice and saw a black man standing a few feet away. He had a handsome face of such perfect symmetry she would have mistaken him for an angel had his eyes not been so dark.

"Ms. Janet would not want you thinking such things," he said.

She rose to his feet. He looked familiar though she was certain she'd never met him before. "Who are you?"

"JB Braxton." He held out his hand, swallowing hers when he shook it.

"What are you doing here?"

"Everyone had to return to the house. I promised Robert I would look after you." He glanced at the ground. "I know how it feels to lose a loved one." He looked up and his mouth curved with a smile that didn' reach his eyes. "So if you'd like to talk…"

She responded to the smile a little ashamed. "I've ha foolish thoughts before."

"Many have. The key is not to let them linger. You mu find a reason to push them away."

"What was your reason?"

He looked startled for a moment then his eyes glinted with humor. "I'm not ready to share my secrets yet." He held out his arm. "Come on. For now pretend the sun is your aunt smiling down on you."

Victoria took his arm and walked from the gravesite without looking back.

Although Robert had given her time off, Victoria went to work the next day. She accomplished all her duties like a machine. She walked to Amanda's room with a load of fresh laundry, but stopped when she heard Nicholas' voice and Amanda's loud sobs.

"Quit crying, brat," he said. "It's not as though your mother died."

"It's not fair."

"Life's not fair."

"She'd always been here."

"Ms. Janet was a good housekeeper. Uncle will get another one."

"Go away," she said in a muffled voice.

"Fine. Waste your tears."

Victoria stiffened more at the callousness of his tone than his words. She remembered being a child when she had to depend on the kindness of others and usually not getting it. She remembered having no mother or father to turn to. Amanda had an uncle who loved her, but he had little time for her and was totally unaware of life's little childhood traumas. Victoria felt her grief slowly melt as a new purpose replaced it. She would be the person she wished she'd had as a child. She would be someone else's strength. That would make her aunt proud.

When Nicholas left Amanda's room and saw Victoria, he smiled. "Hello."

She did not smile back. "Hello."

He held up an object. "I found your earring."

She held out her hand. "Thank you."

He clasped it. "How about a fair exchange?"

"I'm not going to give you anything."

He took a step closer and lowered his voice. "Not even a little kiss?"

"I'd rather eat my own flesh."

"Too bad." He pushed the earring in his pocket. "I guess you won't get this back then." He walked away.

Victoria watched him leave with mounting anger. She would get her earring back and make him regret the day he toyed with her. She entered Amanda's room and rested the clothes on a drawer. She sat on the bed where Amanda had buried her head under the pillows. "Amanda."

The girl turned her tears glistened on her eyelashes. "I'm so unhappy."

"I know." Victoria held out her arms. Amanda fell into them and continued to cry. Victoria gently rocked her. "I know."

At dinner, Amanda sat at the table red-eyed and quiet. Victoria glanced at Mrs. Lavinia Braxton, a handsome woman who moved with the grace of one raised in privilege. Robert's other brother, Jerome, sat next to her. An attractive man with a rugged, arrogant face with a build that almost made his mother look like a child in contrast. He had none of JB's reserve or Robert's impatience. Instead he looked at though he' prefer speeding down the highway on a motorcycle to sitting in an elegant dinning room. Victoria inwardly winced recalling his handshake.

Victoria could feel Robert's eyes on her as she served dinner. She ignored him.

"So, Robert," Lavinia said. "When will you look for another housekeeper?"

Robert shot her a glance. "This is not the time, Mother."

She had the grace to look embarrass. "Yes, of course." She glanced at Victoria. "You can take time off, dear."

"I prefer working," Victoria said, placing the dinner in front of her. She looked around the table then said, "I hope you all enjoy your meal."

Nicholas snapped his fingers when Victoria turned to the kitchen. "You haven't given me my dinner, yet. I suppose you're saving the best for last."

She smiled. "Yes."

Victoria walked into the kitchen and grabbed his plate then poured the contents in Benjamin's extra dish. She entered the dinning room and placed the dish on the floor in the corner. "There you are. Enjoy."

The group stared in stunned silence. Finally Lavinia said, "What is going on?"

Victoria sent Robert a significant look. "I'm feeding my spider."

"Your spider? What are you talking about? Robert what is she talking about?"

"He also took my earring."

Robert sent Nicholas a cool look. "I see."

"What do you mean took?" Nicholas asked. He held at her missing earring. "I found this under my bed."

Her face went hot with the implication, aware that all eyes were on her. She picked up the dog dish ready to hurl it at him then caught Robert's eye and stopped. "That is not true."

"Why do women have such short memories? Remember you—"

Robert set down his fork in a quick, impatient movement. "Nicholas, give her the earring." He gave the command in a soft tone, his voice holding the power and resonance of a low thunder.

Nicholas hesitated then did so reluctantly.

"The next time you try to entertain us, make sure you're funny and tasteful." He sent a significant look at Amanda who was watching the interaction with puzzled eyes.

"What was Ms. Victoria's earring doing under your bed?" She made a face. "I bet you stole it."

Robert said, "Ms. Spenser please take Amanda with you into the kitchen."

Victoria took Amanda's hand and her plate of food then left.

"Robert what is going on?" his mother said. "You can't let her treat poor Nicholas like that. I don't care if her aunt just died."

"I'll handle this."

"But Robert—"

He looked at her; she fell quiet. He wiped hi mouth and laid his napkin down. "Nicholas you hav an hour to pack."

Nicholas leaned back in his chair. "I'm not afraid o you," he said smugly.

Robert rubbed his chin. "Well, you never were very smart."

"I was just teasing her." He glanced around the table. "It was a joke Grandma. Uncle Robert doesn't get a joke."

Robert glanced down and folded his napkin in half. "Where did you find her earring?"

"I just told you."

He crumpled the napkin in his fist. "I knew you when you used to drool on yourself." His cold dark eyes shot across the table. "So don't waste my time."

Nicholas swallowed. "It was in the library, okay?"

"What happened in the library?"

He held up his hands in surrender. "Look, whatever she told you is a lie. She was taunting me. You know how some of them are. They want to be with the boss, so they'll settle for the next best thing. You've got to admit she's a... Look I'm only a guy. It's not like I hurt her or anything."

Rage nearly blinded him as he remembered feeling Victoria's fear and seeing the bruise on her wrist. "You now have twenty minutes to pack."

His mother spoke up. "Robert she's a nobody. You can't take her word over his."

"Actually, he can," JB said. "My own nanny had a few complaints about where Nicholas liked to put his hands."

Nicholas fell forward in disbelief. "Oh, come on! You don't have to play her protector. You know what they're like. They expect it."

Robert's voice deepened. "Fifteen."

Nicholas blinked. "Look if you two have something going on. I didn't know. The others didn't seem so—"

"What others?"

He saw his Uncle's face change into an expression he'd never seen before. It was an expression that scared him. "I'd better go."

Jerome nodded. "The smartest thing you've said today."

Fifteen minutes later, Robert rested against the red corvette as Nicholas put his bags inside. He leaned over the doorframe as Nicholas sat in the driver's seat. "Make sure I never see your face again," he warned softly. "I may find the need to rearrange it if I do." He slammed the door and watched the corvette drive off until it was a red dot in the distance. He turned to Foster who was pretending to water the plants. "Where's Victoria?"

"I think she went to the greenhouse."

"Thanks." He glanced at the hose. "It helps to turn on the water," he grumbled, marching past.

Robert found Victoria in the greenhouse holding up an orchid to the light. "Why didn't you tell me about Nicholas?" he asked without preamble.

She nearly dropped the pot, startled. She set it down hard. "What?"

"Nicholas," he said slowly. "Why didn't you tell me about him?"

Victoria turned the pot around to avoid his eyes. " thought I could handle him."

"What made that change?"

"He was cruel to Amanda and at that moment I wante to hurt him."

"So you know how I feel." He gently brushed her cheek with his knuckles. "You should have told me what happened in the library."

She shrugged, trying to be nonchalant. "He tried to kiss me and I stopped him."

"Did he try any other time?"

"No." She folded her arms and frowned at him. "I can take care of myself."

"If someone's threatening you, you have to tell me."

"Why?"

"You know why. Don't pretend you don't."

"Your mother—"

"I'll handle her."

"Patrice, Nicholas, your mother." She shook her head. "You can't handle everyone for me."

"Why not?"

"Because that's not your job."

He searched her face. "You should have told me about him."

"I couldn't. Not then."

"Why not?"

"Because he's your family and he wanted me for the same reasons you do."

Robert stared at her as though she'd struck him then shook his head with reluctant admiration. "You really know how to hit your target."

"I don't want to hurt you, but if I'm not right then tell me I'm wrong. Tell me that what's between us is more than sex."

His eyes caught and held hers. "It's more than sex."

"How?"

"I don't know. It just is."

She looked away unable to hold his gaze. "What would people think if they found out?"

"I don't care what people think."

"Then why are we keeping this a secret?"

He ran a finger along the rim of a pot.

She knew his silence was an answer. "I can't see you anymore."

"That's fine." It was a lie, but she didn't argue. He'd never ask her to stay and she understood that even though she felt as though her heart was shriveling in her chest.

"Good."

"I guess with your aunt gone you have no reason to stay."

"Yes."

"Except…"

"Except what?" she asked with a bit of hope.

"Except Amanda would miss you."

"Only Amanda?"

His gaze fell. "No."

Victoria hesitated sensing the feelings he would never reveal. "If I stay…"

His eyes flew up. "Yes?"

"It will be complicated."

"We can make it simple."

She felt herself weakening. "We can't keep it a secret forever."

"I know. We won't." He sighed and looked away. " just didn't expect…" He shoved his hands in h pockets. He wanted to change the subject to som thing he was ready to face. He wasn't ready to face losing her yet. "You know I miss your aunt more than I thought. Ms. Janet had such a presence. She was here when grandfather was ill and my marriage was breaking down and when I was dealing with Amanda. I never pictured this place without her."

Victoria reached out and held his hand, feeling his sadness, seeing the compassion and strength that reminded her why she loved him. "I don't want to be someone you'll welcome in private, but deny in public."

"Okay." He nodded and squeezed her hand, but didn't look at her. "I'll handle things."

"What does that mean?"

He lifted her hand to his lips for a featherlike kiss that offered a silent promise. "It means trust me. I won't let you down." He released her hand and walked to the door.

"But what are you going to do?"

He opened the door and called over his shoulder. "Trust me, Victoria. Just trust me."

She watched him go, not knowing whether to worry or feel relieved. She spent a few more minutes in the greenhouse before returning to the main house. She entered through the kitchen.

"You're only hurting yourself," Dana said. "And don't pretend you don't know what I'm talking about," she warned when Victoria turned to her surprised. "I see how you look at him. I've seen it before. Every girl thinks that they're the first. But they're not. Do you think he doesn't know his appeal? Women have been falling at his feet since he could crawl.

"I can't blame you," she continued before Victoria could argue. "If I were younger I might be cockeyed too, but take this from someone who knows. You're like a shiny new toy to him, but your shine will fade." She covered a container and placed it in the fridge. "Remember that."

Robert locked himself in his study, feeling a mixture of anger and relief. Victoria would stay, but she'd compared him with Nicholas. How could she have compared him with that spineless, useless nephew of his? He was different. He tapped an angry beat on his desk. Then why was he so upset? Why did a part of him think she was right? What had he promised her that his nephew hadn't? He shook his head. No, he was different. What he felt for her was different. He wanted her for more than just to satisfy his lust, but what more was there? He certainly didn't want to get married again.

Robert swore, when someone knocked on the door. "I'm not here."

His mother entered the room. "What's going on between you and that woman?"

He leaned back in his chair, tired. He wasn't in the mood for a fight, but from the look on his mother's face it became clear that she was. "Not today, Mother."

Lavinia sat and crossed her legs at the ankles. "I deserve to know what's going on."

"No, you don't. So leave it alone."

"I want to have a talk with her. Bring her to me."

He sat up, angered by her demand. "Don't mak orders. This is my house and—"

"No, this is your father's house. I doubt you'd be able to afford it on the salary you get playing fire chief."

A stab of hurt pierced him. His mother was good at hitting his soft spot—his father's money. Reminding him that he didn't have his father's drive. That he hadn't earned any of his wealth, but had inherited it. He kept his voice neutral, however, used to her careless remarks. "I'm an arson investigator."

"Does it matter?"

"I'm not the only one with a career."

"There are many 'gentleman professions' that you could have selected. You're not like other people. When will you figure that out? And don't tighten your jaw like that. You know there are gold diggers out there. You'd think one wife would have taught you that."

It was a familiar topic he didn't feel like addressing. His voice fell flat. "Is there anything else?"

She smoothed her hair, a ruby ring caught the light. "I want you to get that maid of yours and bring her to me."

"No."

"Okay." She slowly rose to her feet. "Since you won't follow my wishes, I'll do it myself." She turned to the door.

His voice hardened. "I told you to leave her alone."

She spun around and glared at him. When she spoke, ice laced her words. "You watch your tone and remember to whom you are speaking. I have been a Braxton longer than you and if there is one thing this family has in common, it's doing and getting exactly what we want."

Victoria walked to the sitting room with building unease. When Katherine informed her that Mrs.

Braxton wanted to have a word, the slight superior grin on Katherine's face warned her that this wasn't for a casual chat. Victoria found Mrs. Braxton seated on a couch near the window. She chose the loveseat facing it. "You wanted to see me?"

"Yes." Lavinia didn't speak for a long moment then said, "I would like you to tell me about yourself."

Victoria hesitated. "There's not much to tell."

"I doubt that." Her eyes swept Victoria in one assessing glance. "Amazing how much you don't look his type at all. Not that you're not very pretty, but he usually goes for tall leggy types. Not such a well…" She was too polite to finish her uncomplimentary statement and let it drop. "He dated this one woman who I swore didn't have a torso, just legs. But men have a right to their preferences." She shrugged, dismissing any other thoughts. "Since, you work for him so I'm sure you know. He has had his share of women like most men. I expected him to start settling down in his mid-thirties. Everyone was shocked when he married Rosalind. They hadn't dated long and suddenly he announces she was to be his wife. I was worried, naturally. He was still a baby, in his twenties, and only just started taking care of Amanda. I thought he was rushing into marriage to give Amanda a mother, but when I confronted him about it he told me he was in love." She sighed and shook her head.

"I thought my son had taste until I met that woman. Anyone could see from a mile away that she ate men's hearts for supper. But she was beautiful and clever." She twisted the ring on her finger. "Poor Robert was the last one to know."

Victoria hesitated not understanding Mrs. Braxton'

sudden chattiness, but intrigued nonetheless. "What didn't Ro—Mr. Braxton not know?"

"A lot of things. Too many to count. He's smart when it comes to books, but when it comes to women he's out to sea. I blame his brothers for not preparing him better, but then again they too have made some strange choices. I have told them to find women like me: intelligent, attractive, smart, and modest."

Victoria began to laugh until she noticed Mrs. Braxton was serious. She smothered a grin. "Yes, of course."

"It seems they are determined to do the complete opposite. Fortunately, they handle their love lives well. When JB's wife died, he was sad, but he didn't suffer as much as Robert. Robert was crushed when he had to file for divorce. I was relieved. The family was relieved, but we had to scrap him off the floor.

"I don't think I breathed until those divorce papers were signed. I was so thankful those two didn't have children. I did not want that woman to be the mother of my grandchildren. I believe family should handle themselves accordingly. You certainly made an interesting impression with your little altercation with Nicholas." She paused. "Robert's response surprised me even more. It is not like him to take the side of someone outside the family."

"It wasn't—"

Lavinia waved her hand. "Please don't explain. It doesn't matter. Robert has been looking after his nieces and nephews long enough anyway. He's a pushover when it comes to family and everyone knows it. Have you met the triplets yet? No? Well, you will eventually. They are precious. Robert loves them. He will make a good father when he settles down."

"He has done well with Amanda."

"We will see," she said in a low voice. She touched her necklace then said, "I'm taking you out tomorrow." She stood and walked to the door. "So try to find something appropriate."

Victoria remained seated confused by Mrs. Braxton's behavior. At least now she had some information about Robert's ex-wife. She now had a name: Rosalind. And she knew he hadn't wanted to divorce her. That fact tore at her, but she pushed it aside. She had to accept what was.

That evening at the carriage house, Victoria sat on the couch. She hadn't ventured to other parts of the house yet. Places where she'd smile at her aunt, catch her straightening a picture or checking her hat in the mirror. The past surrounded her, reminding her that she was alone again. The living room felt the safest.

A place where the warm memories of her aunt made the house feel less big and empty. Victoria rested her head back and closed her eyes against building tears. If her aunt were here she would know what to do. She would know how to handle Mrs. Braxton and JB and Jerome's curious looks. She felt like such an outsider. She felt ashamed that her feelings for Robert were so obvious for others to see.

When someone knocked on the door, she didn't move. The knocking persisted growing more demanding. She sighed and answered. Robert leaned against the door frame. Behind him she saw an orange sun melting into the distance, brushing the lawn gold and inviting the flower to close their petals. A hawk glided on the horizon a silhouette in flight.

His eyes searched her face. "How are you doing?"

"Your mother doesn't like me," she said answering his silent question.

He came inside and closed the door. He held open his arms; she went into them. "Fortunately, I do." He whispered holding her close. "I like you very much."

She rested her head on his chest. She may be one of many women who have been apart of his life, but now she was the only one in his arms. "I miss her." She couldn't say her aunt's name without her throat closing.

"I know," he said into her hair.

"It feels so lonely here without her."

"Tonight, you won't be alone." He sealed his vow with a kiss, his warm mouth growing more demanding as his hands slid up her blouse. She clung to him not wanting the kiss to end. He pulled away his eyes questioning.

Victoria answered by undoing his belt and lowering his zipper.

Robert lifted a brow and unlatched her bra.

She smiled and unbuttoned his shirt.

"I can undress you faster," he said.

"We'll see." They fell on the couch and stripped each other, letting clothes land haphazardly about the room.

"I win," Robert said waving Victoria's panties like a flag of victory.

Victoria lay back on the couch and opened her thighs to receive him. "Congratulations."

He swallowed, his body tightening at the ready invitation. "I bought my own hat this time," he said slipping on a condom. He came down on top of her, his penetration swift and without grace. He swore feeling embarrassed. "I'm always like this with you."

"Am I complaining?" She tightened around him and arched taking him deeper. His thrusts stoked the fire within her exploding in a climax. She cried out amazed that she could feel such pleasure after her heart had endured such pain.

He wanted to tell her how glad he was that she'd stayed. How much she had become a part of his life. She wanted to tell him how much she wanted to belong to him, how he made her feel less alone. How much she loved him. But neither felt the need for words. They were both hurting and trying to heal, needing each other more than they would admit. They lay still once it was over, exhausted.

"This couch is too small," he grumbled.

"I like this couch."

"I'd like it even more if it were bigger."

Victoria traced a circle around his nipple. "When do you have to go?"

"I don't. They know where I am."

She lifted her head, startled.

He began to smile. "It's okay. You were right. We can't keep this a secret forever."

She sat up and began to gather her clothes. "Everybody knows?"

He watched her amused. "Yes, I told them."

She pulled on her top. "What did you tell them?"

"That I can't keep my hands off of you."

Her eyes widened. "But—"

"I was more tactful of course."

"So Dana and Katherine…?"

"Yes, they know. I'm not ashamed of what I feel for you."

That was true. He lay naked on the couch and what he felt for her presently was quite obvious.

Her eyes slid away before she became tempted to undress again. "Your mother is taking me out tomorrow."

"If you don't want to go, I will—"

She bit her lip then looked at him determined. "No. I will go. I'm curious as to what more she has to say."

He sat up and looked at her suspicious. "What has she said so far?"

"Just how talented and clever Rosalind was."

A shadow of pain crossed his face. "Yes, Rosalind."

Victoria's heart twisted, hearing the depth of sadness in his voice. She changed the subject. "She also told me how you like tall, leggy women."

He lifted a mocking brow. "Seems my preference has changed." He held out a hand. "Come here."

She sat beside him but kept her distance.

"Are you cold?"

"No."

He tugged on her shirtsleeve. "Then why do you have this on?"

"You should go home."

"Oh," he said feigning hurt. "I see. You just use me for sex then toss me out into the cold. I can't even spend the night."

"That's not—"

"Then what's wrong? I thought you'd be happy."

"I am happy, but—"

He kissed her before she could say anymore. "Good." He stood. "Let's go to bed." He walked to the stairs.

"I'm not really tired," she said.

He turned to her. "You're not?"

A smile pulled at her mouth. "No, but you're heading in the right direction."

They made love again. Victoria fell asleep soon after; Robert stared into the darkness. This was right. He didn't care that he preferred the small carriage house to his own. He wanted to be with her and away from disapproving glances.

Dana, Katherine, and Foster couldn't say anything because they were in his employ, but he knew his family would have something to say. He'd left before giving them a chance. His feelings were still too new for him to discuss with others.

He skimmed his hand along Victoria's side amazed that he'd ever wanted anything less than this. Her body was a constant fascination—the soft curves, the taut nipples. He felt himself grow hard and redirected his thoughts. It would be unfair to wake her just because he couldn't get enough. When would he get enough? Would he always feel this way? Would he always have this desire to be with her?

A shiver of panic raced through him. No man should ever be that attached to a woman. It was dangerous. Victoria could leave. He knew how it felt and wouldn't let himself be that vulnerable again. He'd do the letting go, not her. He rubbed his chin. He'd just have to convince her to stay until he was ready to let her go. What did women like? What would impress her? He thought for a few moments then came up with an idea.

Victoria woke up to the sound of banging pots and masculine swearing. She walked into the kitchen and found Robert at the stove.

"What's going on?" she asked.

"Good morning," he said cheerfully. "You're just in time for breakfast."

She stared at him with a feeling of dread. "You're cooking breakfast?"

"Yes. Sit down."

She pulled out a chair. "That's very nice of you, but you didn't have to. I could have cooked something."

"It's no trouble." He placed a bowl in front of her.

Victoria looked down. Gray mush reached the rim of the bowl. She covered her mouth to keep from gagging. "What is this?"

"Oatmeal," he said simply, oblivious to her gasp of horror. "Would you like orange or apple juice?"

"Apple." When he turned to the fridge, she looked around to see where she could dump the contents of her bowl.

Robert handed her a glass and sat down with his own bowl of mush. She grabbed his wrist, as he brought a spoonful to his mouth, afraid he might poison himself.

"When was the last time you had to cook for yourself?" she asked.

He frowned and scratched his head. "I don't remember."

"Which means never."

"Why?" He raised his spoon again.

She snatched it away. He looked at her startled. "What did you use to make this?" she asked.

"Regular oatmeal, milk, cornstarch—"

Her mouth fell open. "Cornstarch?"

"Yes, I heard it's a good thickening agent. My oatmeal came out a little watery, so I—Hey what are you doing?" he cried when she gathered up the bowls and emptied them. She lifted a plate on the counter and saw scrambled eggs with specks of eggshell, and a side of blackened buttered toast. She threw those away as well.

"What a disaster." She put the dishes in the sink. "Promise me you'll never cook for anyone again unless you want them to suffer a slow and painful death." She opened the fridge. "Go watch something while I make breakfast."

"Okay." He left. A few minutes later she smelled something burning. She raced into the living room and saw Robert holding an iron.

"What are you doing?" she asked.

He scowled. "This iron is broken. It burned my shirt."

She covered her mouth to keep from laughing at the expression on his face. "Just put it down and step away."

"But—"

"Put it down. I'll…" She stopped when she heard a loud whirring sound. She briefly closed her eyes as though in pain. "What is that?"

"I saw your hamper was full and put some clothes in the washing machine for you."

Victoria darted into the cupboard and stopped the machine. She opened it and pulled out a shirt that had shrunk two sizes. "No wonder you employ people," she said exasperated, taking more clothes out of the machine. "You're completely useless without help." She stopped when she realized Robert had become very still beside her. She looked at him and regretted her words. "I'm sorry."

He shrugged. "It's okay."

But it wasn't. She'd hurt him by ridiculing all his efforts. "Robert—"

He backed away from her touch. "I said it's okay. I'll be in the living room. Call me when breakfast is ready."

He didn't speak throughout breakfast. Though she had made his favorite scrambled eggs with spring onions and red peppers and cinnamon muffins.

Victoria pushed around her food. "I didn't mean—"

"This tastes good."

The fact that he didn't want to talk about it made her feel worse. She searched the kitchen for a way to make up to him.

"There are a lot of dishes in the sink," she said.

He scooped up his eggs.

"It would be nice to have some help," she said. When Robert didn't respond, she nudged him.

He glanced up uncertain. "What?"

"Could you help me with the dishes?"

He was quiet a moment then pushed himself from the table. " I'll wash and you dry."

She stifled a groan. That hadn't been her plan. "Okay."

She chewed her bottom lip as she watched him add too much soap to the running water. Bubbles rose up, cascading down the front of the sink. He scooped some of the soap up and threw it away.

She turned and grabbed a dishtowel. "I'm sorry about what I said."

"Don't worry…you're not the first person to say it." He handed her a plate that hadn't been completely rinsed off, a thin film of soap still clung to it. She dried it anyway.

"That doesn't mean it's true."

He stopped then rested his hands against the sink. "Actually, it is true." He shrugged. "I know I'm not domestic. I can afford not to be."

"True."

He handed her another soapy plate. "At least I can wash dishes."

She smiled weakly. "Yes, at least you can do that." She scooped up a handful of soap bubbles and pressed them against his face. "But stick to what you know."

He grabbed a dishtowel and wiped his face then whacked her on the behind. "Gladly."

Once the dishes were washed she said, "Now you have to leave so that I can find something to wear."

"No, I don't." The doorbell rang. Robert answered and signed the delivery carrier's electronic clipboard then handed Victoria a stack of boxes.

"What is this?" she asked walking to the couch with her load.

He wiggled his brows mysterious. "Open and see."

She did. Inside she found a lavender silk pant suit, pearl earrings and black shoes.

She ran her hand over the soft material. "It's beautiful."

Robert smiled pleased. "Now you'll fit in where ever my mother decides to take you.

* * *

Lavinia decided to take Victoria to Melior Mansion for teatime. Victoria found herself sitting on a grand veranda with white tablecloths billowing like white sails in the breeze. Lace napkins lay on the table before her with an elaborate tea setting and a three tier tray of delicacies: chocolate covered strawberries, fruit tarts and cucumber sandwiches and pastries that looked like white stones. She emulated Mrs. Braxton's every move, dreading the moment when she would spill her tea or drop her scone and be labeled an outsider. Fortunately, it never happened.

"It is amazing how unlike Rosalind you are," Lavinia said, adjusting the napkin on her lap. She looked out at the great expanse of lawn. "I expected you to be more talkative. Not that I mind you quiet. If someone has nothing to say, it is best to keep your mouth closed."

"I am enjoying myself so much I have little to say."

She inclined her head. "A sensible reply. Has he told you much about Rosalind?"

"No, he doesn't like to discuss her."

"I thought he had gotten over it," she said regretful. "He loved that woman so much it made my heart ache to watch. The Braxton men really know how to love."

Victoria took a sip of tea. *I wouldn't know.*

"She was an artist he met in New York. I told him to stay away from those city women, especially artists. They like to live by their own rules and most of them are plain indecent. But when I spoke to him he was so happy, so I pushed away my prejudices. I flew up there to meet her attend one of her art shows. She did stain glass things.

I call them things because I never quite figured out what they were. They were dazzling and beautiful, but that is all I can say. I bought one and displayed it in my living room. I had to sell it after the divorce, naturally. Robert could not stand to look at it when he came to visit. I could not blame him. I was getting tired of visitors and family asking me what it was." She chuckled. "I tell you, it takes a clever woman to sell something no one can identify. But she was not just talented and clever."

Lavinia poured more tea and added cream and sugar. "She was a shrewd business woman and made money so fast you would have thought she had a machine in her apartment. I liked that best about her. I didn't want some woman marrying my son because of his money." She took a sip. " I did hope things would work out between them. They made such a beautiful couple. Any time they stepped into a room the crowd stared. She was so tall and regal, and he refined and handsome. She had been asked to model once, but she said art was her true passion." She sighed at the memory. "Poor Robert. He loved her so much. If only he had been a little wiser the divorce would not have hurt him so much."

Victoria set her cup down, feeling such envy she wanted to throw it. She envied Rosalind. A woman she'd never known and probably would never meet. She envied her because she had been fortunate enough to hear Robert say, "I love you." She had possessed his love and had hurt him. She envied her regal stature and talented skill. How lucky she was to have once had Robert's love. Perhaps she still had it. Perhaps in the back of his mind she still lingered in his thoughts.

Suddenly Lavinia said, "I'm sure you realize why I'm telling you this. I believe that you are a good sort of woman, but I don't think you're the right one for my son."

I wouldn't have guessed, Victoria thought. "Is it because I'm not talented or clever?"

Her eyes turned to stone. "No. It's because your father killed my husband…"

CHAPTER SEVENTEEN

Victoria raced into the main house feeling as though her heart would crack and bleed all over the floor. She found Robert in the library. "Why didn't you tell me?" she cried.

He jumped to his feet and looked at her alarmed. "Tell you what?"

"About your father."

He grabbed her shoulders. "What about my father?"

Lavinia calmly entered the room. "I told her every thing, Robert. You can try to deny it, but that won't work.

His eyes darkened. "You had no right—"

"I have every right to tell her the truth," she snapped

Victoria fell to the couch all her energy leaving her ice spread through her body. "So it's true? Is that why you never mentioned your father?" Her voice shoo "Because my father killed him?"

He looked at her helplessly. "It wasn't like tha He—"

"Tell her the truth Robert," Lavinia said. "Tell h what he did."

Victoria wrung her hands, wanting to scream. "Why didn't you tell me? Why?"

"Because my son is a good man," Lavinia said. "Because he didn't want you to know how your father destroyed our lives. Because he didn't want to share with you the many years we mourned my husband who was a good and kind man. Robert didn't want to tell you how long it took for my husband to die because your father was a greedy bastard."

"Mom," Robert said firmly. "That's enough."

She continued her eyes pinned on Victoria as her voice trembled with anger. "He had nightmares for years. That's why he left psychology for this fire thing he does. Always searching for answers, but they will never make everything all right. They will never make my husband's senseless death okay." She pointed at her. "You—"

He stood in front of Victoria. "I said that's enough."

Lavinia stopped, surprised by her son's vehemence. "Robert, don't raise your voice at me."

"Vernon Taylor didn't kill my father."

"Yes, he did. He killed all that he was."

Victoria pulled his shirt, desperate for answers. "What happened?"

Robert paused then said, "One of the buildings of my [fat]her's rival went up in flames. My father was indicted [on] arson charges and eventually convicted. Fortunately, [on] appeal they were able to overturn the verdict and he [wa]s released."

"He was never the same after that," Lavinia said. "His [spi]rit was broken. He died a few months after his release. [Yea]rs later we learned that Vernon Taylor confessed to starting the fire for profit. The very same fire for which he'd watched my husband go to prison."

"But he didn't kill him," Robert said.

Lavinia raised her brows. "He didn't kill him? Where was he when my husband was on trial? Where was he when my husband was sent to prison? Where was he when my husband came out of prison with his reputation in shambles?" She looked at Victoria. "Your father burned a lot more than buildings. He burned dreams and spirits. He killed my husband by taking away the one thing he had pride in—his name."

Victoria looked at her with tears streaming down her face. "I know. I live with that fact every day. Don't worry. You'll never have to see me again." She darted to the door.

Robert grabbed her and turned her to face him. "This is why I didn't tell you. I didn't want you to think it was your fault."

She tried to free herself from his grasp. "You must hate him more than I ever could."

He tightened his grip until she became still. "When was younger I did, but my father is dead, and hating yours will not bring him back." Her tears gripped hi heart, he pulled her into his arms, desperate to comfo her. "It's okay."

Lavinia curled her lip. "It's nice to know you're so fo giving of a coward who could watch another man pay f his crimes."

Robert sent her such a look of anger she nearly her tongue. "I said that's enough. I won't repe myself again."

She flashed a cynical smile at the embracing couple. "Fine." She stiffened her back and clasped her hands together. "I think Amanda should stay with me."

He led Victoria to the couch and handed her a tissue. "She's staying here."

"She's reaching the age where she needs a woman's guidance."

"She's staying here."

Her voice rose with indignation. "I will not have her in this house while you carry on with the help! Have you no sense of decency?"

Robert spoke to Victoria without looking at her. "Please excuse us."

"No, please stay," Lavinia said. " Let's hear how your shining knight will come to your rescue. He's good at rescuing women. Aren't we Robert? First your sister then your first wife." Her lip twisted cruelly. "Remember how he thanked you?"

"Yes," he said quietly.

"You let her walk all over you. She could do anything."

"No, she could never hurt me as much as you do." He shoved his hands in his pockets. "I knew she never loved me, but I have to remind myself that you do."

Lavinia stared at him startled by his words. She never intended to hurt him. She loved her baby boy, but she now saw the pain he was careful to hide. She fought against gathering tears. "I don't want to hurt you. I want what's best for you. I wish you could see that."

All she could, though, see was the depths of his feelings for the woman sitting on the couch. He wasn't even aware how he looked at her, the possessiveness in his eyes, and the tenderness of his touch. She wondered if this woman would use him as others had. He was so blind to how vulnerable he was to her. "You were always so stubborn." She sighed, resigned. "So you're serious about your feelings for this…" She gestured to Victoria searching for words. "Woman?"

Robert folded his arms. "Her name is Victoria."

"I know."

"I want you to say it."

"Well for once in your life you're not going to get what you want." She pressed a hand to her forehead and shook her head saddened. "Poor Robert you have more of your grandfather in you than I thought." She looked at Victoria with reluctant admiration. "Well, young woman I congratulate you. It seems your aunt taught you well."

Victoria stared at her confused; Lavinia laughed. "Oh, yes. We haven't gotten to the Will yet. When will that ridiculously hairy man get here?"

"Mr. Englewood was detained due to an emergency," Robert said. "He will be here tomorrow."

Her face brightened. "Oh good. That should prove exciting."

Victoria glanced at both of them. "Why?"

"Because you'll likely inherit the carriage house an enough money for you to live well for the rest of your lif You see your aunt also knew that marrying a Braxton w a good career move."

Victoria turned to Robert. "What is she talking about

When he didn't respond, Lavinia said, "Your aunt to care of his grandfather, then had the presence of mi to marry the dying man and became his rich widow."

"That's not why she married him," Robert said.

"Your grandfather was a sick old man," she scoffed. "Why else would she marry him? Did she love him?"

"Yes."

"Are you sure?"

"She learned to," Victoria said, remembering her aunt's words about the man she married. "She learned to love him very much." Now things made sense—the picture on the side table, the reason her aunt never told her the name of her husband. But why? Why had she kept it such a secret?

"I'm certain her love grew the closer he got to the grave," Lavinia said.

"You can choose to believe that," Robert said. "But you can't deny that his last few years were some of his happiest. Because despite the death of his first wife, his second son, and his illness, he knew how to live with joy. I think after Dad died you forgot how to love."

She turned before he could see her tears. "I have things to do." She left the room.

Victoria moved to follow her. "You have to go after her."

"Why?" Robert asked.

"Because you hurt her."

He sighed. "She's been hurt a long time."

"I know," Victoria said then slipped out of the room.

The sky drizzled a somber rain over the carriage house when Mr. Englewood arrived to read the Will. A tall thick man with a bushy brown mustache that matched his eyebrows, he smiled when he saw Victoria. He held out his hand to her and said, "It's a pleasure to meet you."

"Same," she said.

"Your aunt was a wonderful woman. She will be missed." He tapped his portfolio. "Where will we meet?"

She led him to the study where he addressed the others. Lavinia, JB, and Jerome sat on one side of the room, while Victoria and Robert sat on the other.

Mr. Englewood sat at the desk and opened his portfolio. "Let's begin…"

Victoria glanced at a picture of lilies behind his head. Her aunt hadn't used the study much. The presence of the elder Mr. Braxton lingered in the room with his selection of gardening and finance books and wood sculptures. Her aunt had preferred the living room or kitchen. The kitchen had been the place of her joy and the place of her death. To Victoria it would be the keeper of her memory. A place where she'd cooked their evening meals, filling the house with the scents of plantain, soursop soup, and sizzling fish fritters. She'd remember the sight of her aunt's reading glasses sitting low on her nose as she read waiting for the water to boil or a stew to simmer.

"Well, that was expected," Lavinia said, breaking into Victoria's thoughts.

She blinked. Everyone stared at her. "I'm sorry?"

"You inherited almost everything, weren't you listening and please don't look surprised."

JB frowned. "Mother."

"Imagine your grandfather giving away something on our land."

"It was his land first."

She looked at Robert. "At least she won't have to marry you to get her hands on your money. Unless two million isn't enough."

Victoria jumped to her feet. "Two million? There must be a mistake."

"There's no mistake," Mr. Englewood said. "Naturally, she left a significant amount to charities and had established a scholarship fund for youth in Jamaica, but most of the money was entrusted to you. I can address any questions or concerns you have. I will leave you my card."

"But there must be an error. This can't be right."

"No, it's not right," Lavinia said. "But it's real."

Millions. It did seem a cruel twist of fate that she should benefit from her aunt's marriage. Her father had ruined their lives. She shouldn't inherit what was rightfully theirs. "I don't want it."

They stared at her.

She grew more adamant as the silence lengthened. "I'll give it back."

"Don't be foolish," JB said.

"Didn't you hear how much?" Jerome said.

Robert tugged on her arm. "You're just upset."

"No," Victoria said. "My father did a terrible thing. If I give you the money back it would be a way to atone."

Robert shook his head. "You don't have to sacrifice for your father. Your aunt wrote this Will in good faith. She would want you to be taken care of."

"No, I've done nothing to deserve such a fortune."

"Keep some of the money," Jerome said. "We're not exactly paupers."

"Keep it all," JB said. "Your aunt wanted it that way."

Victoria looked at Lavinia. "What do you think?"

"I think you're a very dramatic and proud woman. You will not do us any favors by treating us like a charity."

Victoria's temper snapped. She stood and went to the door tired of trying to be kind. "I'd like to have a word, Mrs. Braxton."

"You can't speak to—"

"I don't like waiting, Mrs. Braxton."

Lavinia didn't move.

Victoria waited.

A tense silence filled the room.

After a moment, Victoria picked up a vase and studied it. "This is beautiful. Is this very expensive?"

"Of course," Lavinia said, annoyed by her ignorance. "And rare too. It's a—"

Victoria cut her off by tossing the vase in the air. She caught it and looked at her. "Then if you don't want me to break it I suggest we have a word."

Lavinia slowly rose to her feet. "Very well." She walked past her and sat in the living room.

"Let's go into the kitchen," Victoria said.

"I do not sit in kitchens, Ms. Spenser. Now what do you have to say to me?"

Victoria tried not to take offense to the rude tone. She sat in front of her.

"I know you don't think I'm worthy of your son. But I do love him."

"Love?" Lavinia scoffed. "You love his good looks and his money. Perhaps you know his favorite color or what he likes with his dinner, but that doesn't prove anything. Women have been falling in love with my boys since the day I had them. And not one of them was sincere. JB's wife died before he could discover the truth thank goodness.

"Not one of those women knew what love is. Do you know what love is?" She didn't give her a chance to reply. "Love is seeing him when he's miserable with a cold and still being grateful he's yours, it's the quiet moments at dinner when you remember his hair used to be thicker, but you don't care. It's tantrums and laughter—"

"It's being angry," Victoria interrupted. "But never hating him. It's accepting his moods as he accepts yours and it's knowing your heart will not waver with time."

Lavinia stared at her surprised and a bit humbled. "I see. Perhaps you may be different after all," she said with reluctance. She stood. "However, I still don't approve of…" She waved her hand searching for words. "This." She studied Victoria for a moment. "But I think I understand now." Lavinia suddenly sighed and turned away. "No, I know I do." She patted Victoria on the shoulder in a fleeting, absent gesture then left.

Once everyone had gone, Victoria wandered around the house disoriented, trying to grasp how her life had changed. Soon the house became a prison and she walked the grounds wondering what to do next. She ended up in front of the insect ravaged garden. She felt as though her life resembled it. It had begun with such potential only to be ravaged by unforeseen forces. She should feel glad, but couldn't.

She now had a place to stay and money to live on. Why did a sense of emptiness linger? Perhaps she was wicked.

Wicked to want her aunt back more than all the money in the world. Wicked to want to belong to someone because that was what she'd wanted her entire life. She'd wanted a quiet, safe existent with someone she could make proud. She'd wanted to escape her past, but kept running into it. Now every time she looked at Robert she would see the face of one of her father's victims.

Victoria heard someone coming and sighed. She had wanted time alone. JB turned around the corner. "Hello," he said.

"Are you here to discuss the Will?"

He looked surprised. "No."

"I won't tell you what I said to your mother."

"I don't expect you to." He shrugged. "She's really a nice woman once you get to know her."

Victoria sniffed. He sat beside her.

"I don't want to talk," she said.

"You won't have to." He fell silent then said, " Did Mom tell you about Rosalind?"

"She told me everything about her."

"Even how she was Robert's greatest humiliation?" He nodded at her disbelief. "Yes, she did. She was beautiful and talented, but she also made a fool out of him."

"How could anyone make a fool out of him?"

"By publicly showing everyone that she preferred other men to her husband."

"She had a lover?"

"Lovers in the plural. We're scared to count how many. She was an artist, I'm sure Mom told you, but she forgot to mention Rosalind's little projects. She claimed to want to patron other artists so she started selecting protégés.

Robert supported his wife's career unconcerned that they were usually men. The family suspected early that her protégés were much more than that, but we said nothing. Robert had no idea. Then one day he caught her in a very intimate position with one of them. He filed for divorce.

"Through the divorce proceedings he discovered she hadn't been brought up in the middle-class Connecticut neighborhood as she had claimed, but had come from a tenement house in the Bronx. That wouldn't have bothered him because he's not an economic snob, but then he found out that when he'd met her she wasn't making money from her art. She'd had an older man paying all her expenses for certain favors. Basically, she had climbed her way out of poverty on the backs of successful men and he was just another rung on the ladder. I'm not sure if you can understand, but it really hurt him to be married for his money and prestige, and then have his wife completely reject him as a man. He promised himself he wouldn't get caught again."

Victoria pulled at a blade of grass. "Why are you telling me this?"

He shrugged. "I just thought you might like to know."

She digested his words and they sat in silence. Soon Jerome and Foster joined them. Jerome surveyed the area. "So this is the famous garden?"

"It was going to be beautiful," Foster said.

JB looked around. "There's always next year."

Jerome looked at her curious. "So tell us about yourself."

"You know everything that's important," Victoria said no mood to humor him.

Robert came around the corner. "Don't put her on the spot."

"Hey we're just curious, little brother," Jerome said. "You didn't think you could keep this a secret for long, did you?"

JB nudged Victoria. "If Robert doesn't work out, you're free to stay with me."

"Right," Jerome said. "Like any woman in her right mind would want a man with three children."

She stared at JB amazed. "Of course! You're the one with the triplets."

He suddenly smiled. "Yes, all girls." He took out his wallet. "I have some pictures."

Jerome rolled his eyes and groaned. "Don't let him get started. You're lucky he doesn't drag along his camcorder."

JB ignored him and handed Victoria his wallet. She flipped through the photos of three little girls about five years old. "They look like you," she said.

JB studied the images. "They have a lot of their mother too."

"Careful," Jerome warned. "He thinks just because they're cute he can use them to persuade some woman to marry him."

He put the pictures away, uncomfortable. "That's not true."

"Sure it is. It took you two years just to get Christine to marry you and that was because—"

"Quiet," Robert said.

"You don't need to use your children to get a

wife," Victoria said, squeezing his hand. "You're reason enough."

Jerome laughed at the expression on JB's face. "Wow, Robert. You actually found a woman who can make JB blush. Careful little brother seems you've found another woman who knows how to handle men."

A stunned hush fell.

JB sent his brother a quelling look.

Jerome cleared his throat. "Uh, sorry about that."

Victoria stood, sensing the tension between them. "I have to go. Nice talking to you."

The men waited for her to leave then JB turned to Robert. "So?" he asked.

Robert shrugged. "So what?"

"What's going on?"

"I think that's obvious," Jerome said. "Here's my advice. Have all the fun you want, just don't marry her."

JB shook his head. "No, she gets on with Amanda. You should marry her, if only for that."

"She'll take him to the cleaners. Keep her as a mistress. She won't cost much."

"She has her own money. She won't cost anything."

Jerome folded his arms. "When has a woman cost you nothing?"

"I think Victoria's different."

"Why? Because of that grand display earlier? I agree with Mom—a quick show of dramatics and nothing more. She'll get used to having money real fast."

"So, you don't like her," Robert said.

"I didn't say I didn't like her. I like her very much, which means she's probably not good for you."

"Want her for yourself? Wouldn't be the first time."

Jerome narrowed his eyes. "I told you I was never with Rosalind. You don't have to believe me, but it wouldn't be the first time she lied to you."

Robert shoved his hands in his pockets and turned away. "Sorry. I do believe you."

He nodded letting his hands fall. "Good. I'm just offering advice. I think you should be careful."

"I'm very careful."

"Too careful," JB said. "You need to take a risk."

Jerome threw his head back and laughed. "This coming from *you?*" He laughed until tears filled his eyes.

JB frowned. "Ignore the laughing baboon and listen to me. Take a risk."

"I am," Robert said.

Jerome sobered. "If he marries this one, how will he know whether she's just marrying him for his money?"

"Because she now has money of her own."

"And again I say—"

Robert held up his hands. "I'm not interested in getting married again so let's drop the subject."

Jerome shrugged. "Okay. Let's go grab a beer and complain about women."

Robert saw Foster's face. "No, let's get a couple of root beers and catch a game."

The men agreed and piled into his car.

"Have you seen Amanda?" Katherine asked Victoria later that day. Victoria saw Lavinia in the distance and knew Amanda's disappearance would be the ammunition she needed to take her away. "I think I know where she is

Does she always disappear like this?" Lavinia asked,
ning toward them.

Usually," Katherine said. "She has a wild streak that
Braxton overlooks."

ictoria took a deep breath trying to keep her temper.
manda is a sensible girl. She is merely picky about who
spends time with." She turned before either woman
ld reply. "I'll find her." A few moments later she found
anda sitting in her favorite tree. "There you are."

'm not going back inside," she said in an angry
e voice.

Vhy not?"

Because Grandma wants to take me and I won't go."

Your uncle won't let her take you."

He always does what the family tells him."

ictoria watched an ant crawl up the trunk trying to
k of something to say. "I don't think he will this time."

manda fell quiet then said cautiously, "Grandma
sn't like you. She didn't like Ms. Janet either."

Yes, I know."

Vhy not?"

he shrugged. "Just because."

Vell I like you."

was a simple statement, but after the looks from
herine and Mrs. Braxton she needed to hear it. It
le her feel as though she did belong in some way.
a glad."

manda swung her legs. "Are you going to leave now
Ms. Janet is gone?"

ictoria studied Amanda's worried face. "No." She

motioned for her to come down. "Let's go before it gets dark."

"I want to stay out here." She hugged the trunk of the tree. "I want to sleep on this branch and watch morning come."

"It's not safe for you to stay out here."

Her face lit up as she thought of an idea. "You could stay with me. There's plenty of room."

"I've got a better idea. You could sleep on the balcony."

Amanda considered the suggestion then asked, "Will you stay with me?"

Victoria hesitated. "Okay."

Amanda smiled then climbed down the tree. "Great! I'll help you pack."

A half hour later, Robert met them as they came through the front door. "Where have you been?" he asked Amanda. "I come home and Ms. Katherine is in a panic."

Amanda raced past him. "Ms. Victoria is spending the night."

"That wasn't my question," he called after her. "Where are you going?"

"To get Ms. Katherine." She disappeared around the corner.

Robert stared amazed. "I haven't seen her that excited in a long time." He turned to Victoria and began to grin. "So she convinced you to stay, hmm?"

"I only thought—"

"You don't have to explain. You make her happy. Thank you." He bent to kiss her.

She turned her cheek to him afraid someone might see them. "Not here in the open."

He wrapped an arm around her waist. "Relax. I told you they already know."

She turned her back to him and tried to remove his arm. "It still doesn't seem right."

He pulled her closer. "It feels right." He kissed her throat his coaxing lips melting any reservations. "Don't you agree?"

She felt herself weaken and tilted her head giving him further access. "I'm beginning to."

"Do I need to be a little more convincing?"

"Perhaps."

He brushed her hair aside and kissed the back of her neck. "Would this convince you?"

"Maybe."

His mouth seared a path to the curve of her neck. "How about this?"

She grinned. "Definitely."

Katherine came around the corner and halted when he saw them. She drew in her lips. Victoria began to pull away; Robert tightened his hold. "Yes, Ms. Anderson?"

"Your niece has informed me that she wants to sleep on the balcony," she said.

"Yes, I know."

"She wants me to set everything up for her and Ms. Benser."

Robert nodded. "What's the problem?"

She glanced at Victoria. "I think we should discuss the topic in private."

"I don't."

"Very well. Your mother and I don't think it's appropriate behavior for Amanda to have sleepovers with the help staff."

"I'll decide what's appropriate behavior," he said cold and exact.

"Yes," she said with a hint of disapproval. Her eyes slid to the arm wrapped around Victoria's waist. "I'm sure you have a different idea of what that is."

Victoria could feel Robert's anger. She tried to move; his grip became like a steel bar. When she winced in pain, he loosened his hold. "Ms. Anderson why are you here?"

"I was hired to look after your niece and other familial issues," she replied.

"Yes, you were hired. So you're aware that position can change."

She blinked surprised by the veiled threat. "Yes, Mr. Braxton." She held her chin high. "Excuse me."

Victoria shook her head as Katherine's footsteps grew distant. "She's going to dislike me even more now."

Robert tucked a strand of hair behind her ear. "Why would she dislike you?"

Victoria sighed. She didn't feel like explaining it to him. "I don't know. She just doesn't approve of me."

"Don't worry. My nanny was the same way."

Her voice cracked in surprise. "Your *nanny*? Katherine is your nanny?"

"Yes, of course. What did you think she was?"

"I don't know," she stammered. "But she made her role sound so impressive."

"It is impressive. She looks after Amanda and any oth

children that come to the house. She watched Nicholas and Patrice grow."

A nanny. She'd thought Katherine was a social hostess. She'd gone about with all that grace and snootiness to look after children? Katherine suddenly seemed so ordinary she nearly laughed. Everything would be okay.

Victoria didn't consider herself good with children, but Amanda didn't seem like any of the children she'd grown up with. That evening under a canopy Victoria and Amanda set up their sleepover. The scent of a sweet spring evening filled the air. They made popcorn and cotton candy, then shivered over ghost stories and giggled at silly tales, watched a movie on Amanda's DVD, made up songs, and then listened to some.

"I want my magician's cape," Amanda said beginning to stand. "Ms. Katherine knows where it is." She pushed a button on the device that connected to other areas of the house. A few moments later Katherine came into the room.

"Did you need something?" she asked.

"Yes," Victoria said. "We need Amanda's magician's cape."

"It's in the game room."

"Would you fetch it, please?"

Katherine folded her arms and sent Victoria a significant look. "You know where the room is."

Amanda's face darkened like her uncle. "We know where it is, but it's your job to get it for us. Now go."

Victoria stared at her appalled. "You can't speak to a grown woman like that."

Amanda looked at her confused. "Yes, I can. She's supposed to do her job."

"No, you must still treat people with respect."

Katherine spoke up. "Amanda can speak to me in any manner she wishes. You, however, cannot."

Victoria stood and walked to the door. "I'll be right back Amanda. Ms. Katherine and I need to have a few words." Once outside in the hallway, she said. "That was unnecessary."

"I do not respond to the requests of those below me. You may sleep with Mr. Braxton, but I can assure you that's the only position that's changed."

Victoria straightened. "Please fetch Amanda's cape. I will not repeat myself."

"Neither will I." She spun on her heel and left.

Victoria sighed and headed to the game room. She knew her relationship with Robert would not be welcomed, but hadn't expected this. Katherine made her feel as though what she had with Robert was wrong. Perhaps it was, but she didn't care.

"Did Ms. Katherine get the cape?" Amanda asked when Victoria returned to the room.

"Yes," she lied. "Now let's pretend we're goddesses trapped by an evil witch…"

"So is it serious?" Foster asked Robert in the study they went over the monthly ledger.

"Is what serious?"

"You and Victoria."

Robert frowned. "We are discussing business right now."

"I know… and it's getting messy."

He glanced up. "What do you mean?"

"How long do you plan on paying your lover a salary?"

Robert stared at his checkbook, taking reign on his temper. He did not like discussing his personal life, but Foster had a point.

"Ah," Foster said. "So it is serious."

Robert picked up another bill.

"She doesn't need the money anymore."

"Meaning she doesn't need me anymore?"

"I didn't say that."

Robert scribbled an amount on a check.

"Come on, Braxton. Everyone is talking."

Robert sent him a glance. "They can as long as I don't hear them."

"I like her."

Robert rubbed the back of his neck ridiculously glad he did. "My mother doesn't."

"Fortunately, she's leaving tomorrow."

The two men smiled, then Foster laughed and the tense mood broke.

Someone knocked on the door. "Come in," Robert said.

Katherine entered. Foster whispered, "Here's someone else who doesn't like Victoria. Excuse me." He nodded to Katherine then closed the door behind him.

"Yes, Ms. Anderson?"

Katherine sat then said, "I've enjoyed being in your employ for a while now."

"And I've enjoyed having you."

"I liked the structured environment in which you chose

to raise your neice. The staff hierarchy was instrumental to how efficient duties were performed and…"

Robert lost his patience. "Make your point."

"Ms. Spenser feels she has the right to order me."

"What did she order you to do?"

"To fetch Amanda's cape."

Robert stared at her annoyed that she would interrupt him with such a trivial complaint. "And that's a problem?"

"Yes, it is."

"Because she asked you and not Amanda?"

"I understood that the hierarchy in this household included whom should answer to whom. I have never in all my years working here had to fetch something for someone in a position below me."

"The hierarchy has changed Ms. Anderson Everyone is equal."

"I doubt that Mr. Braxton. Every household has its fa vorites." She stood. "There is no need for a reprimand I am giving you my notice."

He nodded. "Very well."

"But be careful, Mr. Braxton some poisons smell sweet

The next morning, Robert found Amanda and Victor eating breakfast in the breakfast nook. "You're bad for th house, Ms. Spenser," he said pulling out a chair.

"Why?"

"Ms. Anderson has decided to leave us."

She looked at him surprised. "What do you mean?"

"She gave me her notice."

"But she can't leave," Victoria said alarmed. "Is s still here?"

"Yes, but it's nothing to worry about. You could look after Amanda until—"

She pushed back her chair and stood. "No, I couldn't."

Robert shook his head confused by her look of panic. "Victoria, you just spent the night with her."

"Katherine is better at this than I could ever be. I have to stop her." Victoria ran to Katherine's room. She'd been inside before.... She found her completing her packing. "Please don't leave."

Katherine folded a blouse. "Why not?"

"I'm sorry I asked you to fetch the cape. We've never liked each other and I let my pride speak...I apologize. I understand that you only answer to Amanda. I'll never ask anything of you again."

She placed the blouse in her suitcase. "It's too late."

Victoria gripped the headboard. "You don't have to leave. Please. I never wanted this."

Katherine sent her a sharp look. "I disagree. I think you've gotten exactly what you wanted. You've successfully gotten rid of every person that could stand in your way."

"You're wrong."

"Am I?"

"You can't go."

"Why not?"

She took a deep breath. "Because I can't look after children."

"Amazing considering the many times you told me how to handle Amanda."

"They were just suggestions."

"I will not stay."

Victoria lowered her voice. "If I were to leave…"

"I would rejoice." Her tone filled with venom. "I regret the day you stepped foot in this house. No wonder there have always been rumors about you and the destruction you cause. Your spirit is as black as the ashes you see. You've created division and turmoil in the short months you've been here. Because of you Patrice and Nicholas are gone, Mrs. Braxton had harsh words with her son, Foster's garden died, and your aunt passed away."

Her voice broke. "That was not my fault."

"Your behavior no doubt placed extra strain on her weak heart. Your aunt was a woman of such character, strength and humility. You were too selfish to know the shame you caused her by flirting with Mr. Braxton. Trying to impress him with your 'gift.' Now she's gone and you have her money to live on. But you'll never be one of them. No matter how fine you teach yourself to speak or what clothes you wear. You'll never belong." She smiled bitterly. "Though I know you will try.

"But Janet wasn't the one you hurt the most. Mr Braxton is your worse destruction. A man who once lived by order and rules, a man respected in his field had been reduced to using the ramblings of a cursed woman in h work. No, Victoria Spenser I wish you'd never come. Yo are ambitious and conniving. If only I had the stomac to stay and watch when he finally learns the truth abo you." She snapped her suitcase closed then left.

Victoria fell on the bed, a stab of anguish festering her chest. No matter what she did she was ultimately co demned. She could leave. She could start somewhe else. Katherine was right she'd never belong.

Robert entered the room and sat beside her. "Victoria?"

She stared sightlessly at the wall. "I couldn't get her to stay," she said near tears.

"That's okay. You can…" He stopped when she shook her head.

"I can't handle the responsibility of looking after children. I don't trust myself."

He didn't understand, but pretended to. "Okay. Then could you just stay in the house a for a time while I try to find someone else?" He reached for her hand, but she pulled it away. She didn't want to feel his touch with Katherine's accusations still ringing in her head.

"What did she say to you?" he asked.

Victoria stared at her lap.

"She was angry, you can't believe anything she said."

"But she meant it."

"She's gone now." He reached for her hand again; she let him take it. "Please stay with Amanda."

"I don't know."

He clasped her hand in both of his, and said gently, "She really enjoys you. We'll all help out, Foster, Ms. Dana, and myself. Even Benjamin."

Victoria bit her lip then said, "All right."

He opened his mouth to say more; then his mobile rang. "Braxton."

"We found the dog," Grant said.

CHAPTER EIGHTEEN

They found the little beagle mix with its throat slashed five blocks from the house in a clearing full of weeds and debris. Local kids playing there had found the dog buried under tires. The sight of the dog bothered Robert. What bothered him more, however, was Victoria staring at the old woman's burned house. She'd been determined to come with him, certain that she could read something from the ashes. Because they couldn't state that the fire was arson, he hadn't been able to come up with a profile of whom they were dealing. Victoria was their best hope.

"Someone wanted her dead," Grant said as they walked to meet Victoria.

It was such a senseless loss of life. "Strange he didn' slice the woman's throat, too. He just left her to die i the fire. How did he know she wouldn't escape?" The stopped and stared at what was left of the house. Th wind scattered ashes across the burnt lawn. "So what d you think?" Robert asked Victoria.

She didn't answer right away. She could feel the lingering pleasure of the firestarter as he'd watched the building burn. As he watched flames burst through windows and devoured furniture. In her mind she saw a photo of Glenn Miller melting. "He didn't like the house," she said. "He thought it was falling apart."

"Why did he leave her inside?"

"Because to him she was just like the building."

Grant swore; Robert agreed. That was not good. If the arsonist was now associating people with buildings they could be dealing with someone with a God Complex. Someone who believed they had the right to choose who lived and who died.

Although they spoke to potential witnesses, they had few leads to go on and had faced the inevitable that this fire would be classified as accidental and considered closed. They followed a potential lead—the victim's habit of pretending she was doing home remodeling and inviting different contractors over. They called a variety of companies and spoke to people who had visited her house, but came up empty.

Prescott splashed water on his face and grinned at his reflection in the mirror. He'd handled the cops well. Especially that Braxton character. He was just as smooth as he'd appeared on TV. He wasn't the kind of guy that meant what he said. He liked to let his big words and fancy clothes intimidate you, but he wasn't intimidated. They probably taught Braxton to talk that way in those private schools the rich send their kids to.

Prescott wiped his face with a face cloth. He liked Braxton's partner, though. What was his name… Elliot. Yea, Elliot. He seemed like a guy he could relate to. A guy who knew how it felt not to be able to afford a day off, that a buffet was the best way to stretch a thin budget. Elliot knew how it felt to be crapped on by people who had it easy in life.

Yea, he didn't mind answering Elliot's questions, but he felt sorry for him. He even felt a little sorry for Braxton. Poor guys. They really were baffled. He hung up the rag then left the bathroom. Why had the cops needed to talk to him, anyway? He'd thought they'd classified it as an electrical fire. What made them think it was something more? Perhaps he shouldn't have killed the dog, but he knew it would be lonely without its owner. He'd done it a favor.

Maybe the dog hadn't tipped them off. Maybe that psychic they used…what was her name? Yes, Victoria Spenser—Vernon Taylor's daughter. Arsonist Extraordinaire. Wow. To think she lived in his county. Perhaps there was more to her skill than anyone suspected. She probably had her father's skill with fire. No doubt Vernon had taught her a few things, had shown her some tricks.

He tossed the face cloth down on the counter. She was pretty and smart. She might even be impressed by the way he'd learned to manipulate fires. He'd love to talk to her. He felt a sudden adrenaline rush. He'd really love to talk to her…and soon he would.

Robert twisted and turned in his bed. Hampton. The little dog's name was Hampton. He didn't know why that bothered him so much. Why the sight of the dog lingered in his mind. He'd seen worse. Perhaps because the dog was a visual reminder of how the firestarter's mind was deteriorating. His violence was escalating. If they didn't catch him soon, he'd take another life.

Unfortunately, they were no closer to stopping him. He knew Victoria was just as frustrated as he was. He pounded his pillow then sat up. The case wasn't the only thing that frustrated him. Victoria slept only a few doors away. He wondered what she was wearing. It didn't matter what she was wearing. He'd picture her naked anyway. Or imagine her wearing just a garter belt. Red, no blue. He liked the color blue.

He lay back and stared up at the ceiling. She was probably asleep anyway. No, she wouldn't be asleep. She was probably thinking about the house. Something about the house bothered her. He didn't like the way she'd been staring at it. As though she were taking the death of the woman personally. At one point he'd felt as though he could read her feelings as though they were his own. He'd felt a desperate need to solve the case. To atone for something.

He groaned and threw his pillow on the ground. Great, now he was beginning to lose it. There was no special tie between them. He was just very good at observing people and decoding their emotions. He had to get some sleep. He couldn't function this way.

He pushed the sheets aside and got out of bed.

Victoria stared at the strips of moonlight that cast a pale, unearthly glow on the floor. The room felt large and alien. She enjoyed the comfort of the sleigh bed with its silk sheets and the sight of the gilded mirror on the wall, but what fascinated and terrified her the most was the fireplace. A large fireplace with an intricate stone mantle almost swallowed the main wall. She wondered what it would look like with a fire burning inside. She had found a box of matches that had been left on the mantle, but she could never trust herself to start a fire. She had buried the matches in a drawer. At times like this, however, in the silent night, she wondered…

Victoria gripped the sheets when she heard footsteps outside her door. The door swung open and she recognized the figure that came into the room just by his stance. She sat up as the figure came towards the bed. "What are you doing here?"

"Move over," he grumbled.

She did. "You can't stay here."

"Why not?" He waved a dismissive hand. "Forget it. Don't tell me. I don't care." He climbed into the bed and drew her close. He rested his head on her chest and sighed satisfied. "There, that's better." Within seconds he fell asleep.

Victoria toyed with the tight curls at the base of his neck. Yes, he was right…that was much better. She pushed away thoughts of the fireplace and fell asleep, too.

"You don't need to worry about the gallery," Victoria told Ms. Linsol, the new housekeeper. She was a woman from Barbados who carried herself well and had attractive, fine sculpted features. Aside from her good looks and grace, however, she was Katherine's complete opposite. She was a woman eager to learn and eager to help in any w possible, even taking Amanda out on occasion. She made everyone feel at ease. Victoria was about to give more instructions when Foster burst into the room. "I don't believe it," he said.

The two women stared at him. "What happened?" Victoria asked, concerned when she saw tears in his eyes.

"You did it, Vicky, you did it."

No one had ever called her Vicky before. Victoria usually wasn't fond of nicknames, but coming from him the name filled her with pleasure. "Did what?"

"The garden. Haven't you looked? I know you've been busy and all, but I thought you'd at least glance at it."

"What's wrong with it?" she asked cautiously.

"Nothing's wrong with it. It's blooming." He ignored her puzzled look, grabbed her hand, and led her outside.

He stopped in front of the garden. "Look. Just look at it. Isn't it beautiful!"

It was a labyrinth of blue. The garden looked as though all his ideas and sketches had leapt off the page of his imagination in full Technicolor. He had layered the plants tall to short and varied their tones from sapphire lackspur to violet-blue lisianthus to spanish blue-bells nd finished off with pretty blue perennials and annuals. weet scents filled the air as the flowers warmed themelves in the sun.

"You've done well, Mr. Foster," Ms. Linsol said.

Victoria threw her arms around him. "We won!"

He laughed and clumsily hugged her back. "Not so st. There are still other houses that may have gardens tter than this."

"I doubt it."

Victoria drew away when she heard the shifting of gravel as a car came up the drive. She turned and saw Robert stepping out of his SUV. Her heart overflowed with joy and she ran to him, stopping before she threw her arms around him. Though everyone now knew what was between them, she still felt awkward showing it. She skidded on the stones and crashed into him.

He steadied her. "Slow down. What's wrong?"

She beamed at him. "The garden survived! We're going to win. The rain must have helped the treatment work," she said in a breathless rush.

"What?"

"The garden survived. Look!"

Robert looked past her and his mouth fell open. He slowly walked towards Foster in amazement. "I don't believe it. It's a miracle."

"Named Victoria." Foster grinned at her.

"I didn't do it alone," she said, not wanting to take all the credit. "You both helped."

The men ignored her.

"I thought that mix was a bunch of nonsense," Foster confessed.

"I know. A total waste of time," Robert added.

"But hey she was determined and said that you wanted to do it so I figured let's give it a go."

"I thought I'd be indulgent. She was so deter mined, I wasn't sure I would get her out of my offic until I said *yes*."

Victoria spoke up. "Now wait a minute—"

"I was almost glad the rain came so that it would work."

Foster nodded. "Yea, it would have saved her the humiliation just in case the treatment didn't work anyway."

She folded her arms. "It was—"

Robert winked at her. "You're free to start undressing at any moment."

Her hands fell to her hips. "I'll save that for the judges."

The two men gaped at her alarmed. She laughed.

Robert quickly recovered. His voice was harsh. "If your fingers even brush against your buttons, you're fired."

She laughed harder. "I'll bet they're all women anyway. Although some women—"

He scowled. "I'm not kidding."

"They'll be too busy looking at the garden anyway. I bet all the other gardens will look like weeds compared to ours."

Robert rested an arm on each of their shoulders. "You both make me proud. I want to thank you for a job well done."

She leaned her head against him. "The judges won't want to leave."

Foster nodded. "If we don't get First Place, we darn well better get second."

She shook her head. "This garden deserves nothing but First."

Melinda's eyes felt raw after hours of staring at the computer screen.

"You need to give yourself a break," Grant said.

"A break? I think I'm ready to quit." She'd spent hours on the phone attempting to find CHC. When that resulted in nothing, she had searched the computer for chemical retailers and container manufacturers in the city. When she found nothing in the city, she expanded her search to the state, then the nation, and, finally, the English-speaking globe. Still nothing. "This is fruitless."

He massaged her shoulders. "You'll find them."

She sighed, relaxing under his hands. She still couldn't believe how quickly she'd gotten used to him being in her life. He still smoked too much, had a sick sense of humor, and bristled at the sight of authority, but she liked him. She liked him a lot; she liked his kisses even better. Who would have guessed a man with such a dirty mouth would have such sweet lips? She glanced at them now and had to hide a grin, very sweet. "Fifteen more minutes then I'll stop and treat you to breakfast."

"Sounds good." He dropped a hand to the front of her blouse.

"That isn't my shoulder."

"Sorry my hand slipped."

"If you don't move it, it might get arrested."

He slipped a finger inside her blouse. "It's been arrested before."

She slapped his hand away. "Find something to keep yourself busy."

"I have."

"Besides me."

"Oh." He sat down and glanced at his watch. "Fifteen minutes starts now." He rested his head back and pretended to fall asleep.

Melinda didn't think she'd find much in fifteen minutes but kept up the search anyway. After ten minutes, she moved to shut down her computer when CHC came on the screen: Canadian Hazardous Chemicals.

"I found it," she said in disbelief.

Grant lifted his head. "You did?"

"Yes."

He fell to his knees and held his hands together as though in prayer.

She looked at him and laughed. "What are you doing?"

"I'm having a religious moment. Our prayers have been answered."

She printed out the information, then dialed the number. She got a busy signal. When she tried reaching Braxton she got the same. She hung up the phone frustrated.

"Don't worry we'll get them," Grant said, grabbing her jacket. "Let's get something to eat."

She wasn't in the mood for a heavy breakfast so she grabbed coffee and a bagel, then returned to the office and called again. No answer. She sat back and glanced around the empty office. Grant had responded to a call, so she had no one to talk to. She flipped through a magazine, then dialed a third time. This time a woman picked up the phone.

"Hello," Melinda said. "I'm special agent Melinda Brenner with the Bureau of Alcohol, Tobacco, and Firearms in the U.S. I need information about some of your shipments to Maryland."

The woman didn't reply.

"Hello? Hello?" Melinda glanced at the phone wondering if she'd lost connection. "Hello? Are you still there?"

"What kind of information do you want?" the woman asked.

"I'm interested in a large delivery of about three hundred five-gallon containers of acetone last March."

"You're a DEA agent?"

"No, I'm with the BATF."

"I'm sorry, but I can't provide you with any information."

Melinda sighed. "Okay, then I'd like to speak to your supervisor."

The woman hesitated then said, "I'll get in touch with the owner and have him call you back in a few minutes."

Melinda hung up the phone and waited. She frowned when the receptionist told her she had a call. She had given the lady at CHC her direct line. "Take a message," she said.

"The caller said it's important," the receptionist insisted.

"I'll call them back."

A few minutes later her phone rang. "This is Daniel Ruskus of CHC. I understand you're interested in some information?"

"Yes," Melinda said. "I'm interested in a shipment of a large quantity of acetone sold to a purchaser in the Haltson area."

"Sorry, but we don't manufacture chemicals. Only chemical-safe containers."

"All right. Did you ship a large number of five-gallon hard plastic containers to Maryland within the past three months or so to a single customer? The name CHC is on them."

"One moment."

Melinda heard typing, but had the feeling that Ruskus was stalling for some reason.

"We recently had a similar inquiry from another agency in the U.S.," he said.

"Who?"

"I've been instructed not to say. I was also instructed not to mention their inquiry to anyone else, but if you're with the BATF…"

"Did you have the information they wanted?"

"We shipped 250 of that particular container to a warehouse in Maryland for a company called umm…I have it here somewhere…"

Melinda tapped her pen irritated. He was stalling again.

"I found it. Techno Technology." He gave a shipment date.

It was one week before the building had burned. Just what she needed. It was now clear that the discarded CHC jugs were concentrated in the Techno Technology section of the warehouse for a reason. They had shipped the jugs to a warehouse only a few miles from the burned warehouse, but how had the containers ultimately ended up full of acetone inside the building? she wondered.

"Who signed for the shipment?" she asked.

"A customer by the name of Josef Haddad."

Melinda tapped a finger against her forehead in frustration. Why did that name sound familiar? After ending her conversation with him, Melinda got a call from the office receptionist again. "Melinda the same man is on the line. He says he's from the DEA and he needs to speak to you."

She picked up the phone and identified herself.

"Hello," the man said. "I'm DEA agent Doug Frank. It's no coincidence that I'm calling you now. Ruskus just informed me that you called him. I think we need to talk."

Doug Frank wasn't pleased. It seemed that Haddad and his cousin had slipped away from their house with more than two hundred gallon containers full of acetone and delivered it to the warehouse while they were under surveillance. The two agents sat with Melinda, Grant, Robert, and DEA supervisor Doug Frank in Frank's office.

He informed them that they knew nothing about the fire or Haddad being the subject of criminal investigation until CHC had informed them about their query.

"We thought we were onto a coke lab," Doug said. "Haddad rented two Ryder trucks. He used the first rented truck two weeks before the fire to purchase twenty-five fifty-five gallon drums of acetone. It was that transaction that caught our interest."

"So you started surveillance," Grant said.

"Correct. The following week Haddad rented another Ryder and picked up 250 jugs from a warehouse in the south of town that had been delivered by CHC. We traced CHC the same why you did back to Techno Technology. We were convinced there was a drug lab inside the residence. But we didn't have sufficient probable cause for a search warrant."

"So they were able to slip away," Robert guessed.

He nodded embarrassed. "That's why no agen

followed either the Ryder or van when each left the residence separately during the afternoon of the fire.

"At six that evening, agents searched the truck for signs of cocaine, but didn't find anything. Three hours later a police detective working an off duty job guarding the warehouse district spotted a van nosing around the area. The detective pulled the van over. There was only one person in the vehicle and the partition blocked his view of anything in the back.

"The detective took note of the van's tag number and learned it was the same van under surveillance. The driver handed over his driver's license that identified him as Basam Haddad. The detective noticed some papers and a CB radio lying on the vacant passenger's seat; however, nothing appeared suspicious. He ran a R&W—records and wanted—on the man's name. Haddad came back clean."

"They always do," Grant said.

"Unfortunately, so did the house when we executed a search warrant. No acetone, no CHC jugs, no coke. Nothing. It had all disappeared, as well as Haddad and his cousin."

"Yes, we discovered that, too," Robert said.

"Since they haven't claimed insurance we can't prove intent to defraud. Possessing acetone isn't a crime."

"But with all this money at stake, you would have thought Haddad would be camped out waiting for the insurance claims to pay off," Melinda said.

The group fell silent knowing one thing. Haddad and his cousin were smarter than that.

CHAPTER NINETEEN

"I don't think it's about cocaine," Robert said to Grant and Melinda at lunch.

"It's about insurance," Grant said.

"I'm not sure it's that either."

Grant frowned. "Then what do you think it is?"

"I think we're missing a piece of the puzzle."

"What else is there?" Melinda asked.

"The third man."

"What third man?"

Grant spoke up. "Victoria said—"

Melinda held up a hand. "Stop right there. While I respect her skill, whatever that may be, there's no sign o there being a third man. And even if there was, until w get these two, we don't have anything to link him. So unti Victoria can 'see' a man's face or name I don't want he visions part of this investigation."

Victoria wasn't presently seeing anything except th garden winning First Place. Her high hopes for th

garden faltered when the Great Gardens judges arrived:
two men and one woman who sported polite smiles, im-
passive glances, and vague statements. They asked Robert
and Foster a few harmless questions, made references to
the layout then said they'd be in touch.

"At least that's over," Robert said as the judges piled
into their car and left.

Victoria frowned. "They didn't even look excited."

"They want to be impartial."

"That one lady judge said it was 'interesting',"
Foster said gloomily. "You know that is the kiss of
death. It's probably the color selection of the daffodils and hyacinths."

"And the day is sort of gray," Victoria said, looking up
at a sky that couldn't get any brighter.

"We did our best," Robert said, turning to the house.
"All we can do now is wait."

With each passing day Victoria's hopes perished. She
had imagined that the judges would be so impressed by
the garden that they would call the same day or at least
the day after. Three days later, however, Robert hadn't
heard a word. She sat on the stone step of the house
looking at the fireflies and the sliver of moon high in the
darkening sky. She remembered how much fun she had
when she was back home catching *peenywallies* and using
them as lanterns as they walked to and from different
houses for church. Those days seemed far away. That girl
was so different from the woman she had become.

She turned when she heard something making its way

through the grass. Robert came towards her holding a rose—in his teeth.

She jumped to her feet, her heart pounding. "We won?"

His face split into a grin.

She ran and leaped into his outstretched arms. He spun her around until the moon and fireflies melted into one.

He stopped and gazed down at her. "We did it," he whispered.

"Yes, we did."

He picked up the flower he'd dropped and handed it to her.

She raised it to her nose then searched his eyes. There was such smoldering emotion she had to drop her gaze. "I wish Aunt Janet were here."

"Me too." He sat on the front step and pulled her down next to him. "My grandfather loved nights like this. When I was younger, he would wake me up in the middle of the night and tell me he had something to show me. It was always the same thing and sometimes I would grumble as I followed him downstairs to the garden. He would lie down on the grass, gaze up and say, 'Look at that!' as if the night sky were a new and brilliant discovery. I could never understand how he could have the same amazement each time. But now I do." He turned to her. "Because every time I'm with you, I'm in awe."

Her cheeks grew warm. "I wish I could have met your grandfather."

He rested his elbows on his knees. "You two would have liked each other. Like you, he didn't fear anything."

"Oh, I fear lots of things."

"You don't let the fear stop you and that makes all the difference. No matter what obstacle he faced, my grandfather didn't stop trying to live life to the fullest. He'd had a hard life as a young man, but nothing made him bitter."

She thought about his mother's anger and shook her head. "I'm sorry about your father."

"You don't have to apologize."

"But I do. I may have gotten a new dress or dinner at my favorite restaurant because of what your father was accused of. I can't make it okay and I never will, but let me just tell you how sorry I am that your father was taken from you. And when you want to, you can talk about him all you want. You don't have to keep him secret just because you think it will hurt me."

"My father." His voice shook, he steadied it. "He reminded me of an oak tree. Impressive. Strong. He and my grandfather were both strong. I don't know how they did it."

"Yes, you do."

He began to smile. "My resident psychologist. How do I know?"

"Because you live the life you want no matter what other people say. You're here with me even though—" *My father was a murderer.*

"Let's not discuss it anymore. It was something that happened when we were both kids. Besides the night is too beautiful for painful memories."

She waved the rose under his nose.

He grasped her hand. "What are you doing?"

"Every time you smell a rose, I want you to think of this night and how you felt."

He brushed his lips against hers. "I don't need a rose to do that." He abruptly stood. "You'd better rest so you'll be ready for tomorrow."

She pricked herself on a thorn and sucked her finger. "What's happening tomorrow?"

"The media arrives."

She frowned, confused. "But they'll want to take pictures of the garden not me."

He turned. "Victoria, even a prize winning garden could not compete with you."

He was right. The photographers and journalists that crowed his doorstep the next day instantly fell in love with her. Probably more for the gossip columns than for the garden, Victoria handled it with grace, enchanting them with the stories of how she had saved the garden from ruin, Aunt Margaret's flower shop, and her journey to America. The journalists scribbled down her every word as the photographers tried to capture her allure—her rich cocoa skin, abundance of hair, and full figure—on film. They took some pictures of Foster and Robert, but it was obvious to everyone that she and the garden were the main attraction. By the end of the day her throat felt sore and every time she blinked she saw flashbulbs.

"I'm glad that's over," she said, collapsing in the kitchen.

"I think you were wonderful," Ms. Linsol said.

"But it's not over yet," Dana said.

Victoria wearily lifted her head. "What?"

"There's the party."

"What party?"

"Mr. Braxton is hosting a garden party. He usually does so this time of year, but this one is going to be even more important. He'll have influential people from all over and wild card tickets."

Victoria yawned. "Wild card tickets?"

"For a price, some of the public can attend. But most people will be from the organizations he belongs to. Everyone will get to see the garden."

She rubbed her tired eyes. "Are we supposed to serve the food?"

"No, it's entirely catered. We're guests. It's unorthodox, but he doesn't care."

She sat up horrified by the thought. She would be surrounded by people like Lilah, the woman she'd met at the restaurant, and others who had lots of money and education. People closer to Robert's world than she could ever hope to be. "But I don't need to go. Why would I need to be there?"

"Because you helped Foster with the garden," Ms. Linsol said.

Dana sent her a significant look. "Victoria, we both know of all the people in this house he will expect you to be there."

Her mind raced through the meager selection of clothing hanging in her closet. "But I have nothing to wear."

"Buy something. You have the money."

She paused. She'd buried herself in hiring the new housekeeper and possible nanny that she'd pushed the reality of the money aside. She still cringed at the thought of spending it. Though others had not known about her aunt's marriage they seemed more accepting of Janet's hidden wealth than Victoria could be. It wouldn't hurt to buy a new dress. Unfortunately, she had no idea how to go about shopping for a dress.

She went into a store and bought the first suitable dress that caught her eye: A flowery print dress with lace at the trim. It was expensive so Victoria felt certain it would suit.

Amanda saw it hanging in the laundry room as Victoria ironed the clothes.

She grimaced and pointed. "What is that?"

"My dress for the party."

"You can't wear that."

"Why not? I think it's lovely."

"I think it's awful." Amanda snatched the dress off the hanger. "I'll be right back." Victoria began to protest, but she was already gone. Amanda returned a few moments later, looking pleased with herself. "It's all set."

Victoria stared at her. "Where's my dress?"

"I'm donating it to Goodwill," she said simply.

"Wait a minute—"

"I can't wait." She unplugged the iron. "We're going shopping. Foster is taking us into town and Uncle gave me the money." She waved her credit card with pride. "I showed him how ugly your dress was and he raised my limit."

"You have a credit card?"

She shrugged. "Sure. Doesn't everybody?"

* * *

Foster drove Victoria and Amanda to a little boutique tucked in the side roads of town. A personal assistant waited for Victoria with a selection of dresses already picked out. Victoria went through an assortment of pleasant conservative styles, which Amanda soundly rejected.

"You look like my teachers," she grumbled. When the assistant brought another dull selection, Amanda lost her patience. "She wants something beautiful so that my uncle will fall in love with her."

The assistant hesitated, surprised by her bluntness, then nodded and returned the clothes.

Victoria looked at Amanda, her cheeks on fire. "Why would you say such a thing?"

"It's true, isn't it?" She folded her arms and twisted from side to side, grinning. "Now they'll know what you need."

"You could have said I wanted something beautiful. You know I don't want your uncle to fall in love with me."

She toyed with one of her pigtails. "I know you like Uncle Robert and he likes you."

"Yes, but—"

She sent her a sly glance. " And I've heard Ms. Dana talking."

"She's always talking."

"But this time it was interesting."

Victoria sighed exasperated as curiosity took hold. "What did she say?"

"They said they knew how much he liked you when Uncle made Patrice leave because of you. He's never done that before."

"Patrice chose to leave on her own."

Amanda didn't listen. "I'm so glad he made her leave. I told you she was gross, didn't I? She used to make Ms. Natalie clip her toenails. And she'd always call me 'Poor Mandy' because my parents are away. But making Nicholas leave was the best. He likes to pull my hair when no one is looking. Once I put jelly in his shoes, but he had so many, he didn't even notice."

"Does it make you sad that your parents aren't here?"

"No. They send me lots of postcards. I wish Uncle would get married though."

"Why?"

She shrugged. "Just 'cause." Then she smiled at Victoria in a way that made her uncomfortable.

Victoria sighed relieved when the assistant came back with new dresses for review. She looked at the new assortment and knew Amanda wasn't far from wrong. She did want to buy a dress that would make Robert fall in love with her. Something that would make him stop, stare, then announce his undying love.

She finally found the dress she hoped would do. A translucent blue dress of shimmering layers of silk with an accompanying shawl. She loved how the silk hugged her body and caressed her skin. At another store she bought black slingback shoes. Then off they went to the hair salon where Amanda, or rather her uncle, had already scheduled an appointment. She had her hair put in a soft upsweep of twists.

"You're gonna look beautiful," Amanda said as they drove home. "I wish I could come to the party."

"You'll be bored," Victoria said. "It's a grown up party."

"How come grown-ups have all the fun?"

"Who says we have all the fun?" Foster said from the driver's seat.

"You do," she insisted. "I can tell."

"I'm going to tease you about this moment when you're older."

Amanda rested her chin on the back of his chair. "I'll be too busy having fun to care. I'll be going to parties, shopping, traveling."

"Sit back," Victoria said.

She turned to her. "Will you visit me before you go to bed?"

"It may end late."

"I'll wait up." She clasped her hands together. "Please. It's only fair I get to see you all dressed up. And you have to tell me everything that happens."

She squeezed her hands. "Okay. I will."

The evening was perfect for a garden party. The tart bite of winter had gone away and summer was pushing through the buds of spring. The array of colors in the garden looked spectacular in the glow of the setting sun. People moved through the heady scent of bell-flowers and petunias that mingled with the smoke from tiki lanterns. People oohed and ahhed over their surroundings with permanent smiles on their faces. Victoria's smile was beginning to fray, however. For the past hour and a half she had exchanged pleasantries until it became a strain.

She tried to remember what her aunt would say, how she might behave, but that didn't help. Everyone looked

so well-dressed and sounded so articulate and knowl-
edgeable. She had the strange urge to act like Amanda
and find a place to hide. She felt embarrassed not
knowing what to say or how to act.

This crowd was unimpressed by her, unlike the
media who had made her feel like a celebrity. She
hadn't expected the crowd to fawn over her, but she
had hoped for more than bland smiles and cool dis-
missals. They knew the truth about her. She wasn't
apart of their world. She remembered how Uncle
William would scold her when guests came over. On
the rare instances when he'd let her out of the room
to meet them. *Don't drag yuh feet, cover yuh mout when
yuh cough, mind your manners*. It didn't matter how she
behaved, however, they all still whispered about her.

Her grand entrance had also been a disappointment.
She didn't see Robert anywhere when she had arrived at
the party, and she still hadn't seen him almost two hours
later. Hadn't he even planned to see her? she wondered.
Perhaps he thought she would enjoy herself. How little
he knew her if he thought she would find this stuffy
crowd enjoyable.

She glanced across the garden and saw someone
looking as uncomfortable as she felt. Foster wore an olive
suit that could have benefited from an iron. He scanned
the crowd like hunted prey as he tugged on his collar for
the tenth time in half an hour. She walked toward him.
An attractive black man with thinning hair and a big
smile blocked her path. "Victoria Spenser?" he asked.

"Yes."

He held out his hand. "I'm Prescott Delaney."

She shook his hand overwhelmed by his enthusiasm. "It's a pleasure to meet you."

"The pleasure is all mine. I was glad I could scrape together the money to come here and meet you."

She didn't know what to say so she just smiled.

He glanced around. "This place is amazing. I'm just a regular guy you know. This kind of thing isn't me, but I had to come." He lifted the end of her shawl. "You're an inspiration."

A sense of unease rippled through her, mingling with a hint of excitement. Something about him didn't feel quite right. She kept her smile in place. "Thank you."

"I am a contractor. I know a lot of people who could use your expertise." He pointed. "I see the trellis could use repair. I gave Braxton my card."

"We'll remember to use your help."

His gaze measured the length of her. "You're prettier in person. I saw you on TV both times. So how do you handle crowds like this?"

"I'm sorry?"

He lowered his voice to that of a conspirator. "I know about you. About your gift. You sense things right? You don't have to answer that... I know you're involved with the recent fire investigations. So do you think the old woman's place was an accidental fire?"

She sent him a look. "I think you already know the answer to that."

He stepped closer. He smelled like vanilla a safe, wholesome scent, that didn't seem to suit him. "It was arson, but they don't have any leads yet. I know this because they asked me questions about it. I'd been to the old lady's house. She'd wanted a window seat built. So what do you think?"

She glanced around eager to escape. "I don't think this is the place to discuss that."

"Where would you like to discuss it?"

She took a step back. "Since you gave Mr. Braxton your card when my schedule is free I'll know how to reach you."

"Yes, that's right." He shook his head then said, "Crazy bastard if it was arson."

She looked at him, trying to read his eyes. "I don't think he's crazy."

"You don't?"

"No, he's too clever for that."

He appeared thoughtful for a moment. "Not everyone would think that. I don't. I know about fires…my father was in construction. He used to help build those indestructible 'burn buildings' fire departments use. Now they got scientific gadgets or video-game stuff. It's not the same you know? These investigators need to be in the action. They need to feel the heat and smoke and find out the personality of a fire, how it works. Don't you agree?"

"Yes."

"I hope you catch him."

She fought to keep a pleasant expression. "Thank you."

When he made no move to leave she quietly said, "Excuse me." She walked past him, but soon realized Foster had disappeared. Now she had no anchor in this sea of people. She saw an empty bench and made her way towards it, hoping to get there before someone else had the same idea. She was about to sit when she spotted Robert. Her heart leaped.

He stood out of the crowd like a palm tree among hibicus. Even across the garden his magnetism hit her. She tugged on the fringe of her shawl debating on whether she should wait for him to notice her or if she should go to him. She took a step in his direction, trying to think of casual things to say, but people surrounded him and she didn't want to join the group. When would she ever feel as though she belonged?

She wrapped her shawl tight around her and discreetly left the party. She headed to Amanda's room. A hand covered hers as she climbed the stairs. "Has it stuck midnight?" Robert asked, his deep voice stirring feelings within her.

The warmth of his hand melted her insides. She halted paralyzed, afraid that if she moved or breathed he would disappear and the moment would end. "No."

He moved up a step behind her. "Then you can't leave yet."

"I have to," she said woodenly, trying to ignore the cologne that floated around her.

"Why?"

He sounded so ordinary that she turned to him. Her heart nearly stopped. He looked devastatingly handsome in a black suit that accentuated his rich skin and killer smile. He seemed extra large, extra arrogant, and completely out of reach. He was every much the eagle compared with her butterfly. She had money now, but still didn't belong in his world.

He snapped his fingers in front of her face. "Victoria?"

"You look wonderful."

"So do you. Come back to the party. You don't have to be afraid."

She started, remembering her talk with the man who smelled like vanilla. "Who said I was afraid?"

He shrugged. "I just felt..." He stopped, frowned, then shook his head. "Forget it." He held out his hand. "Come on."

"I'm tired."

He laughed. "Yes, some of them are pretty boring, aren't they? A room full of stomach pills." He studied her as much as she did him, but whatever thoughts he had, he kept to himself. "There are people I want you to meet."

"I've met all the people I can stand."

"Yes, thank you for not slicing anyone with your tongue, I wouldn't want blood dripping on my flowers." He lowered his voice. "Let's sneak away then."

"I have to visit Amanda."

He smiled resigned. "So she wants you all to herself? If only we all could be so lucky." He turned and left.

CHAPTER TWENTY

Amanda sat wide-awake on her bed when Victoria entered her room. She gushed over Victoria's dress and asked questions about the party, wanting Victoria to describe in detail, what people where doing, wearing and eating.

Victoria told her about the waiters and their trays of champagne, miniature tarts and salmon, and the overheard conversation of a professor comparing society to an ant colony. She described several of the women's outlandish clothing. She stopped when someone knocked on the door.

They looked at each other confused.

"Are you expecting someone?" Victoria asked.

Amanda shook her head. "No." She made a face. "It won't be anyone interesting."

The person knocked again. "Come in," she said.

Robert entered with a tray of cheesecake covered in strawberries. He had a plate for each of them.

Amanda bounded towards him. "What are you doing here?"

He set the tray on her desk. "I brought dessert, hoping I could persuade you to let me stay."

"You've come to visit me?" she asked shyly, but pleased.

"Yes. Foster told me you wanted to join the party."

She looked away embarrassed. "Yea, but Ms. Victoria's been telling me all about it. Do you like her dress?"

Robert's eyes traveled to her as she sat on the bed, the large glass doors that led to the balcony framing her like a picture. "Very much," he said in a low tone.

"I'm glad." Amanda sat on the bed and bounced up and down. "We had an awful time trying to find one. It almost took forever because the woman kept bringing out these boring dresses, but then I said—"

Victoria covered her mouth. "Then we got this dress."

"You chose very well," he said.

Amanda smiled with pleasure. "You look very nice, too."

He bowed. "Thank you."

"Can we eat now?"

He handed them a plate then sat on the ground and Amanda sat next to him, peppering him with questions that he calmly answered. Victoria sat across from them as Robert teased Amanda about being a pest. Then she and Robert took turns telling stories until Amanda fell asleep, her head resting on his thigh. She watched him tenderly brush hair from her cheek.

"You love her very much," she said.

He glanced up surprised. "Sure. She's my sister's kid."

Victoria knew his feelings were more than that and wondered when he would admit that fact to himself.

Robert smiled in memory. "I remember the first day I brought her home. I was terrified. Anytime I wanted to pick her up I made sure there were pillows around in case I dropped her." Robert put Amanda in bed then invited Victoria out on to the balcony. Jazz music floated up to them mixing with the scent of ivy. In her mind she saw drifts of smoke from the tiki lamps mingle with the moonlight. She thought about the recent fires and felt an unmistakable high.

"What's wrong?" Robert asked.

"What do you mean what's wrong?"

"Something is troubling you, and don't give me that look—just answer the question."

She gripped the railing. "I met a man."

Robert's face became a hard mask. "What did he do? Is he still here?"

She grabbed his arm as he turned to leave. "It wasn't like that. He was very polite. He was also very interested in the recent fires."

"That's common. I get that a lot. People find out I'm an arson investigator and suddenly the want to know what a burned body looks and smells like."

"It seemed more than casual interest. I don't know…it may be nothing. He said he gave you his card."

"I get a lot of business cards and hand them over to Foster."

"I need to see them."

They retrieved the cards from Foster and shifted

through them. Victoria seized one. "Prescott Delaney. That's him."

"Hmm…his name sounds familiar."

"He said he talked to you. You questioned him about the fire."

"Oh. It's not uncommon for potential witnesses or even suspects to develop an unhealthy interest in a case. Since he doesn't stick out in my mind, he probably came out clean." He saw the concern on her face and sighed resigned. "Okay I'll try to find out more."

She slowly smiled. "Thank you."

Unfortunately, despite his search there was nothing suspicious about Prescott Delaney.

Prescott would have been thrilled if he'd known he'd captured Victoria's interest. He glanced out his window at the summer evening. It had been weeks since the garden party, but he was still high from his meeting with Victoria, Vernon Taylor's daughter. He couldn't believe he'd gotten the chance to meet her. She was all he thought she would be. Such pretty brown eyes. He'd researched all he could about her. She loved fire as much as he did. That gave them a special connection no one else could understand.

He wondered if she knew he was the firestarter for whom the investigators were looking. He doubted it. Prescott turned from the window and sat on his couch. He wanted to see her again. He didn't know when she'd be free to discuss the fires with him. Maybe he could convince her to use him to build something. He'd love to do something to impress her.

He turned on the Channel Six news. A pretty brunette came on the screen.

"It's been over four months since a fire ravaged a local warehouse and investigation has fallen flat. Despite their psychic guidance, the investigators have few leads, little evidence, and no suspects…"

Prescott watched with growing anger as he listened to the reporter's offensive tone. Who the hell was this woman? He read the name on the screen. *Susannah Rhodes.* Susannah sounded like such a nice, elegant southern name. One would have thought she'd grown up with more manners, but those ambitious women always seemed to have more balls than breasts.

Susannah Rhodes… oh yea…he knew about her. He was surprised she was still working. Years ago she was just a washed up lush the tabloids liked to capture in embarrassing situations. Amazing the type of people the public gave second chances.

Prescott flexed his fingers as a headache slowly grew. You'd think she'd be more grateful for this chance to educate the public. Instead, she had a disdain for the community and even her audience. Just because she was pretty didn't mean she was better than others or had the right to be disrespectful of the people who risked their lives to keep the county safe. Just where would she be if anything happened to her? He began to grin…

Grant balanced on the back legs of his chair as he sat in Robert's office. He glanced at Melinda, who had on her focused face. Personally, he'd rather do something else. He was sick of the warehouse fire case. The Techno Technology company still hadn't filed an insurance claim, athough all the other companies in the warehouse had. When he'd gone to inquire about why, the insurance agent looked at him confused. He hadn't even been aware that one of their clients had been involved in a fire.

Grant sighed. Aside from that, there were no signs that Haddad planned coming out of hiding any time soon. Through reconstructing the TT cargo they learned that the company didn't have the high-quality electronics from Singapore and China they had listed. Instead, they had a lot of cabinets. It was a nice façade…like a warehouse stacking empty boxes to look full.

"So how much is the real value of the destroyed merchandise?" Robert asked.

"It was all a scam," Melinda said. "They listed the value one price, but it's possible to get an identical version at any discount store. I'd say the real loss is about twenty thousand dollars."

"They had a six hundred thousand dollar insurance policy."

Grant clasped his hands behind his head. "I'd say the answer is obvious. Insurance fraud."

Robert shook his head. "Unless someone benefits or attempts to benefit from it we can't prove a motive for arson."

"Since Haddad has verified his custom documents he might have bribed someone to get the cargo in the U.S."

"I already thought of that," Melinda said. "The government refuses to use the manhours to find out more about our man and his activities."

Grant let his chair fall on all four legs, before succumb-

ing to the temptation of banging his head against the wall.
The conclusion stared them in the face. Either they solve
the case themselves or let the arsonist go free.

After Grant and Melinda left his office, Robert grabbed
a bunch of old files and began going through them.
Unsolved cases were not uncommon in his field, but
something about this case nagged at him. He'd gotten two
questions answered about the warehouse fire. First
Haddad may have entered the building hidden in a crate.
That was how he'd gotten in undetected by the alarm.

Second, though the warehouse owner, Ms. Warren,
continued to state that no acetone was stored in the warehouse they were able to determine that TT, Techno Technology, had an unmarked padded crate delivered as
coming through customs. That meant that because it was
shipped within the U.S., its contents were not noted. Unfortunately, the source of the delivery was left off surviv-
ng records.

Robert flipped through the OPEN files, then stopped
t one that sent off warning bells. The Magruder
rocery store fire. It had occurred three years ago and
ad eerie similarities to the warehouse fire. It involved
large loss and was an acetone fire. Robert went
rough the two-page witness list. He saw that Grant
nd Melinda had run background checks on all the wit-
esses. They had either met them in person over had
oken to them over the phone. The current employ-
s had been questioned face to face. Robert went
rough the list until a name jumped out at him.
ddad. The file listed him as a disgruntled employee.

Like most arsonists, Haddad had come out clean on the background check. He'd worked at the grocery store only three weeks, but he had clashed with the manager and most of the employees. Robert began to smile. Two fires and one man—that was not a coincidence. They'd broken through their dead end.

He called Grant then Melinda.

"I knew he sounded familiar," Melinda said pleased. "We've got our man."

"Except for one possibility," Robert said.

Her voice fell. "What?"

"Our man might be dead."

CHAPTER TWENTY-ONE

Victoria saw fire in the distance. Flame-orange leaves rustled, ready to fall to the ground. A brazen wind tore some from their branches, as the hand of autumn staked its claim. She'd spent months on this land yet still felt like a wanderer. She found solace in the greenhouse now that the garden bed needed to rest. She'd been disappointed when Robert found nothing on Prescott, but felt relief at the absence of fires. She'd come close to a regular life.

She tucked a strand of hair behind her ear. She'd had it stylishly trimmed and cut. It wasn't the only change in her life. She now ate with Robert and Amanda. She remembered her first meal at the dinning table.

Dana had smiled at her as she placed a dish on the table. "It's going to be a lovely meal, Victoria."

Robert lifted a brow. "What did you say?"

"I said the meal…" She abruptly stopped and looked apologetic. "I'm so sorry Mr. Braxton I forgot." She turned to Victoria. "I mean it's going to be a lovely meal, Ms. Spenser."

Victoria dismissed the address. "You don't have to call me that."

"Yes, she does," Robert said.

"Robert, I worked with her."

"And now you don't. It's a sign of respect. You used to call me Mr. Braxton."

She smiled. "I also called you a lot of things behind your back."

"You were wise enough not to let me hear them."

"I don't mind calling you Ms. Spenser," Dana said.

"It's not right," Victoria said.

Amanda spoke up. "How about Ms. Victoria like I do?"

Robert sighed. "Fine."

Victoria turned from the window and laughed in memory. She sat in front of her fireplace and held a match. She bit her lip then struck it and watched it burn. She quickly blew it out, the stream of smoke lingered. Like the smoke, she felt like she was lingering. This wasn't truly her home, but neither was the carriage house. She felt a sense of restlessness and uselessness.

The words of the reporter from Channel Six still stung, but they were true. Her visions hadn't helped the investigation. She thought about Pastor Fenton saying that she would never find a man who would have her, that she would never have children. How Katherine had accused her of being cursed. If Robert knew all about her past what would he say?

He'd showered her with gifts. Her closets bulged with clothes she'd only seen in fashion magazines. She even had jewels that she kept in a safe behind painting of a famous aviator. She'd visited Rober home in Georgia. He'd given her so much, except for the one thing she craved.

She sighed. How could a woman be so greedy? She lit another match and watched the flame come to life. So many things could succumb to such a tiny light. She could understand the firestarter how he could watch in awe as something burned. At times she wondered if she were her father's daughter in other ways. Dangerous ways. She heard footsteps and blew the flame out. She opened a window and tried to wave away the smell of smoke when someone knocked. "Come in."

Robert came into the room and sniffed the air. "Are you trying to start a fire?"

Her eyes widened. "No, I was just—."

"It's okay if you can't start the fireplace. You don't have to pretend that you do."

"The fireplace, yes of course. I thought about using it then changed my mind."

"Why?"

She shrugged.

He added wood then lit a match and stoked the fire into life. "There."

"Thank you."

It glowed red in the dim light of the coming evening. Robert stared at it wishing he had more to say. He felt as though he were losing her somehow. She'd probably grown tired of him. *You're too intense,* Rosalind used to say. *Where's your sense of fun and adventure?* He glanced at Victoria her fine clothes made her look different than the woman he'd first met. As though some that spirit that had drawn her to him had left her. He felt like a collector keeping a butterfly in a cage. His heart ached with a selfish pain because he didn't want to let her go, but knew one day he would have to.

Melinda walked into her bathroom and halted at the sight of the green toothbrush next to hers. She picked it up and went to Grant who stood in the kitchen chopping vegetables for dinner. He wasn't the greatest cook, but he loved chopping things for her. She saw the cigarette in the ashtray on the table. He used to smoke and chop, terrifying her that she'd find ashes in her salad. She'd convinced him to stop.

"What's this?" She waved the toothbrush.

He took it and held it upside. "I don't know. It's a mystery."

She rested a hand on her hip. "I mean what is it doing here?"

"I plan on spending the night."

"Yes, I know. It won't be the first time."

"And since I don't expect it to be the last time I thought I'd have a toothbrush handy."

"I also noticed a razor, some aftershave, and mouthwash in the bathroom."

He returned to chopping celery. "Uh huh."

"Are you trying to move in?"

A smile quirked the corner of his mouth. "Not yet, but give me time."

"Don't I get a say in this?" Her phone rang before he could reply.

"I just saw the living dead," a voice said. She recognized it as an agent who had been watching the Haddad house.

She gripped the phone "What does that mean?"

"We found Haddad."

Melinda hid her shock when Josef Haddad came into her office. He didn't have a single scar. No missing fingers or discolored skin. Instead he was an exquisite little man with cool manners.

"Sorry it took so long for me to get in touch with you," he said. "I had a business situation to take care of."

"For months?" Melinda said.

"I've been traveling extensively."

"Where were you the night of the warehouse fire?" Grant asked. When Haddad looked blank, Grant reminded him of the date.

He shrugged. "I don't know. It was so long ago." As interrogation progressed it became clear Haddad would not reveal anything. He slowed questioning by repeating statements and giving flippant answers. "Do I look like I've been involved in a fire?" Haddad said after a while.

"No," Grant said. "But we'll be talking again." After he'd gone Grant said, "He's a cool character."

Melinda rubbed her temples. "He's infuriating. His mother taught him well."

"We need the weak link."

They both began to smile then Melinda said, "I'll contact his cousin."

Their suspicions proved right. Basam sat in the room is large eyes making him look younger than his years. He dgeted as his eyes darted between them. Melinda used s nervousness as an edge to set up a grim scenario. "We n prove your cousin was involved with the fire. We have an officer willing to state that you were near the scene of the fire. You will both be charged with arson with intent to defraud. Your aunt and sister will also be implicated. However, we may be able to help them if you help us. All you have to do is tell me what happened."

Basam took a deep breath…then did.

It was an arson-for-profit scheme that seemed fool-proof—inflate the value of the imported goods, burn them, then make a claim to the insurance company for the inflated value. They'd broken down the gallons of acetone into manageable five-gallon CHC jugs.

"Why did you order CHC jugs when you could have obtained unmarked jugs locally?" Melinda asked since it was the jugs that lead investigators to them.

"I don't know," Basam said, "Josef thought it was a good idea."

They'd smuggled the jugs full of acetone into two huge crates and Basam delivered them as a routine shipment for storage at the warehouse before the fire that night. Josef was hidden inside the crates with the acetone. He was confident because he'd done it before with the Magurder grocery store fire several years earlier. Josef had stayed after hours to pour gasoline and acetone around and set the place on fire. Six months later he'd accepted a job to burn down a fabric store. He'd hidden inside and escaped out back before that building went up.

The night of the warehouse fire he'd snuck inside with a hot plate that was to be used as a timer and walkie-talkie to communicate with Basam. Everything was on schedule, then something ignited the acetone early before Josef could escape.

Grant nodded in understanding—most people under-estimate the volatility of acetone's fumes.

"He was blown out the door," Basam said, his voice shaking in awed remembrance. "I couldn't believe it. We were supposed to be safely away with a strong alibi before the building caught fire. I was certain he was dead, so I left."

Melinda said, "But he wasn't dead."

"No, he wasn't. It was a miracle that he made his way to us in the early morning. He looked like a monster. Blackened strips of skin hung from him. His nose and ears were burnt."

The family rushed him to the hospital where he'd checked himself out and slipped through the cracks. A couple days later he and Basam flew to Latin America in search of a top plastic surgeon to reconstruct his damaged face. They'd obviously found a miracle worker.

Grant and Melinda left the room. "Call Robert. Let's bring Haddad in. This case is closed."

Robert wasn't so sure. "What about the third man?" he asked Grant over the phone.

"There was no mention of a third man. Basam said it was just him and his cousin."

"Victoria mentioned a third man."

"I know, but she wasn't sure about his role. She mentioned someone watching. Maybe he got off seeing the building burn…that isn't a crime. I don't think he was involved."

"She said he was. She wouldn't have mentioned him if he wasn't important."

Grant gripped the phone thinking about the cigarette

he'd smoke when he ended this call. "Look, I'm not against anything she said, but to tell you the truth I'm sick of this case. I would like to see it closed. It was hard enough getting this far. We have nothing that would connect a third suspect and if there had been someone else, Basam would have said something. He doesn't seem the loyal type."

Robert sighed.

"If there is a third man, he won't stay quiet long."

"Yes, that's what bothers me."

Susannah threw up her hands exasperated. "Will you give me a break?"

Foster sat stoic in her living room chair. "You're slipping. Your last three reports have been skewed and mean spirited, especially your report about the fire investigation. You've done this before and it hurt people."

"I didn't hurt anyone."

"That report was unfair."

"That report was a simple 'Do you remember when' piece, and it was weeks ago. It's called news."

"It was slander."

"I didn't use any names. I just reported the truth. Everyone knows your precious boss has nothing on the warehouse fire, and that was months ago." She poured herself a drink and swallowed. God why had she even let him come over? Probably because of those damn blue eyes. They made him seem so harmless...but he wasn't harmless—he was a nag. If only he could understand how cutthroat her business was.

The viewers liked a woman with an edge, a woman who

cut through the crap. Her producer had loved the stalled investigation story, debunking psychic hoopla was what news thrived on. Add some police incompetence, and you've got the public's attention. The public loved to see their civil servants screw up. She sniffed. Civil servants my ass…they had the audacity to spend her tax money on some New Age crap and still hadn't gotten anywhere.

Foster took the glass from her. "How much have you been drinking?"

She ran a hand through her hair. "Enough to quench my thirst. I'm fine. Okay?"

"The pain won't always be there."

She turned away. "I don't want to hear it."

He set the glass down. "Your mother died from this. You don't want to do the same."

She folded her arms. "I don't plan to."

"Come to the next meeting."

Her lips became a thin line. "Look, just because you lost your daughter doesn't mean you have to father me."

Foster stared at her as an old hurt gripped him. She was right. Tanya was gone. She would have been near Susannah's age if… No he couldn't start the *What ifs* again. He felt a fresh pain that time had yet to ebb. Alcohol used to numb it for him, but he'd taught himself to feel the pain, then let it go. There was a power in letting go. He wished Susannah knew that. She had talent, but he couldn't save her. He had to let her go. She'd have to reach bottom just as he had.

"You're right." Foster grabbed his jacket.

"Hey look you don't have to be angry," she said with remorse. "I didn't mean—"

He stopped and stared down at her, his eyes piercing hers. "I'm not angry. I'm sorry." He opened the door. "You know how to reach me." Foster jumped in his car and slammed the door. He'd lied. He was angry. Angry at himself for caring. Angry that he needed Susannah to succeed so that he wouldn't feel like a failure. He pulled out of the driveway.

Prescott watched him leave.

CHAPTER TWENTY-TWO

Candlelight flickered casting shadows on the dining room walls. It bounced light against the crystal glasses and china plates. Victoria glanced around the table at Robert's partner, Grant, and his companion, Melinda Brenner. She stared at the luxurious meal Dana had prepared to help them celebrate the case of the warehouse fire, but as Victoria watched Grant light a cigarette she felt a restlessness that threatened to diminish any joy. The case wasn't solved. The firestarter was still out there.

Benjamin whimpered beside her. He stared up at her with large brown eyes.

"Does he need to go outside?" Grant asked, glancing at the dog.

"No," Robert said. "He can get out if he wants to."

Victoria struggled to concentrate on the conversation. She watched the candlelight flicker, swaying like a charmed snake. Benjamin nudged her with his wet nose. She touched the top of his head letting the silky hairs of his fur run through her fingers. It calmed her.

She gasped, as a searing pain struck her in the middle of the chest. She toppled to the ground.

They rushed to her side; Robert lifted her to sitting position and rubbed her back. Grant and Melinda looked at her helpless. "What's wrong?" Grant asked.

She couldn't speak. She needed all her energy just to breath. She felt the heat of flames as the clawing fingers of a monstrous fire gripped a home, its teeth gnawing and devouring with such ferocity she wondered if she were going mad. All her senses felt as though they were melting together. She tasted blackness. She saw the roaring; she heard the heat. This fire was a riddle meant for her. There was no attempt to hide the fact that it was arson.

She closed her eyes trying to read the language of the flames. It spoke of evil—not revenge or hatred, but madness. Its creator had escalated to the one level she had feared. The level to which her father had descended. It wanted to take her, too.

Robert stroked her forehead. "Talk to us."

"It's a house fire," she gasped feeling as though her lungs would burst through her chest. "Someone's inside. But it's too late."

Melinda looked at Robert. "What is she talking about?"

"The fire."

"Tell us more," Grant urged.

Melinda sent him a look of disgust. "She can barely breathe yet alone talk. She needs to lie down."

"We need to get this information before she forgets it."

"Can't you see that she's suffering?"

Victoria buried her face in Robert's chest. The roar of the fire drowned out anything else. She had to remember the feelings weren't hers. She couldn't let them claim her. Soon the power of the vision faded and she could see the fire and not feel as though she were being consumed by it. She glanced up at Robert and immediately understood why.

Somehow he was channeling his energy through her, making her stronger than her vision. Whereas her skin felt cool to the touch, his burned, beads of sweat grew on his forehead. She knew she had to control her feelings before it grew again and overwhelmed them both. She took a deep breath and slowly distanced herself from the vision until her feelings were her own again.

"It's over," she said.

Robert looked exhausted. "Are you okay?" he asked.

"I'm fine." She wanted to ask "Are you?" but knew he wouldn't welcome the question.

"What the hell just happened?" Grant said then took a long drag of his cigarette.

"You saw what happened," Melinda said. "Don't ask silly questions."

He exhaled. "I know about her...I didn't know about him."

Robert frowned. "What are you talking about?"

His hand trembled as he took another drag. "I didn't know you saw them, too."

"I didn't see anything."

"But you felt something, right? You nearly made the air pop. You—"

"It was nothing," Victoria said, before Grant could continue.

Robert opened his mouth to respond then his mobile rang.

* * *

The death of Susannah Rhodes hit the front page of the morning newspaper and became the main story on TV. She received all the attention she'd craved in life as though the price of her life had risen in the ashes of her death.

Robert shifted through the ruins of her house...only the walls remained. He studied the burn patterns and scrutinized the area. He saw a definite coning pattern: The way a fire spreads from one point out in a fanlike pattern. There had been cigarettes and alcohol, but he didn't think they had started the fire. This was no accidental fire, and he'd comb the house to prove it; however, there was no need. The pathologist later confirmed his suspicions. He gave Robert unwelcome news.

"Her lungs are clean," he said.

Robert stared down at the body and swore. Clean lungs meant that she hadn't breathed any smoke. She had been dead before the fire reached her. An outsider wouldn't have seen past the blackened body to clues that lead to the cause of her death. Fortunately, the pathologist saw through the disguise and identified stab wounds. One pierced her lung. Another went right through her.

A task force immediately sprung into action, but no matter how many witnesses they spoke, to everyone came up clean. At the site they had no knife, no footprints... nothing to link anyone to the crime. Robert was quickly losing hope, until Grant called him.

"You're not going to like this, but I had to warn you."

Robert stiffened. "Warn me about what?"

"We've got a suspect."

"Okay. What's the problem? We can finally get closer to discovering the name of this bastard."

Grant hesitated. Robert heard him inhale and pictured him standing outside of the station smoking. "Someone saw a car in the driveway before the fire. They got a license plate and we came up with a name."

"Who?" he asked impatient.

Grant sighed. "It's Foster."

Two officers arrested Foster as he drove up to the house. With no reliable alibi and plenty of opportunity to commit the crime, he became the state's number one suspect. The news hit the papers. The assistant of a prominent person suspected of murdering a local reporter was definitely newsworthy. Robert skimmed over the news article in disgust. The brass above had taken him off the case until the fervor died down. Besides, having his name in the paper didn't help the image of the department.

He knew a lot about image and how important it was to maintain it. He glanced up when someone knocked on his open office door. Caprican entered with a malicious smile. Robert resisted the urge to grab his extra shovel in the corner and remove Caprican's expression.

"How are you doing, Braxton?" he asked.

"Doubt you would care, Caprican."

"No, I doubt I would." He sat.

Robert glared at him. "What do you want?"

"I came to give you a little advice. You don't seem to now how to hire people. First you had the psychic daughter of a known arsonist and now an ex-alcoholic suspected of killing a reporter."

Robert folded the paper.

"Amazing how much this case is like another I know."

"Foster doesn't gain to inherit anything from this."

"No, but there are other motives, or are you going to ignore them? I know you like to ignore evidence when the opportunity suits you."

Robert leaned back in his chair. "Are you finished?"

"I'm sure you'll follow all the rules so that you'll get to the truth and not let any personal prejudices influence you."

"I'm not on the case."

"Of course, but that wouldn't stop you from helping another guilty man walk free."

"If you want to be able to walk yourself, I suggest you get out of my office."

Caprican stood. "Good luck, Braxton. See you in court, unless you arrange for a different outcome. I know you have connections in high places." He left.

Robert drummed his fingers on the desk. Foster was only a suspect. Opportunity wasn't enough to charge someone with a crime. Though investigators were tossing out possible motives, most of them didn't stick. Without one, Foster could go free. That was the problem. Robert knew Foster had a motive. A good one. If anyone discovered it, it may be enough to indict him.

He swore. Caprican had a point. Did he circumvent the system and assume Foster was innocent and keep the information he knew to himself, or use the system to prove the truth? Did he put his trust in the system he worked in?

* * *

Victoria stood in the grocery store aisle and read the recent news headline in disgust. The picture they painted of Foster turned her stomach. They have the wrong man, she wanted to scream, but she knew no one would listen.

"Awful isn't it?" a voice said behind her.

She turned and saw the man from the garden party. She couldn't remember his name, but did remember her suspicions about him. "Hello."

"Prescott Delaney," he said, holding out his hand.

She shook it. He had large, rough workman's hands. "Yes, I'm—"

"I remember you," he cut in. "I was at your garden party."

"Oh, yes."

"So are you free yet?"

She felt a sudden chill. "Free for what?"

"We were supposed to talk about the arsons." He tapped the newspaper. "We both know he didn't do it."

She licked her lower lip then said, "Do we?"

"Sure. You said you'd check your schedule."

She reminded herself not to show fear. "Yes, I remember. I've been busy."

"Sure you have. But you're not busy any more are you? This recent fire must have shocked you and confused the investigators. Fires are good at keeping secrets. Are you?"

An ugliness spread throughout her and for a moment she thought she would be sick. That instant she knew she stared into the unrepentant eyes of a killer. Had her father's gaze been so cold?

He smiled, pleased by her look of understanding. "Impressed?"

She nearly choked. "Yes. Very."

"You must be very curious. We need to talk. Don't you think?"

She controlled a shiver and tried to keep her voice neutral. "Yes. I will call you."

"I'll be waiting." His friendly mask fell as his tone turned to ice. "Don't disappoint me." He tipped an imaginary cap then left.

That night, Victoria paced her room. "Why won't the police do something? They are investigating the wrong man."

Robert watched her from the bed. "They have to follow the clues where they lead and right now they lead to Foster."

"But I told you about my conversation. We know who the culprit is." She threw her hands up frustrated. "We have a name. It's Prescott Delaney. He practically challenged me to turn him in."

"I've already checked him out—twice. He has a solid alibi. There is nothing to link him to this crime. There's nothing to link him to the warehouse fire, or the restaurant fire, or anything else, and the police can't arrest a man based on a hunch."

"You know this is more than a hunch."

Robert's patience snapped. "I need evidence. Hard facts."

"Find something. Arson investigation is not an exact science. You could—"

His tone fell flat. "No, I couldn't."

She stared at him amazed. "You won't bend the rules even if it means a murderer could walk free? Is that how the system works? As long as you're clever enough, you can do whatever you want until you get caught?"

"You should ask your father that question."

Victoria staggered back as though he'd struck her. "That's unfair."

Robert pushed the sheets aside and sat on the edge of the bed. "Life's unfair. That's why we have rules. When you start to bend the rules, when do you stop? It will be too tempting not to stop until the rules mean nothing to you anymore. You'll live by your own rules. That's why we have criminals. They have their own rules. I won't start down that path. Checks and balances are the rational man's only defense to anarchy." He took a deep breath. "You don't really want me to do what you're suggesting. Evil breeds in deception."

She narrowed her eyes, her tone hard. "Then maybe I am evil because I will do anything to put this man in prison and if you won't help me…"

"I won't."

Victoria turned and opened her closet and grabbed some clothes.

Robert closed the closet and forced her to look at him. "You need to trust the system."

"I don't," she spat out. "I don't trust it. What do they need to indict him?"

"Enough evidence to prove motive and opportunity."

"Do you they have both?"

He hesitated. "They have opportunity."

"But no motive." She sighed with relief. "So without a motive they can't go any further."

"Right."

She clasped her hands together. "Good then he's safe."

"No," Robert said in a low voice. "He's not safe."

Victoria looked at him curious. "Why not?"

His eyes held hers. "Because he does have a motive."

"No, he doesn't." She turned away.

"Yes, he does." Robert stood in front of her determined to make her face the truth. "Foster had a motive. Enough of a motive to get him indicted."

Victoria shook her head. "He's innocent. He didn't do it."

Robert stared at her amazed. "Don't you care what the motive is?"

"No because that doesn't matter." She bit her lip thoughtful. "Does anyone else know about this?"

"No."

She lifted a suggestive brow and rested a hand on his bare chest. "Then no one needs to know."

His muscles constricted at the gentle touch of her fingers as they slid from his chest to his stomach. He could feel a growing, carnal hunger rise. His entire body tensed, waiting for a release that wouldn't come. He couldn't respond to her as she wanted him to. It was dangerous to weaken now; dangerous to both of them. For a moment, he allowed himself to linger in her gaze, her silent request clear. Her loyalty to his friend made him want her more.

He swallowed, resisting the urge to lean closer, to press his mouth against hers, to feel the softness of her body against him. He took a deep, shuddering breath. His will had to be stronger than his lust. "You want me to keep what I know a secret."

"I want you to protect your friend. You'd betray him by exposing anything about him that could get him into trouble.

"My job is to protect the innocent. If foster is innocent he'll be fine."

"Your father was innocent."

Robert's gaze darkened. He moved away from her touch. "Don't bring him into this."

"You brought my father into this."

He stared at her his heart aching as he felt the distance growing between them. "I guess we'll always be on different sides of the law."

"One man already paid for the crimes of another. Do you want to repeat that?"

"My father's trial occurred at a different time. The type of investigation back then had relied to much on 'hunches.' We now have experts…"

"We have a more scientific way to skew the truth," she challenged. "People are scared. They want someone to put away and they don't care who it is."

He clenched his teeth desperately wishing she would understand. "I've spent my entire career trying to help change this system and now you want me to betray the oaths I've made. The system is there and it can work. I'll get Foster a top attorney."

Victoria flashed a mocking smile. "If you're going to toss money around why not pay off the judge and jury as well?"

He stared at her a long moment then said, "Don't push me, Victoria."

She grabbed the front of his shirt and stared up at him with pleading eyes. "I know you want to use Foster to prove your ideals. I know you need to believe that your father's death was for a reason. I know you need to believe that because of what happened to him, you were able to change the very system that failed him, but you can't. The system hasn't changed because people haven't changed. You said your father was a strong man yet what happened to him destroyed him. Foster isn't strong. He won't be able to handle the pressures of a trial. You could push him towards the bottle again."

He removed her hands and walked to the window. "If anyone found out I kept information I could lose my job."

"So what?"

He stilled. "What do you mean by that?"

"Your job isn't that important."

He slowly turned to her. "You mean I don't need it, right?"

"I know you like your work, but—"

A gathering fury raced through him, but he kept his voice level. "*Like it?* Do you think it's some sort of hobby I do to fill my time? My job is what I do. It's who I am. Do you expect me to disgrace my name, my oaths and my fellow officers just because I can afford to?" When she didn't reply his voice hardened, commanding an answer. "Do you?"

She waved her hands helpless. "I just don't know... don't know," she said then let her gaze fell.

He turned back to the window and rested his hands on the windowsill. His tone deepened with disgust. "If that is the case, you don't know me very well. I live by standards and those standards are not flexible."

"But you could—"

He spun around, his eyes blazing, "I will not bend!"

The passion of his words crashed against the walls like the memory of an echo, mingling with the sound of a soft wind brushing past the window.

Victoria grabbed her suitcase and said quietly, "Neither will I."

The next day, Robert sat in the diner he and Grant had visited the night of the warehouse fire. The night before Victoria had entered his life. He stared out the window, but saw nothing. He felt the weight of what he must do. He had only one course of action, no matter how many people would disapprove. With a good defense Foster could get a nonguilty verdict like Andy Tracts. He believed that. He had to.

The chef, Sebastian, came out from the kitchen and sat at his table. "You're making me look bad."

Robert turned to him. "What?"

He gestured to Robert's plate. "I've burned your meat as requested and you haven't even touched it."

Robert glanced down at his uneaten steak. He pushed the plate away and rested his arms on the table. "I've been coming here a while, haven't I?"

Sebastian nodded. "Yes, unfortunately."

He ignored his teasing. "What kind of customer would you say I am?" He held up a hand. "And don't flatter me."

"I don't think I could." Sebastian thought for a moment, adjusting his large glasses, then said, "I'd say you were demanding, but honest. You treat the waitresses well. You're a cordial, but exacting man. Predictable."

Robert nodded at the apt description. "What if I were to be flexible and order a medium rare steak."

Sebastian's eyes lit up at the possibility. "Yes?"

"And I tasted it and didn't like it. Would you like me to lie and tell you that I did like it?"

He shook his head. "No, I'd be disappointed."

"Why? Wouldn't the lie make you feel better?"

"Well, your word wouldn't be worth as much if you lied. It would lose its value." He shrugged. "Besides you tell the truth. Lying wouldn't be like you."

Robert paused then said quietly, "There are times when a man must lie or at least not reveal the truth to save a friend."

"A true friend would know that even an honorable man can't lie about certain things."

"Why would that be?"

"Because an honorable man believes in a higher good. Silence has its place, but it will be your conscious that screams."

Victoria stood in front of Susannah's burned house draped in a wool coat and scarf as the wind scattered leaves on the ground.

"A nice puzzle, isn't it?" Prescott said.

A part of her hadn't expected him to come, but knew arrogance would force him here. She understood his a rogance as much as she despised it. Arrogance provided a nice shield when you lived on the margins of life. Her father hadn't been an educated man or important, but he had the power to destroy, and that made him feel greater than he was. Prescott was arrogant enough to think he would never get caught. She would use that flaw to her advantage. "Yes, it's a good puzzle," she said.

"The warehouse fire was better."

"Why?"

"Because of the acetone. Those two clowns had no idea how it worked." He laughed. "They didn't understand its personality. That guy Josef had taken a nice arson-for-hire job that should have been mine. I always thought it would be cool to be an arsonist for hire like your father." He briefly frowned. "Anyway Josef beat me to the job, and then when I heard about his insurance fraud scheme I thought I'd watch and see what happened. Anything could set off acetone fumes. A pilot light coming on in the coffee area or a frayed electrical cord or an electrical switch." He smiled in memory. "Something came on and the building went up. What a beautiful sight. Poor guy was still inside. Heard he lived, though, but he's no longer a concern of mine."

"What about the old lady?"

"Probably a hot plate turned into a detonator or a frayed cord. You can make anything look like a malfunction if you're clever." His watched beeped. He glanced at it and swore. "I have to go. We'll talk more later."

"Yes." She turned off the recorder in her pocket, trying not to smile.

* * *

An hour later, Victoria stared at Robert stunned. "What do you mean it's not enough? I got a taped confession."

Robert shook his head at the tape recorder lying on his desk. "Prescott didn't admit to anything. The DA would laugh at a tape like this."

"He described how the warehouse fire burned and the old woman…"

"All speculation."

"Speculation? He mentioned acetone and a hot plate that's important."

"He didn't say 'I did it.' That's a taped confession."

Victoria grabbed the recorder and began to turn. "Okay, then I will—"

Robert jumped to his feet and seized her arms, forcing her to face him. "No, you're not going to do anything. Stay away from him. He's dangerous. He's not worth the risk."

"Foster's worth the risk."

He searched her eyes then shook his head in amazement. He'd seen that expression before. "This isn't about Foster. This is about you and Prescott."

"No, it's not."

He ignored her. "I think a part of you likes meeting with him. A part of you is attracted to what he is. Maybe it's even more than a part. Perhaps you just want to be with him because you relate to his sense of justice more than you do mine. It wouldn't be the first time a woman found herself attracted to a dangerous man." Rosalind loved them, craving the excitement and challenge they promised her. It had only taken several months before she had become bored with her safe, boring husband and found the company of other men. He hadn't known it then, but he wouldn't be blind again.

Victoria had a wild, untamed freedom he could never grasp or tame. He knew she would leave him before he had the chance to let her go. "Just admit it."

Her gaze didn't waver. "I only want to catch him."

"At what price?"

"At any price."

He turned and sat on the edge of his desk. "No, that price is too high."

She took a few steps towards him then stopped; her voice became a persuasive whisper. "But you haven't spoken to anyone yet, have you?"

He paused. "No." He shook his head at the hope in her eyes. "But I plan to."

"You'll kill him."

"He's strong."

She pounded the desk. "And what if he's not? What happens if you're wrong? What happens if the system doesn't work or Foster isn't strong? What will you do then?"

"The system can work."

"The system is made up of men and men are not fair. They lie."

"And you expect me to lie to?"

She clasped her hands together as though in prayer. "I expect you not to say anything. Please."

"I have to."

Her hands fell to her sides in defeat. "Fine."

He grabbed her arms before she went to the door. He

pulled her towards him until their noses nearly touched. "You have to trust me."

"I do trust you, but I don't trust them. I don't trust the men of your system: the connivers and manipulators and the hunters and the weak-minded. My father was better than them all."

Robert rested his forehead against hers and closed his eyes. His voice was barely a whisper. "Please don't do this to me. Don't make me choose."

Victoria heard the anguish in his voice; it echoed the pain in her heart. She cupped his face. "You already have." She took a deep breath feeling as though her insides were crumbling, but she refused to fall apart. "And so have I." She brushed her lips against his then took a step back.

Robert didn't release her. He drew her close and deepened the kiss sending her sensations spinning under the assault of his persuasive mouth and seductive hands. For a moment she surrendered, wanting only to be with him, but she knew she couldn't. She pushed him away and fought back tears.

"Victoria, please." He reached for her again, but she slipped out of his grasp and went to the door.

"I'm sorry." She turned the door handle then stopped. She removed her earrings then placed them in his palm. "I want you to have these."

He stared down at them confused. "Why?"

"Because I love you and I want you to remember that." She swung open the door then raced out the room.

The brilliant red, gold and yellows of the leaves turned a dusty brown as autumn lengthened. Robert sat in his study thinking of Victoria's last words to him. She'd said she loved him, he didn't believe her. How could she love a man she didn't understand? A man she didn't respect? Since Foster's indictment no one in the house spoke to him. He hadn't noticed how his staff had begun to feel like family. No doubt Victoria had told them about his choice and they'd turned against him.

He didn't blame them. Foster was one of them. It didn't matter that he'd gotten Foster a top legal defense team. Spending money was no great risk.

He sighed when someone knocked on the door. "Come in."

Foster walked into the room. "I need to talk to you."

Robert studied him; his skin looked pale, his face older. Though he'd prepared himself for this moment it still caused pain. He hadn't realized how much he'd considered Foster a friend. No, he was much more. He admired him. He'd fought valiantly against his alcoholism and had rebuilt his life. The one thing his father had not been able to do. He was the man he wanted to be and now he would lose him. "I understand if you would like to leave my employ."

Foster sat. "No. You had to tell them about Tanya, Braxton. I don't blame you."

"Why not? I blame myself."

"I blamed myself for Tanya's murder, but I couldn't change anything. I blamed Susannah's report for tipping off the suspected murderer by sharing information to the public that the police didn't want anyone to know. Then I saw her at one of my AA meetings and I wanted to save her."

"They never found the guy. The DA will use that same

defense now, stating that her recent reporting about my investigation made you snap."

"I did go to see her about her reporting, but I didn't kill her."

"I know."

"I used to drink so I wouldn't have to face life. This case is forcing me to face my past, and I've found out that I am strong enough to face it. That's because of you."

Robert felt his throat tighten. "I will do everything in my power to help you."

"You've already done enough. I know that you and Victoria are at odds because of me."

Robert shook his head. "It's not you. It's our belief of what's right and what's wrong. We can't seem to compromise."

Foster hesitated. "I don't want her taking unnecessary risks because of me."

He narrowed his eyes. "What do you mean?"

"She told me that she plans to talk to that Prescott character."

He felt a chill come over him. "Why?"

"She wants him to go after her."

Victoria set down her fork and smiled at Prescott. His wide smile shone white in the dim lights of the restaurant. It wasn't a fancy place like the ones to which Robert had taken her. Lobster didn't appear on the menu, and there were no personal waiters or separate wine lists; however, it didn't need those things. Its calm earthy atmosphere made customers feel at ease.

She sipped her drink and glanced away from his

intense gaze. She was used to it. He was in awe of her and she didn't wish to discourage it; however, she shouldn't have accepted his invitation to dinner, but a part of her couldn't resist the challenge. A part of her that was drawn to his confidence, drawn to the way he treated her as though she were a queen. He rushed to open a door or hold out a chair for her at every opportunity. When he spoke she listened as though he had bewitched her. She felt alive in his company; she felt as though anything were possible. That she could do anything.

He knew how it felt not to belong…how it felt to live on the fringes of life and battle the shadows. He understood the dark side of her. There was nothing she needed to hide from him, unlike Robert…

She took another sip of her drink, feeling the cool liquid slide down her throat. She was here for him. She would catch Prescott somehow and make sure that Foster went free. Unfortunately, he had a clever way of speaking without revealing anything she could use. She sent him a sidelong glance, a shiver racing through her recognizing the dangerous game she was playing. Her firestarter was clever about a lot of things. If she didn't handle this right she could fall into her own trap.

CHAPTER TWENTY-THREE

"What the hell do you think you're doing?" Robert demanded when Victoria answered her door.

Victoria ignored how her heart leapt at the sight of him. She folded her arms and blinked bored.

He took hold of his temper and said in a calm voice. "Foster told me what you're up to."

She shrugged. "So?"

He clenched his teeth. "This isn't a game, Victoria. Prescott is a dangerous man. He's killed two people... you could be next."

Her voice remained quiet. "I know."

"You can't do this."

"I have to." She turned away.

He followed her inside and slammed the door. "Why?"

She spun around. "Because I prefer to die than watch him kill another innocent person and see it in my mind I have to stop him. No one stopped my father and look what he did. If no one stops Prescott he will get more dangerous than you'd ever imagine."

"I can't let you do this."

"You can't stop me."

"Yes, I can."

A malicious little smile touched her lips. "You can try, but you will not stop me."

"Don't underestimate me, Victoria."

She raised a mocking brow. "I'm not."

He saw the challenge in her eyes and felt the same challenge in his soul. She was almost everything he was not, but he knew he was staring at his equal. He understood her and knew that she understood him. He could fight her, he could destroy her, but there would be no victory in such a triumph. He'd prefer spending his energy pursuing another prey; even if that meant losing everything.

"Okay," he said in a hoarse voice as though the words were being ripped from his throat.

She frowned. "What?"

He sat on the couch and looked up at her, a cold and ominous determination bright in his gaze. "I'll get him for you. No matter what it takes. I promise you'll get him."

It was his eyes rather than his tone that made her shiver. The predatory nature she'd first sensed when she met him shone clear in his gaze. His words of assurance should have warned her, but instead left her feeling cold and hollow inside. Yes, he could get Prescott and destroy him, but he could also succumb to the darkness within himself and might never recover. She knew there was a certain threshold from which one could never return. She couldn't allow him to make that sacrifice. "But you said that with your job—"

"I'll resign tomorrow."

"No."

He stared at her bewildered. "Why not? You wanted me to do it before."

"I was wrong. I can't let you give up what you love or who you are because of me. I love you as you are. I don't want you to change. I'm not worth it." She shook her head with bitterness. "If you knew the truth about me…"

"You say you love me?"

"Yes."

He pulled her down next to him his voice urgent, but gentle. "Then trust me. I know everything I need to know about you and I know what I'm doing." His voice deepened with conviction. "I will never let anything happen to you."

She stepped away from him and wrapped her arms around herself. "Do you know why some people think I'm evil? It's not because of my visions."

"Tell me why then."

She swallowed as her stomach twisted in knots "Because I killed my cousin. I was about seven and we were playing with matches. I loved matches and fires. We would light candles and set leaves and paper on fire even though adults warned us not to. One day when I was supposed to be watching him, I lit a match and it caught the bed clothes on fire. Before I knew it the entire room burst into flames. I got out; he didn't."

His voice softened. "You were a child, Victoria. You shouldn't have been watching him anyway."

"That doesn't matter. At times I wonder if I wanted him dead. I didn't like him. He wasn't kind and I hated his parents, but he hadn't deserved to die because of me. I've always felt I should have died in that fire because I have no reason to be alive. I know that catching Prescott is what I'm meant to do no matter what the cost."

"I'll get him for you." Robert gently wiped her tears. "Give me time."

"It's too late."

"What do you mean?"

"I had dinner with him one night and I made him very angry…"

Victoria knew Robert couldn't protect her no matter how he tried. She had a destiny he couldn't control. Victoria lay in the bed staring at the ceiling as Robert slept next to her. He'd done so for the past week because she refused to stay in the main house and he refused to leave her alone here. Prescott would strike anyway…she just had to make sure to sense him before he did.

She glanced out the window and saw the bold red slashes of a rising sun. Had she stayed up all night? She glanced at the clock. It read 2 A.M. The red slashes morphed into the sight of flames. She sat up in bed and sniffed the air. She didn't smell smoke. Where was the vision coming from? Had he chosen another house to spite her? A sense of dread nearly made her sick. She leapt out of bed as her thought raced with possibilities. He wouldn't, but she knew he would.

She thought about her father who had killed eighty people in one night. Prescott was as dangerous as that. He would find the perfect way to hurt her. She couldn't afford to be too late this time. She looked out the window and saw what she feared. Brilliant red flames devouring the main house.

She shook Robert awake. "Call the fire department," she said racing to the door.

He came instantly wide-awake sensing her panic. "Victoria wait—"

She didn't. She ran outside, her thin nightgown a poor shield against the cold air as the frozen grass stung the bottom of her feet. She had to wake them. The alarm would not sound he'd make sure of that. And Benjamin... she couldn't think of what he may have done to him. She only knew he'd get pleasure out of burning them in their beds as her father had his victims. She could feel his pleasure through her panic.

What a glorious blaze! Prescott watched in the distance proud as flames consumed the Braxton mansion. Vivid orange-red flames shot into the dark night, cackling and clawing, tossing ash and bursts of light into the sky. *Victoria do you see what I have done?"* He wanted to laugh and shout out her name. The sight aroused him and he could feel a hard bulge push against the front of his trousers. A painful, yet sweet ache. This sight was prettier than any woman could be. This blaze would make the 'Breaking News' on TV and would be plastered cross the front of every newspaper. He could see it now: *Local Arson Investigator's Home Turned to Ashes.* And they would never trace it to him. They would say the cause was a careless accident in the kitchen. Everyone knew that most fires started there.

His body trembled as the psychic orgasm ascended. *Oh yes.* God it felt good. For a moment he rested his hand there and moaned. He wanted Victoria to see this. He wanted her to be with him. She would understand. It would nice to have a woman around for a change. To find a place of release between her thighs after experiencing such a high. Yes, Victoria had made him angry that night at dinner by taunting him. By saying that no one could be as good as her father. Now he had proven her wrong. He'd gotten the better of an arson investigator; her father had never done that. He laughed, satisfied.

His arousal grew more intense as he thought of the fire and Victoria, his breathing more labored, desire increasing to a level he couldn't control it. He removed his trousers and gripped his hardened penis. He rested one hand on the tree to anchor himself, his knees growing weak as the movement of high right hand quickened. Finally the release he needed exploded through him and he groaned deep in his throat and surrendered. When he was through, he rested his forehead against the trunk, oblivious to the cold wind racing past his backside and the now limp organ in his hand. He sighed. Next time he'd be inside Victoria and it would last longer.

He started to stiffen again at the thought, but this time took control of his desire. He pulled up his trousers then glanced at the house again, his ears alert for any telling sounds of danger. Fire trucks would be coming soon and he didn't want to be spotted. He shoved his hands in his pockets and glanced toward the cottage house. No doubt Victoria could feel his rush. She could sense his pleasure. He wondered if the experience had been good for her too. He hoped so. Suddenly, his joy turned to dread as he watched a figure in a night dress race toward the building. *Victoria!* What was she doing? She knew better than to enter a burning building.

For the first time horror gripped him. He knew that was exactly what she meant to do.

He raced toward her, shouting her name, but she disappeared inside before he could stop her.

Victoria burst into the house; the heat of the fire seized her skin. Thick smoke blinded her and attacked her lungs. She darted up the stairs and rushed to Foster's room. She shook him awake. He stared up at her groggy.

"Get Amanda. There's a fire."

She entered Ms. Linsol's room, it lay empty. Relieved, she turned back to the hall and saw a large flame grab a wood railing causing an overhead beam to fall. She looked down into the space below and saw the living room up in flames. Feeling that heat, she backed away until she was flat against the wall. Soon she felt Prescott's presence. She saw him coming toward her like a demon from the underworld.

He stopped a few feet away, his face a mask of rage

"What the hell do you think you're doing? You're not supposed to be in here."

"You were supposed to come after *me* not them."

He smiled his teeth frightfully white in the thickening haze. "I did. I did this all for you." He held out his hand. "We'll talk about it later. Come on. I'll get you out of here."

She made a sideward movement. Something was wrong. She felt it in the air. "You shouldn't have done this."

"I shouldn't have done a lot of things."

The smoke was darkening fast; soon she wouldn't be able to see him, he would just be a voice in the blackness. The fire was speaking to her, but she couldn't interpret its message. Something was wrong. "I don't think—"

He made an impatient gesture. "Come on Victoria, don't make me angry."

For some reason she was glued to the spot, paralyzed by terror. From what, she couldn't tell. "I can't."

"Trust me, I'll never let anything happen to you."

She slid to her knees, a wave a dizziness washing over her. Hadn't Robert said those very words to her? "You have to leave."

"Not without you."

"Victoria!"

Anger pushed through her paralysis at the sound of Robert's voice. What was he doing here? He was supposed to wait outside. He was supposed to be safe.

"Victoria!"

"Don't say anything," Prescott warned. "Come on. We don't have time."

She pushed herself from the wall, moving toward the sound of Robert's voice. "I can't leave him here."

"He'll blame you for this. Can you face that? He doesn't understand you like I do."

The truth of his words hit her like a back draft. He was right. Hadn't she been blamed for her cousin's death in Jamaica and her aunt's flower shop going up in flames? Robert had every right to hate her now. It was her pride that had put his family in danger and had caused him to lose the inheritance his father had left. Without speaking she headed down the hall. Satisfied, Prescott followed her.

Then she sensed a warning and began to move quickly. Though Prescott hurried his pace it wasn't fast enough. The floor groaned beneath his feet and then gave way. His eyes widened in shock as he fell through the floor. He grasped the edge, his legs dangling over the inferno below. The arms of the flames reached for him.

"Victoria!" he screamed. "Victoria! Help me!"

The sound of his cries raked at her heart. She could not watch him die. She tied her night gown around a pole, anchored herself against it and reached for him. She knew he could pull her to her death, oddly she felt no fear. She grabbed him, but wasn't strong enough to hold him. Her muscles strained and trembled, and she bit her lip not wanting to shout out. She felt as though her shoulders were being pulled from their sockets. Pair shot up her arms as sweat streamed from her forehead and down her back.

The flames below began to move and sway while the room seemed to go from large to small then back again.

"Don't let go," he said, his nails biting into her flesh. She could feel her skin tearing under his hold and the slow trickle of blood that followed.

She squeezed her eyes shut. "I don't think I can hold you."

She heard the low groan as the pole began to give way and loud rip of her nightgown as it began to tear upper her side. She wouldn't be able to pull him up. She looked into his eyes. His dark brown eyes reflected the look of horror and pain on her face then shifted to mirror something else: the sight of a man with no heart. A man full of evil, an evil as tangible as the flames below him. He would never release her. If she didn't save him, he meant her to die too. "I can't hold on any longer." She tried to release him, but he held on tighter.

"Don't let go," he said in a low voice was had become eerily calm. "We were meant to be together. This is our destiny."

"Victoria!" Robert called.

The pole gave a low ominous moan; she could feel her body slowly sliding across the floor closer to the edge. "Robert! Help me!"

She felt him appear at her side no longer able to see through the smoke. He crawled low on the ground holding a wet face towel over his nose and mouth.

He removed it and told Prescott, "Grab my hand."

Prescott shifted his gaze to him and said, "I can't."

Robert tried to remove his deathlike grip on Victoria, but failed. "If you don't release her, you'll pull her down with you."

"You can pull us both up, but I'm not letting go."

Robert wrapped his arms around Victoria's waist and lifted her toward him, when Prescott's head came into view, he grabbed Prescott's belt and lifted him up.

Prescott collapsed on the ground gasping for air.

Robert seized one leg of Prescott's trouser and forced it up. He grabbed the gun Prescott had hidden there then put it inside his jacket. Prescott sent him a venomous look; he ignored him. "Stay low," he ordered. "We're going to crawl out of here. Follow me."

Victoria forced herself to crawl though every time she rested on her arms, pain ripped through her.

Robert led them to the far west wing where the smoke cast a hazy fog, an illusion of safety as the fire rumbled behind them. The arm of the fire had yet to ascend there. Robert touched a door then opened it. He didn't make it inside. Prescott hit him on the back of the head with a marble statue he'd grabbed from a floor stand. Robert fell to the ground.

Prescott pushed him over and grabbed his gun. He then looked up at Victoria. At first she stood paralyzed then ran. He lunged at her and grasped her wrist.

"Let me go." She struggled to free herself. "We can't leave him."

He dragged her behind him. "We don't need him now."

She held on to a column, but her arms were too sore for her to hold on. "I am not leaving him."

Prescott pulled her angrily towards him. "Don't upset me again." He touched the barrel of the gun against her forehead. "You'll do exactly what I tell you to do."

She shivered inside, but showed no fear. A denser smoke began to fill the corridor. Stars began to dance in his eyes as a faint feeling slowly encased her. "I can't leave him."

"You will. We'll never be free with him around. Don't you understand? We need to escape."

"I won't go with you."

He softened his voice and used the nozzle of the gun to trail a tender path alone her jaw. "I don't want to have to kill you."

She boldly stared back. "I'm not afraid of death."

"Then this will be easy." He cocked the gun. Before he fired, their was an explosion of shattering glass as the fire reached the third floor landing with its arched window pane. Startled, Prescott fired, but missed her. She twisted away from him and rain. He fired again. She felt something rip through her side and fell to the ground.

Prescott rolled her body over and knelt beside her as blood seeped from the wound. "Pity," he said then pressed his lips against her mouth and raised the gun again. Before he could aim she hit his kneecap with the edge of the candleholder. He cried out in pain and dropped the gun. She reached for it, but he grabbed her hair and yanked her back then struck her. She stumbled and fell lying motionless.

Prescott rose to his feet and looked down at her in

disgust. He didn't have time to kill her now; he didn't know where he was and needed to find a way out. The smoke was burning his lungs and if he didn't get out soon, he knew he'd be dead along with the rest of them. Victoria and Braxton would never regain consciousness. He glanced at their motionless bodies then made his way down the hall.

He dashed up some steps, fighting dizziness and nausea. Once he reached the landing he placed his hands against the walls to guide him. To his surprise one wall moved slightly inward. He shoved it open, entered and then halted. Instead of the sight of moonlight seeping through a window he found darkness. He turned back to find the door then heard a hollow sound beneath him. He dropped to his knees and felt the ground. His fingers brushed across a latch. Relieved to find a way to escape, he grabbed the latch and lifted it.

Victoria slowly pulled herself to her knees, cradling her side. Her head ached, but fortunately the bullet had only grazed her. Suddenly large hands grabbed her. She cried out in fear and pain.

"Victoria, it's me." Robert said, his voice close to her ear. "Where is he?"

"I don't know."

"That's okay. I need to get us out of here."

Crawling on their hands and knees Robert led them to a far room. Once inside Victoria grabbed several sheets off the bed and stuffed them under the door. Robert opened the window. He reached under the bed, grabbed

n escape ladder, which was in every room, and attached
to the windowsill.

Victoria felt her knees buckling, her lungs constricting.
I don't know if I can make it."

"You'll make it," he said without sympathy. "Because
ou're going first and I don't plan to let you die."

"I'll follow you."

"Would you prefer I push you out? I think the fall may
urt."

Fueled by anger she descended the ladder. When her
eet touched the ground the world began to spin. Robert
rabbed her before she hit the ground. He lifted her up
nd carried her a distance away. When Amanda saw
hem, she dashed madly towards them.

"You're hurt," she said, tears streaming down her face.

Victoria managed a smile. "I'll be all right."

Amanda didn't believe her and began to sob.

Robert fell to his knees and took her in his arms. "It's
kay. We're all safe now."

Foster and Ms. Linsol, followed by Benjamin, soon
ppeared from the other side of the house. Ms. Linsol said
enjamin had saved her life. She had followed him out of
e house. Soon the sound of sirens pierced the air.

Victoria stared at the burning house with anguish.
he was cursed. Destruction followed her everywhere.
he tried to shrug off Robert's arm from her shoul-
ers. "This is all my fault. He was supposed to come
fter me not you. Your beautiful home is turning into
shes. Now all that you love is gone."

He kissed Amanda on the forehead then turned to her

his heart in his eyes. "No, all that I love is right here in my arms." His mouth stopped any protest and soon she had none to offer. She drank in the essence of him, reveling in the warmth of his kiss, and the strength of an embrace that held her with a possession she found exhilarating. She truly belonged to someone, not out of obligation, but because someone had chosen to claim her.

She kissed him back, matching his possession, promising to be the guard of his heart, the shield of his honor. He smelled like ashes and soot, but no longer would the smell repel her. No longer would the past hold her captive; it, too, had burned in the flames.

Robert drew away and gazed at her with such love, tears filled her eyes. "Rest your wings butterfly," he whispered. "With me you're already home."

Days later fire investigators found a body in the Safe Room, charred beyond recognition.

EPILOGUE

Victoria lay in the hospital bed, cradling her new son as Amanda peeked over her shoulder.

"He's so beautiful," Amanda said in awe.

"Do you think he'll open his eyes?" Foster asked.

Victoria smiled down at him. "He probably will like sleeping like his father."

Amanda glanced at her Uncle who rested his head on his hands on the other side of the bed. She lowered her voice. "Will Uncle Robert be okay?"

"No," he grumbled. "Uncle Robert will not be okay. Uncle Robert wants to kill who ever came up with the concept of sympathy pains."

Victoria affectionately patted him on the head. "You were wonderful."

Robert groaned. "God, the first three months were hell."

"I didn't have morning sickness."

He lifted his head and glared at her. "I know."

She bit back a grin.

He held his head as though still in pain. "And twelve hours of labor."

Victoria looked down at Winston. "I think he's worth it."

Robert looked up at Foster, Amanda, and Victoria. To outsiders they probably made a strange picture. An older white man who was more father than assistant, a niece that he considered his daughter, and a woman who saw more than others could realize. What an odd family, but it was his family. His eyes fell on his son and he felt a warmth of pride spread through him. "Yea, it was all worth it."

ABOUT THE AUTHOR

Dara Girard is the author of *Table for Two, Gaining Interest* and *Carefree*. You can visit her website at www.daragirard.com.

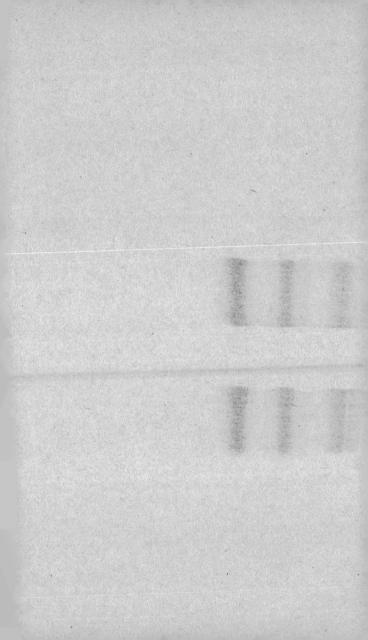